CROSSING BLADES

ARCTIC TITANS OF NORTHWOOD U BOOK ONE

HAYDEN HALL

Copyright © 2023 by Hayden Hall

All rights reserved.

ISBN: 979-8-8563-0133-4

No part of this book may be reproduced in any form or by any electronic or mechanical means, including information storage and retrieval systems, without written permission from the author, except for the use of brief quotations in a book review.

Cover photo by XramRagde

Cover design by Angela Haddon

Edited by Sabrina Hutchinson

Written by Hayden Hall

www.haydenhallwrites.com

❀ Created with Vellum

About the Book

This year is my last chance to take the Titans to victory. I cost us the cup last year, but I'm not making the same mistake again. And I'm determined to get drafted by the end of this season.

The success I anticipate is built on three years of razor-sharp focus and hard-earned respect. Not to mention how much of my personal life I sacrificed for hockey. The Titans trust me to lead them and I won't betray that. Nothing could possibly go wrong.

Until the former love of my life and current arch nemesis, Cameron Martinez, skates back into my life. His very presence throws me off balance. His intense gaze and aggressive, dominant, and possessive streaks feel like a lasso pulling me toward him.

It only takes so many shared showers and locker room encounters before I'm too weak to continue resisting this pull.

But we both know there is no future for us. Our ambitions have always left a trail of ruin and heartbreak in their wake. Why should this time be any different?

Except I can't think straight when he's around. And every private moment we share makes me forget why I'm even here in the first place.

Prologue

RILEY
Three Years Earlier

I took a deep breath, finding comfort in the warm familiarity of his musky scent after the thrill ride that had us both still panting for air.

Cam's eyes were closed, but his long, black lashes quirked as he abruptly held his breath.

As I lifted my gaze to his tousled, black hair, tingling ran straight into my toes and I curled them, swallowing down a moan that was bursting with pleasure. He exhaled with a groan, exhausted from his acrobatics. I'd never realized how bendy our bodies were until Cam pushed us to our limits. Warmth was still rising and splashing through me. And it would keep tingling for the rest of the day. Hell, I'd still feel it tomorrow, no doubt.

I loved our Sundays.

They were unofficial, but you couldn't find a more predictable thing in my calendar. It was the same every week.

> What's up?

>> Not much. Just hanging.

> Alone?

>> You know it.

Silence. He was texting, erasing, texting again.

>> Wanna come over?

> On my way.

And every Sunday morning, while my parents and my brother were at church, Cameron took me to hell and back. Every Sunday, we acted like we'd just thought of it.

We didn't talk about what it meant, but we didn't have to. There had never been that much need for us to talk. I knew what drove him out of his home and what he was running from. And guess what? I loved that I was his shelter from the storm. He ran to me. Whenever the shouting was too much to take, he found his quiet place next to me.

Cam quirked up one corner of his lips as I ran my fingers down his bare, sculpted torso. I'd been looking at that torso for longer than I could remember. I'd gazed at it since I knew I preferred male torsos. Maybe longer. Sharing the locker room all our lives meant I'd seen him stripping down to his underwear practically since the day we'd met. And even more so since our first hockey practice. But it was only ten months ago that I'd seen him this way. Open. Willing. Up close.

My fingertips traced the middle of his six pack all the way to the edge of the cover that was over his crotch.

Cam shared a wolfish grin. "Don't tell me you're horny already."

I so fucking was. The truth of it stretched my lips wide and I looked away from his deep brown eyes just as they touched my face. "No," I insisted, my voice cracking.

Cam snorted. "Right. And I believe you."

"I'm not," I said, mock firmly.

He shoved his hand under the sheet and found me swelling. I throbbed at his touch and Cam laughed out loud. "Liar."

"I didn't lie," I said. "You used your voodoo witchcraft to get me hard."

"Voodoo witchcraft?" he asked, incredulous. "They're called abs, dude."

"They're called abs, *dude*," I mocked him.

He only laughed harder. "You'd know if you bothered to actually work out, *bro*," he teased.

I punched his shoulder, showing him the power of my training. Besides, if all we had done today in my bed wasn't considered a power-workout, I didn't know what could be. Our laughter died down and Cam exhaled slowly, looking at the ceiling.

I closed my eyes and waited. Any moment now, he would ask me to fire up my PlayStation and play *Star Wars Jedi: Fallen Order*. He would then proceed to complain that the game was made with only one point of view and that it was acting morally superior to the order-bringing Empire. To which I would act horrified that I would have sex with a Palpatine supporter.

The thoughts tugged on the corners of my lips.

It was as inevitable as needing to inhale that I would fast-forward to the coming fall and all the things it would bring. And my smile only grew wider.

"Huh?" Cam muttered next to me and I realized I had lost myself in thoughts again.

"Nothing," I said softly.

Cam snorted. "If nothing can get you grinning like that, I'd love to see what something could do to you."

I lifted my arms and slipped my hands under my head, twining fingers. Maybe I could ask him while he played *Fallen Order*. It was true we never talked about big things, this one was too big to ignore. We were finally leaving Holland, Michigan. We were finally getting away from the prying eyes of our families. Well, my family had prying eyes. Cam's only shouted, as far as I knew.

It was weird that we hadn't talked about it yet, though. The huge elephant in the room. And I was nervous about bringing it up first because it could make me look needy and I didn't want that. I wasn't needy. I just knew what a good deal was. I'd known it instantly; as soon as we had received our acceptance letters, I had known what the ideal arrangement would be.

We should be roommates at Northwood University.

It only made sense. We had been friends — I'd even say best friends — for half our lives, and we'd been having sex for months. We had been teammates throughout high school and we would continue to be teammates at Northwood. *Arctic Titans* for the win. We were both going on a hockey scholarship, so it was obvious we wouldn't be parting ways any time soon.

Not that I wanted to rush things.

We had a good thing here. I could keep this going for ages. We didn't need to make it official. Hell, we didn't need to have sex every week, either. I could totally go on like this and have my best friend with me when we embarked on the next chapter of our lives.

But when I looked at Cam, my heart throbbed softly and a fear of something changing clawed at my guts. Talking about anything important had gotten harder the longer we had been intimate. Or talking about anything at all. My tongue was tied and my palms were sweating. The sneaky little voice inside my head kept telling me he would just scoff and shake his head if I said something stupid or sentimental.

I scanned his face. He seemed so peaceful, gazing at the fluorescent stars glued to my ceiling. It was nearly noon and they weren't glowing, but he'd slept over enough times our entire lives, long before we'd turned our sleepovers into something better, that he knew what they looked like at night.

He was all sharp lines and angles. There were no curves on his handsome face. Straight nose, pronounced Cupid's bow, thin lips with sharp outlines. Even his eyes were narrow and his eyebrows flat when he wasn't frowning. Everything about him whispered of caution and alertness. He was deadly elegant like a young tiger.

Cam looked around, then spotted his underwear on the floor where he had thrown them over his shoulder. It had been a dorky move that had made me laugh. He was swift in getting out of the bed and picking them up, then putting them on. When that was done, I fully expected him to fire up my PlayStation, but he hesitated. "Your folks are coming home soon," he said.

I checked the time on my phone. "Yup."

He nodded, still hesitating, but I wasn't sure what was up. He knew my folks wouldn't mind it if they found him here, playing games. They'd pretty much made it clear they had given up on me. In their eyes, I had chosen to chase a rubber disk on ice. It was far from a noble profession like my brother, a doctor, pursued. If I spent my Sunday morning gaming, it wouldn't faze them. So long as they didn't know what sort of sinful bliss had preceded it, we were good. And I was very careful that they would never find that out. That was why I got up and dressed too, then made a round to clean up all the evidence from my room.

"Riley," Cam said so quietly I almost thought I had imagined it.

A creeping sense of foreboding tickled the inside of my stomach. "Huh?" I asked without looking over. I was in the middle of wrapping up the used condom in toilet paper. Why wasn't he playing the game already? That was how our Sundays were supposed to go.

"Can you stop doing that?" he asked.

"I gotta clean this up before they return," I muttered flatly. Why was he acting strange? He knew the drill.

"It can wait a minute," he said.

I held my breath and tucked the wrapped up condom inside the nightstand's drawer. "What's up?" I asked as I turned around. Cam was wearing his shorts and sleeveless T-shirt, his sculpted arms making me drool. His hair was messy in a stylish way, making him look like a bad boy through and through.

"We should talk," he said, his tone impossible to decipher.

I swallowed. He must have figured out that I had been forging plans for us. "Er...yeah," I said, mentally running through my options. Honesty. That was the best way to go. "I've been thinking," I started, hesitating a moment, then remembering to grow a pair. I lifted my chin. Facing against a dozen beefy guys on ice never scared me. Looking Cam in the eyes rendered me a disintegrating mess. "Since we're both going to Detroit, I think we should be roommates. I'll bring my PS." I tacked on that last part without thinking. It sounded like I was bribing him with my gaming console.

Cam's jaw stiffened.

I knew that look. It was usually the look with which he arrived, not the one he wore after sex. It was the look that followed his parents shouting the roof off the house. "Riley..."

"I mean, they have a team house, right? We'll be living in the same house anyway. It's not like we can afford a place to rent." I snorted. My heart rate was quickening. "And we already know each other. It's better than having to get used to someone else's routines." I was deliberately avoiding the very thing I wanted the most.

I wanted to be there when he exited the shower, skin flushed and hair tousled. I wanted to be there when he studied so hard his eyes turned red and he pushed himself away from the desk with a tired sigh. I wanted to witness the moment his breathing changed when he fell asleep, then again when he woke up. Most of all, I wanted to be the thing he saw first every day, even if I slept across the room.

We'd been dancing this careful little dance for the better part of the year. I never brought up what I wanted next because we had the same destination in mind. There was always time for that kind of talk later. We first needed to get away from our families and settle in at Northwood.

Cam's eyebrows flattened and panic soared through me.

"I know we can make it work," I blurted. "It'll be fun. We can play games, study together, fuck whenever..." I choked a little as I dangled this opportunity in front of him, but he was stiffening all over and I knew I had already lost whatever this battle was about.

I was so fucking stupid.

As if sleeping with me was a lottery win. I was good enough for a small town kid who wanted some fun. But that was the extent of my worth in bed. Or anything, really. The only thing I knew how to do was chase that rubber disk. And even that, Cameron Martinez did better.

"Cam," I said.

He sucked his teeth. "Fuck, Riley."

The words rang through me until my fingertips vibrated with anticipation. "Wh-what's going on?"

He closed his eyes and exhaled, then opened them and looked into mine. "We can't..."

A quiver ran through my lower lip and I pursed them both to hide it. "We can't what? Be roommates?"

"It's just..." He looked away, up, then to my left, then into my eyes again. "We can't turn this into a...relationship."

"That's not..." But I knew it was. That was my endgame. Even if I'd never said it aloud, I knew it in my heart. Cameron Martinez was my endgame. "We're not..."

He cocked his head as if to challenge me to say it. "Riley, we're not a couple."

"I know that," I said, a frown creasing my brow. "I never said we were. I'm talking about a solution to a practical problem. But if you want to share your room with some random stranger, be my guest. I don't care."

He held his breath and stared at me for a few heartbeats. Then, he said softly, "I won't share the room with anyone."

I snorted. My family was barely afloat financially — probably because of unwise purchases like a PlayStation 4 or the massive flatscreen mounted to the living room wall — but Cam's were always one step from bankruptcy and one snide look from shouting their throats out. He wasn't getting his own place in a million years. He'd end up in the team house just like me. "Why? You could share the room with me, Cam. It's not a fucking marriage proposal. We're a good team."

"That's not gonna happen," Cam said flatly.

I shook my head in disbelief. "Why?" I demanded in outrage. "You'll end up with some random guy in your room. Why not a friend? I could be that guy."

Cam closed his eyes as if not to see me. It was only after the words were out that I truly understood. I wished I had closed mine too so I wouldn't see him either. "You can't be that guy, Riley. You're going to Detroit. I got accepted in Santa Barbara."

It took me a long moment to understand the words that he had just said. A car engine outside my room alerted me that we had less than a minute of talking openly before we had to pretend we were just hockey friends. "What?" I whispered, already tuning myself for the company of my family in the house.

"I'm not going to Detroit," he said.

My frown deepens. "You applied to SBU?" I asked.

He nodded, opening his eyes and looking at me emotionlessly. It was like arguing with a shark. There was nothing there. Not even hatred. Just pure survival and perseverance of the strong.

"You never said," I whispered, my voice trembling with hurt and rage at this betrayal.

He shrugged like it was nothing. He didn't have to

defend himself. One of us was clawing desperately for a chance that wasn't there; the other was stating facts. We both knew who was walking out of here victorious.

"Cam, for fuck's sake," I hissed as Dad killed the engine in front of the house. Car doors opened and shut. "Are you serious? You applied halfway across the country and didn't say a word." Not to mention that he was, actually, accepted at Northwood, too, but was choosing the other one.

He inhaled quietly, his chest rising. "I gotta go there, Riley," he whispered when the front door opened and three chattering people entered the house. "I wanna be far away from everyone."

"Including me," I stated bluntly.

He winced for the briefest of moments, then deadened his expression again. "I'm sorry."

"Oh. Great. We're good, then." I partially turned away from him.

"Riley," he said.

I didn't answer.

"You don't get it." His tone was far more accusatory now and that felt like a goddamn glowing rod of iron branding my ass.

"I don't get it?" I spun to look at him, my eyes stinging. I wasn't going to give him the satisfaction of seeing me cry, so I blinked fast and bared my teeth. "For years, I followed you, Captain, and never doubted you. Everyone told me to give up hockey and do something with my life, but I persisted. It was just you, me, and hockey. And nobody except you gets it. They all think I'm a failure. Just another dumb guy skating on ice. I know what it feels like when you want to run away, Cam. I've been dreaming of running away for years and it's finally here. I just never realized I'd have to do it alone."

Cam bit his lower lip and looked down, his body swaying shortly toward me like he was going to hug me. I wasn't sure I'd be able to survive it. Instead, he whispered: "I'm really sorry."

And that was it.

Cameron Martinez turned to the door and walked out without a goodbye.

Somewhere on the other side of the house, he was greeting my parents on his way out. It was a horrible reminder that I needed to march out of the safety of my room and eat my lunch with them like everything was normal.

They didn't know. They could never know what had just happened to me.

And I had to sit with them and pretend like nothing had happened. Like my soul was intact and pieces of my heart weren't scattered all over the place.

My fingers trembled as I rushed to my bedroom door and shut it, inhaling deeply and holding that breath for as long as I could. It slowed my heartbeat, but it did nothing to the welling sob in my chest.

I bit my lip until I could taste iron, then growled and channeled all my emotions into anger. Anger I could use. Anger was good. It burned and purified. It killed when it needed to.

Like a rotting limb, I needed to amputate this brimming sadness and the only way I knew how was with hatred. It was the easiest one to find so quickly. So I did.

On the other side, numbness awaited.

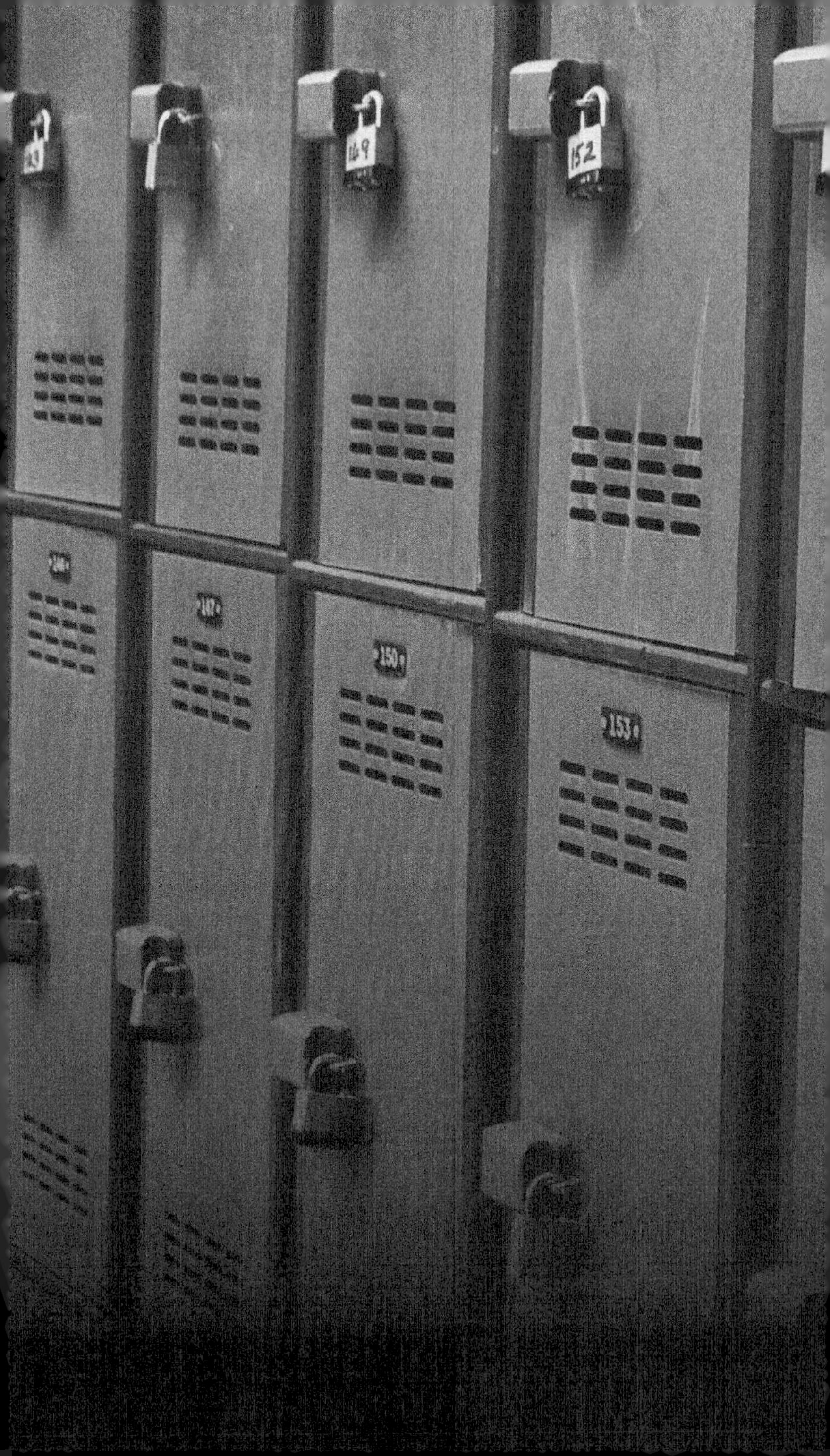
152
150
153

ONE

Riley

You knew you accomplished something if it hurt like hell. And today, it hurt like hell.

I tore off my shoulder pads, muscles searing. The scent of sweat and ice filled my nose as the team shuffled around the locker room. Sticks were clattering here, helmets bumping there. There were more than a few satisfied grunts as the guys filled the space of the locker room and experienced the same sort of high I did.

I was peeling off my scratched knee pads when a hand slapped my shoulder and shook me. "Awesome work, Cap," said the familiar voice of my roommate and assistant captain, Caden.

"Right back at you." The gleam on his face that came with sweat and pride was there as usual. The guy was bursting with talent and energy. One year into college hockey and Caden had proved himself to the point that Coach Murray named him my assistant, to my delight, at the end of last season. Today, Caden had soared like he was trying to prove something. "Keep it up and I see captaincy in your near future."

Caden lifted his hands shyly and shook them. "I won't mutiny while you're around, Cap."

A snort from my left caught my attention and I shot a glare at Beckett. "Knock it off, Partridge." It was true that my time was running out. I had captained the team last year and we had gotten so close to the championship, only to fall short of bringing home the cup. This was my last shot before graduating. And that meant handing over the reins at the end of this season, hopefully with a cup to show for the time I had spent as an Arctic Titan.

"Hey, if you like guys sucking up to you, Cap..."

"Seriously, Partridge," Caden growled and Beckett grinned, lifting his hands in surrender and stepping back. "Ignore him," Caden said to me.

I sucked my teeth. "You ignore him. He's just being provocative."

Caden snickered and nodded, then marched into the shower. I was the last to get there and the last to leave, stopping at Coach Murray's office on my way from the drills.

"Good job, Son," Coach said from his desk, typing something at the computer before lifting his steely, determined gaze to meet mine. "If you keep up the team spirit like this, we may take home that cup."

The sting of last year's defeat appeared in me. It had been my loss for the entire team. I'd had it. I'd been skating through the Breakers' defenses, feeling like I was at the top of the world. I'd seen the victory before me and it had blinded me to their sneaky little bait and switch maneuver.

"You gotta stop beating yourself up over it, kid," Coach Murray said, his voice pitched high and raspy, but always the most dominant in the room. We shared a quiet moment of understanding, then Coach moved onto the reason he had invited me in here. "Over the rest of the week, we'll have four new team members joining the Titans. I want you to bring them up to speed."

My eyebrows trembled for a brief moment.

Coach brushed one side of his mustache with the back of his index finger. "Unofficially, of course. Show them how we do it at Northwood. Gym, drills, rink. Walk them through it, son. They'll respect you for it."

A sense of unease uncoiled in my stomach. Showing some freshman where the gym was wouldn't earn me a great deal of respect. Besides, I wasn't so sure I deserved anyone's respect. Least of all for showing them the campus map.

Coach's gaze was intense, eyes narrowing in expectation.

"Yes, Sir," I said, realizing it had been a while since it was my turn to speak. "I can do that."

"Of course you can, Brooks." Coach gave a firm nod that served both as encouragement and dismissal, so I headed out of his office and made my way toward the team house. It was on the other side of our campus for the very obvious reason of the rink needing a fairly large space in the east-most area.

The entire campus sprawled over a massive plot of land. It was almost a world of its own. On my way back from the rink, I had to pass administration buildings and the great library. Beyond them, entering the heart of campus, lay the bustling student center with coffee shops, work and study spaces, and restaurants. Each way you went, there were faculty buildings for different departments. Once the semester actually started, this whole area would be swelling with students grabbing coffee while running late to their first lectures. It was only beyond these that several kinds of accommodations were placed. Dormitories with single beds and shared rooms; fraternity and sorority houses where the wildest of parties took place; and team houses for hockey, football, and baseball teams. In practice, it was a disorganized mess of people running around; but it also somehow worked like clockwork. Like a beating heart, the campus milled with students and staff scurrying up and down the paved paths, cutting across green lawns, and, on hot days like today, flocking to the shade of old oaks, ashes, maples, and elms. Some outer paths were often dotted with early risers who love a good run instead of coffee. I knew because I was one of them.

I turned right after passing through the much more subdued student center — only a fraction of students populated campus in these weeks before the semester kicked off, and it was mostly us on sports scholarships who needed the early drills and getting back into shape — then made my way to our team house. With ten occupied bedrooms and two guys per room, ours was the biggest of the team houses on campus. It was an old colonial revival house with red-and-brown brick walls, a large wooden front porch, gray-tiled roof, and white window shutters hanging from white frames. The lawn was large and, thankfully, not left to us to tend, so it sported blooming roses in full health. A feat none of us would have been capable of.

My muscles still hurt as I approached the front door and filed in. The rest of the team was already shuffling around. Beckett was in the fridge, mixing one of his calorie bombs. No doubt he would be at the gym for the better part of the afternoon. With the body he had, I didn't need to look at his schedule to know how much of it was blocked for exercise.

Being the only openly gay guy on the team, I made it my priority to never look at other guys in this house. Especially not the ones as straight as Beckett Partridge, who happened to have somewhat lower levels of respect for my captaincy. Besides, I was supposed to be keeping their spirits up, and not making them uncomfortable in the locker room or their campus home. Nobody could ever say I'd done anything like it. Not even Caden, who I knew was exploring his sexuality because he'd pretty much told me so.

I kept my personal affairs well and truly outside the team house.

Partridge ignored me benignly as I made my way through the open plan ground floor, then climbed up the stairs to the room I shared with Caden. It was a sparsely decorated place with two beds, two desks, two chairs, and two wardrobes. A bean bag in one corner and a private bathroom door in the other were the only luxuries we needed or wanted. "All good?" Caden asked, turning from the desk to look at me. "What did the coach want?"

I rubbed the bridge of my nose and tossed my duffel down at the foot of the bed, then exhaled. "Just...babysitting duty."

Caden snorted. "It could be worse." He was reading my mood and I was pretty sure he knew what exactly bothered me.

"Yeah. Of course." I sprawled on my bed, staring at the plain white ceiling. "I'll just take them around the house, show them what's what. Show them a bit of campus, where the gym is, where the swimming pool is. That's how great men are forged," I finished sarcastically.

"Dude," Caden said pointedly. "You're the captain for a reason. This isn't a punishment."

I gritted my teeth. Perhaps I needed to hear it spoken in order to realize that was precisely how I'd felt. Or, worse still, how I thought I should feel. In the minutes following our defeat, there had been a groan of disappointment, but nobody had said a negative word to me. It was like I'd dropped a nickel, not a championship.

Perhaps I needed someone to lash out and blame me to my face. Instead, they were shrugging it off, and the weight of their concealed disappointment was more than I could bear. Every single relationship I had with teammates in this house strained a little. Except with Caden, to be fair, but I wondered if that was because he felt a sense of responsibility, too. Not that he should have. That last miss was all on me, but Caden was my right hand man and he was honorable as fuck. Sacrificial, even.

"If only it was," I muttered, more to myself than to Caden.

He scoffed, then cleared his throat. "I'll give you this one," he said in the end. "You get to feel sorry for your ass tonight, Cap, but that's it. We need you."

My ears perked and I couldn't help but share a ghost of a smile. I still had a whole year ahead of me and tonight showed that the Titans still had some grit left in them. *Spit the blood out and get back up.*

I tucked my hands under my head, fingers twining, and felt a deepening sense of relief. Maybe there was a way to do this, after all. Sure, our team had its south and its north poles; sure, we didn't always get along. Beckett and Caden would be the first to tell you, playing as a team was not always intuitive. Often, it took extra effort just to play alongside someone. But we shared the same goals and nearly all the same values.

We had a fighting chance.

As I exhaled with a little more pressure lifting off my chest, I felt Caden's gaze on me.

Just as I looked at him, he bit his lip. "Er...actually, the first of the new teammates is already here."

"Oh. Okay." I sat up, not sure how to feel about this. Was I the last one to find out? The guy could have come around to see us doing drills if he was around. But it didn't matter. "I guess I should go and make a good first impression." A half-smile touched my lips.

The intrusive voices were quick to remind me that I had no actual business acting like a guide or a mentor to anyone. I had always been everyone's second fiddle. An afterthought. The son of a doctor; the brother of a doctor. And this feeling was never far from my heart.

But I clenched my fists and hopped out of the bed, then marched out of my room. The first floor hallway was quiet, so I headed downstairs. The ground floor was not exactly our place of congregating. We also had a basement that sported vintage arcades, table soccer, lengthy sectionals, a surround sound system, and a well-stocked fridge that may have pushed the lines of what was allowed. Most of us weren't that hardcore in party-going, but we were all known to kick back with a cold one.

As I reached the ground floor, I found Sawyer Price scowling over his phone. Our legendary goalie and the guy you didn't mess with, Sawyer lifted his dark gaze from his phone and greeted me with a grunt.

"Have you seen the new guy?" I asked, not wasting my breath on asking if something was up. Nothing was up with him; he just had that resting bitch face. The fastest way to anger him was to pester him with questions on whether he was angry already.

Sawyer thumbed in the direction of the basement. "Getting cozy already."

Ah, a cocky freshman, I decided. I couldn't exactly blame the new guy for feeling like he was at the top of the world. He had scored an athletic scholarship at Northwood U and was on a highly respected hockey team. A thing like that went to your head. But it did inform my approach.

Cocky freshman who thought they were irreplaceable tended not to react well to any sign of a condescending tone. But they also couldn't be left to their own devices. That was how rookie mistakes were made out on ice.

I thanked Sawyer, who was already glaring at his phone again. By his standards, he was having a tranquil afternoon with some peace and quiet, I thought.

When I marched down the creaky wooden stairs, I held my breath. *Be the captain they think you are*, I whispered to myself. *Lead them. And if you can't, pretend that you can. They will follow. Just keep it the fuck together.*

I inhaled, feeling a zing of motivation, a glimmer of hope. I could do this. I could fucking do this.

I turned at the foot of the stairs in the basement, holding a deep breath of air in my lungs to pump myself up and inspire this new guy to join in the camaraderie and brotherhood of the team.

Our basement lounge was well lit and not particularly crowded. Most of the guys were out already or napping after the drills. I quickly scanned the room, spotting Tyler and Sebastian playing table soccer on the far right end of the room, and Paxton lecturing them. Ahead of me, Beckett Partridge wore a coy smirk that reminded me of his uncle, Nate Partridge, who is hockey royalty and, according to some, the reason Beckett was even here. Beckett was a good player, but he wasn't the best as he imagined. But that train of thought stopped abruptly because Beckett directed his gaze over the newcomer's shoulder and met mine. Amusement rose on his face so quickly that I sensed something being wrong before my brain could register the cold, cruel facts.

One, this guy was no freshman. He was tall, broad-shouldered, with a wide upper back and strong curves below his waist. Those legs had been skating on ice for much longer than a few high school years.

Two, his unruly black hair should have been enough to fill in the rest.

Three, the cold gaze over his shoulder as he turned his head was as murderous as on the day I had last received it.

My stomach dropped into the abyss. My throat closed and I wheezed, then gave up on breathing altogether. The elegant swing of his shoulders, hips, and finally feet, turned my new teammate to face me. In all the years that had gone by, and after all the firm decisions never to look him up and to always push him out of my mind, my first thought was that he had grown more beautiful than humans should have been allowed. The cowlick at the back of his head made him look tardy in that annoyingly cute way. His thin lips were as defined as they had ever been. The Cupid's bow was so pronounced that I could almost feel it under my lips after three years.

"Cam," I whispered through my strangled throat.

His expression was as flat as if he was facing a street sign. "It's Cameron, actually." He allowed for a beat of silence in which a surreal hypothesis took root in my heart. Did he not know me? But the corners of his lips quirked and he added, "Brooks."

My heart split through the middle as my lips pulled back over my teeth. "No. Way." The growl was so filled with hatred that it sounded unnatural even to my own ears. "No fucking way," I said, louder.

Cameron Martinez swaggered lazily toward me. The sharpness of his features seemed deadly, like he could cut through me with a mere look.

"What's up, Cap?" Beckett asked slyly. "You look like you saw a ghost."

I narrowed my eyes at him. "None of your goddamn business, Partridge."

He winced and stepped away, leaving me alone with Cam — sorry, *Cameron* — on this side of the room. I was acutely aware of the deadly silence falling over the guys at the soccer table. "What are you doing here?" I hissed quietly, although I was sure they could all hear me. "You're not... This can't be happening."

"I'm afraid it's happening, Brooks," Cameron said flatly, never blinking, never letting his gaze waver. He stood like a monolith against the most violent storms. He was unmoved and unchanged. If anything, he was only hardened by the time that had passed. "You better believe it because we have drills starting tomorrow."

Anger spiked in me before I could truly recognize it and deal with it internally. "You're not fucking telling me what we have tomorrow. I'm calling the shots around here." Cold terror washed over me as I blinked and saw a glimpse of the remainder of my college hockey career. I was going to have Cameron Fucking Martinez on my team. The guy who had tossed me aside like I was a sock he jizzed in and didn't wanna bother washing. The guy who had left me like our years of friendship had meant nothing.

And they hadn't.

I had decided so on the day he walked out that door.

"Well, then," Cameron said with a pointed nod in my direction. "I'll put my trust in you since you're so cool-headed and composed."

I snorted. "Screw you, Cameron."

"I stand corrected." He shrugged, corners of his lips trembling in amusement that made me want to grab his face and squish it until smirking was the last thing he thought of.

What we should have gotten were freshmen with inflated egos who would do drills with us, but sit on the bench when we played against the Breakers next month. With Cameron here...

I didn't want to imagine it.

My position had already been out of balance. I didn't need Cameron Martinez tilting my axis further.

Taking a step forward, I inhaled and discovered a woody, smoky scent radiating off his tanned skin. *Fuck. Him.* "I'm the captain here," I hissed, bringing my face up close to his.

That just made him stretch his lips and bare his teeth in a sinister smile. "Really? Because you seem to think you're the head coach, but you're acting like a child who dropped his lollipop."

Fury I had never known was in me blazed as I grabbed Cameron's T-shirt in my fists and yanked him up close, his torso bumping against mine. But all I did was provoke a deeper grin on his face.

"Are you going to hit me, Brooks?" he asked.

Sudden movement around the soccer table stopped

abruptly, as if all the guys were on alert but unsure whether to step in. I held Cameron until his minty breath touched my face and his amused look pierced through my soul.

Every bit of me shuddered as I released him, staring into his cold, brown eyes and discovering what I had known was there all along. Naked contempt. There was so little of my friend in there that it might as well have been a totally different person.

The Cameron Martinez I had known years ago was still gone. He wasn't coming back. And living with that fact had been easy so long as this creature wearing Cameron's body was half the country away. But to see this person, who looked identical to my first and only flame, here, disregarding me, soon rendered me into that gullible, delusional boy I had been on the day he had broken my heart.

I turned on my heels and marched right the fuck back to my room, the whispers and chatter that erupted in the basement as I'd shut the door behind me still rang in my ears. Caden only needed to look at me once to know not to ask.

Instead, he shut the notebook, snapped his fingers to get my attention, and gestured at the door of our room. "Let's go for a run."

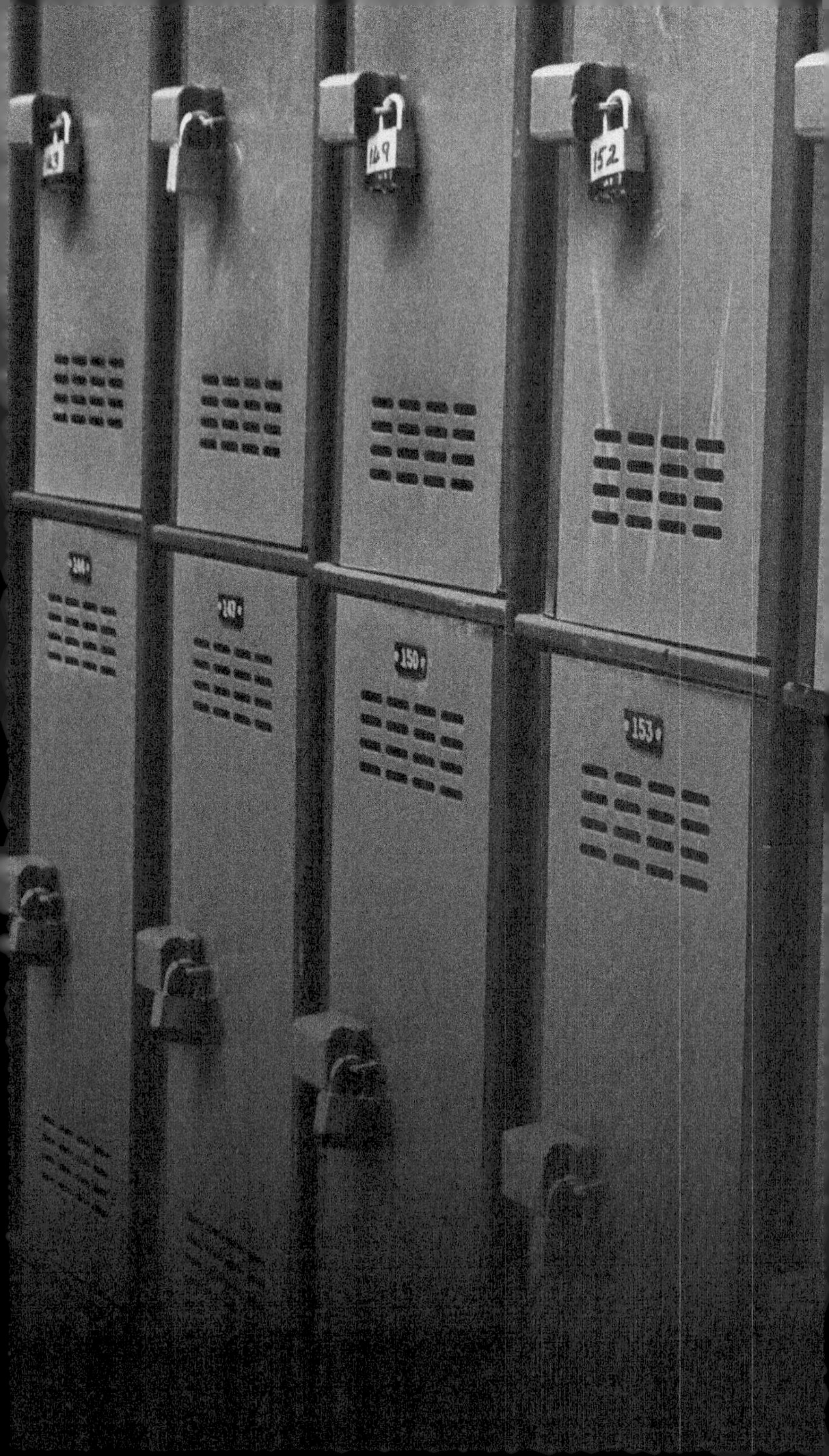
149
152
150
153

TWO

Cameron

I TINGLED ALL OVER.

It was like I'd touched a bare wire. The shock coursed through my veins as I wiped the smirk off my face. The blaze that stayed behind him was so much more than I had expected.

I cocked my head at the basement door when Riley slammed it shut and needed a moment before I realized Beckett Partridge was coming up to me with a lazy swagger. "That went well," he said.

I snorted. "He's not who I expected." I examined Beckett's amused expression and wondered for a moment how he'd gotten me to spill the beans in the first hour of knowing him. He'd sauntered in and slapped my shoulder, then warned me that the captain was coming soon. He'd tried to also warn me about the said captain's temper, but I'd stopped him there and said I already knew. One thing led to another and I'd told Beckett pretty much everything.

"How long did you say it's been? Three years?" Partridge asked.

"Three years," I mused aloud. It felt like it could have been thirty. His reddening face so near mine was etched into my mind, though. It was pressed into my memory as vividly as when he had been bringing his face up close for a whole different reason. But that was ancient history.

Still, my fingertips itched and my breaths were shaky, though I hid that well from Beckett and the rest. Riley Brooks had had his bombastic exit and it left me struggling to think. Those blue eyes were like ice ablaze and his blond hair floppy, falling over the faded sides of his head. He was bigger, too, and definitely stronger than he had been then. And that temper... Phew. It was a recent development.

A small part of me was cocky enough to think I had contributed to its making. Then again, if Riley was so petty that he would be bitter over a hookup that ended for purely geographic reasons, then maybe the temper had been in there all along. He just needed a trigger.

Beckett slapped my shoulder in what was plainly becoming a signature move for him. "You wanna know what I think? You still have a chance."

I couldn't help but laugh, albeit grimly. "Yes, because that was the face of pure longing and lust."

Beckett shrugged. "I've seen harsher flirting."

And I'd seen people hating each other for years of marriage. But I said nothing. It wasn't worth wasting my breath on. Instead, I slid out of Beckett's hold and made my way up to the ground floor where my room was. Thanks to an uneven number of guys living in the team house, I had a solo room, which was a nice fucking change from where I'd been holed up for the past three years. It was even nicer compared to the tiny, crowded place I'd called my home for most of my life. The only downside was that it would probably get pretty noisy around meal times because it was right off the kitchen, but that was a small inconvenience.

The corners of my lips dragged down as I remembered those days. They were inevitably leading to other memories that had no place being revisited now that I lived in the same house as Riley. Keeping a cool head was all that separated me from total ruin.

But that was easier said than done. Riley Brooks had always had the ability to push my buttons. Even if it was just a little, it was enough to tip me over and make me act out. I'd always teetered on the edge. The first hike in volume in my parents' arguments always sent me storming out of the house, seeking refuge in Riley, as a friend, at first. But, as inevitably as taking a breath, that had turned into something far more intimate and problematic.

I managed to pack Riley up and tuck him away in the back of my mind for the rest of the day. The trick was to stay in my room and pretend I was busy unpacking and reviewing all that was still ahead of me. A second chance at hockey and a shot at the NHL.

Moving to Santa Barbara had seemed like such a great idea three years ago. To be far away from Mom and Dad and their endless, useless wearing off of their throats. To get a clean start without all the baggage. To begin meeting guys without feeling like a street dog that got adopted by a nice family. I'd yearned to be a person of my own and it got served on a silver platter.

It was only that the person I got to be was not a nice guy. I was envious of those flashy socialites and competitive to a fault. I got into arguments with everyone who dared to give me a side look. And, slowly but surely, I grew sick of myself.

But here I was, trying again.

By the time I was done setting myself up in the room, the space around me looked only slightly different. I added a few of my hockey trophies to the shelf and sorted notebooks on the desk, filled the closet with my clothes, and stuffed the bathroom with cosmetics. But when I looked around, it could have been anyone's room. There was no me in here. Not that it mattered. For one year, I could live in a barn's attic.

As for Riley, I didn't see him until the next morning. I had only just gotten out of bed. Waking up in a new place left me confused and I needed to saunter out to seek coffee. I stepped out of my room and felt air drain out of my lungs.

Riley, wearing a pair of gray sweatpants and a sleeveless, white T-shirt was closing the door of the room at the top of the stairs and I groaned. It was barely dawn and he was already glowing like a fucking sunflower while I looked like a hobo who owned nothing but a single pair of shorts.

"Oh." It was a flat, emotionless way of greeting me.

I jerked my chin in reply.

His eyes blazed with fury, although I wasn't exactly sure what he was fuming about. Still, his gaze slid down my bare torso as he came down to the ground floor, then passed inches away from me. The large, open plan floor included a spacious common room and a kitchen with a massive island. I pulled back behind it, leaving him on the other side, but I could feel his gaze on the back of my head. It was as though he was deliberately moving slowly just so the weight of his staring would burden me.

I pretended not to notice and got busy replacing the filter in the coffee maker.

Riley's steady movement behind my back flustered me, but I pursed my lips and poured water into the tank, then searched for coffee in the cabinets. He wasn't leaving. Instead, he just stared at me from the other side of the long kitchen island. The longer he stared, the clumsier I got with the cabinets.

"What?" I asked, shutting one of the cabinets and opening the next, where I finally found the precious powder.

"What 'what?'" His voice was rough and groggy. Was this seriously the first thing he did in the morning? A jog? *Jesus Christ, what a show-off.*

I exhaled, shut the lid on the coffee maker, and pressed the button our lives depended on. Then, as calmly as I could, I turned on my heels and faced him. "Wipe your chin, Riley. You're drooling."

His cheeks burst into flames and his black eyebrows contorted. "You're such an asshole."

"You're the one who's staring," I taunted. It wasn't like I expected a warm welcome when my move here became imminent. I'd always known that being around Riley was a necessary evil. And I had accepted it as the price of a second chance at greatness.

"It's just beyond me that you would do this," he said in a restrained tone.

"Actually, having coffee first thing is a very common habit throughout the world." Mine was dripping merrily into the glass pot.

"Ha-fucking-ha." He added a slow clap for good measure. "I'm talking about transferring to Northwood in your final year. What'd you do, Cam? Ran someone over in Santa Barbara?"

My face flattened and eyes deadened. "Cameron."

Riley rolled his eyes. "Eminent Mister Martinez."

"No. Cameron is enough," I pointed out. I wasn't a child anymore and Riley had no reason to use my shortened name. Cam had been a different person. Cam had been a coward. Cam had let other people push him around for way too long.

"That fact you're not answering makes me think it's worse than that," Riley said, crossing his arms on his broad chest.

"One, you have no idea who I am or what I went through. Two, we're not friends anymore, Riley, so don't bother. And three, aren't you on your way out?" I turned away from him after counting it on my fingers and watched my coffee dripping.

"You come onto *my* team and cram yourself into *my* house, after years of silence, and you expect me to just...go along? You're ridiculous. And worse, you are cruel." His tight voice was enough to pull me back around.

"Why am I cruel? Because I don't want to share my business with someone I knew in high school?" I knew that this stung. But it was better for him to learn this lesson early on.

"That right there," Riley said, his voice audibly hurt. "That's what's cruel, Cameron. I'm not just someone you knew in high school am I?"

"What would you call it?" I asked in an expressionless tone.

"I dunno, Cam," he huffed and I winced. For a moment, I thought he was taunting me, but then I realized he wasn't even aware. "Someone you knew in high school sounds about right."

There was silence for a while and I filled it by pouring coffee into my mug. It was too hot to drink right away, so I stared at it before lifting my gaze to meet his. "Aren't you supposed to bring me up to speed around here?" It was a cheap trick to get this conversation moving and get Riley to leave.

Something went out in his eyes and he stared at me in silence for a moment. Then, he pointed his finger away from us. "Rink's that way," he said, then dragged his finger to the right. "Gym's that way. Consider yourself at full speed."

"Great job, Captain." The sneer in my tone was unmistakable, but it did the job. Riley stormed to the fridge, grabbed a bottle of water, and rushed out of the house for his morning run.

The first half of the day went by uneventfully. Despite Riley's half-assed directions, I found the rink without problems. It wasn't like Santa Barbara, where all the facilities were scattered around the city. This campus was a city of its own. Or, at the very least, a town. If I never left it for the rest of the year, I wouldn't get to explore all of it. Not that I was Dora the goddamn Explorer looking for adventure. At most, I might look into bringing a guy or ten over once in a while.

Old habits die hard.

Drills were nothing to write home about that day. Coach Murray did several rounds of pairing us up to practice standard moves and maneuvers. We were trying out each other's positions, which resulted in me playing defense most of the morning. It wasn't my preferred position. I didn't have it in me to wait in the back and protect the ground. I was an attacker by nature or design. My place was in the thick of it, hard checking and getting myself into danger. I'd been badly bruised more times than I could count, and still, the warmth of swelling flesh was the most comforting sensation I knew.

So to say that I underperformed today would be the understatement of the century.

On the bright side, I lowered everyone's expectations so that our first scrimmage next week might bring a few surprises. I also knew that these drills with swapped positions weren't all that important. Not when the true battle of wills and skills began. The idea was to broaden your understanding and have the basic set of skills for emergencies. And those boxes I checked.

But try proving that to the almighty captain. Despite nods of affirmation from the head coach and both assistant coaches, Riley stormed the locker room after practice and directed his glare at me. It was even worse that the locker I got was right next to his.

Sweat was covering his face and tousling his blond hair when he removed his helmet. I was already stripping down to my waist by the time he growled, as if he expected some kind of an apology for something.

"What?" I barked at him.

Riley's eyes narrowed until there were just slits of glowing blue coolness. "What the hell was that?"

Other guys were filing into the showers while I sat on the bench to take my skates off, but because Riley towered over me, I decided to keep the skates on instead. Slowly but surely, I rose and gained a couple of inches on him. *Who's towering now?* "Those were drills. Can I help you with anything else?"

"Is that why you transferred?" he asked. "Or was it

the attitude that nobody wanted to put up with anymore?"

I scoffed and cocked my head to the side. "Are you giving me crap for shitty defense drills? You do realize we have defenders here, right? Or should I explain team structure to you real quick?"

"I'm not sure you understand team structures," Riley said. "For one, I am the captain of this team."

"So you keep saying from the top of your lungs," I growled back. Then, after a moment of staring into each other's eyes, I jerked my chin forward. "For your information, I transferred because I wanted to be in my home state. And before you ask, it's not because I missed a special someone." That did it.

The hurt expression on his face was impossible to misunderstand. His airy voice was barely more than a whisper. "Like you're capable of anything special, Cameron."

And I felt the sting of that because it was true. "Do you really want to do this now, Riley? We were two teenage horn-dogs in a small, crappy town. Then, we grew up. Can you move the fuck on?"

"You're kidding. Me? There's nothing to move on from. It meant nothing. It just revealed to me who you are." But the way his face flushed with heat revealed him as a liar. "And I don't like that person, Cameron. So excuse me if I'm not bursting with joy that you're on my team."

"Mm. But it's not your call, is it? And here I am." I spread my arms a little, letting my gaze linger on his face as he scanned my torso and stepped back.

"Yeah," he said. "Here you are. And I can't do shit about it. So, please try to be professional out there."

"Yes, Sir." He took the mocking as intended, then spun away from me to undress. And I wished to hell I'd taken my skates off earlier because I was stuck watching Riley Brooks peel off his uniform one piece at a time.

Keeping my gaze in the opposite direction was excruciating. He tore off his shoulder pads and knee pads, he pulled his jersey over his head and tossed it into the locker, and it went on and on.

Really, I had no interest in him. None at all. I'd wronged him plenty, but he had been no angel, either. And this thing right now, this crazy, primal desire to glance over my shoulder and see his broad back, was nothing other than a symptom of a long, dry spell mixed with deadly curiosity on what my quasi-ex looked like today.

I kept that in mind when I made myself walk into the shower rather than explore the rippling muscles on Riley's back.

Cold water was exactly what I needed after two hours of drills and one hot minute of Riley all up in my business. I soaped up, rinsed, and dried quickly, then put my clothes on and hurried from the arena to the team house.

I needed to get away from everyone for a minute. From him, most of all. I needed a breather to remind myself of what I'd signed up for. Riley was just a bump in the road. I'd known he would be hard to work with after what had happened between us. This wasn't news to me. Except, I had blocked him out of my mind so successfully that I had never considered what day to day life would look like with him around.

And now that I was here, I needed to act the way I'd meant to. Like it didn't fucking matter.

Because, at the end of the day, it didn't. Not truly. We

had only even gotten together because we had had no options. I'd needed a place to hide and someone to look after me and he'd needed someone to make him feel like he was worth a damn. It was pure luck we had only been eighteen. If things were like that now, we would be the most toxic pairing in the entire galaxy. And it didn't help that he was always ridiculously hot. To the eighteen-year-old me, it had been like winning the lottery. The only other gay guy in town was my hot friend. How lucky had I been?

But it couldn't go on forever. And especially not long-distance, had we tried.

I'd always known he would end up hating me, one way or the other. And I'd always known how to make sure that happened on my terms. But seeing that hatred in every look he sent my way irked me to my marrow.

Something about Riley Brooks made me want to bark back.

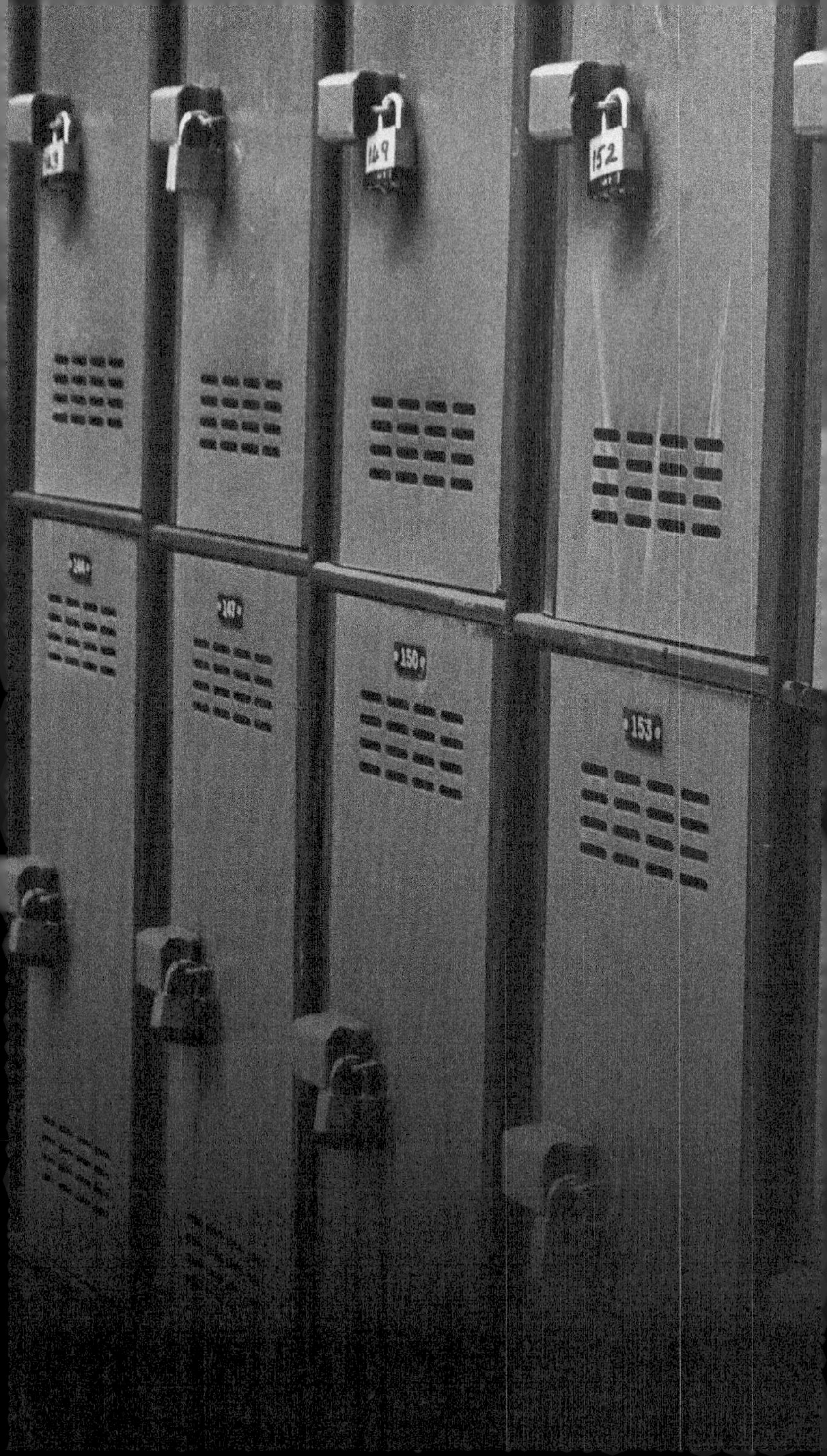
149
152
150
153

THREE

Riley

By the end of the first week back, several things became certain. One, Cameron was an irreparable, heartless asshole. Two, all he was capable of displaying were sarcasm and contempt. Three, we were not a good team like we had been in high school.

When Coach Murray paired us for power play drills on Friday, we were a travesty. The other newcomers seemed to have more grace and skill than the two of us.

It was no surprise that Coach Murray wanted to see me after the drills and I shot my coldest look in Cameron's direction because this was his fault and I was about to get the lecture for both of us. It wasn't fair. The only upside of this entire week was the fact that Cameron hadn't spoken to me since Tuesday and I managed to avoid direct contact pretty successfully. Aside from a few words of instruction on ice, we hadn't interacted.

"Coach? You wanted to see me," I said as I pushed the partially cracked door open and entered Coach's office.

"Brooks," he said, his voice pitched high and nasal, but pinning me to the spot.

"Coach, I can explain," I said, dropping the act and diving head first into it.

But Coach was still two steps ahead of me. He lifted his hand to stop me right there. "I can put two and two together for myself, thank you very much. Let me guess. You don't click together. Maybe you don't like each other. Maybe you're competitive."

I pursed my lips.

Coach lifted an eyebrow. "You knew each other, I hear."

I rolled my eyes. "Barely."

"That's not what I hear," Coach said, his tone giving me no indication as to how he felt about this. I only knew his disappointment at our terrible performance today. "But we're not here to deal in gossip."

I held his gaze while narrowing down the search for the one who spilled the story. Beckett, no doubt. But it was the fact that Cameron so easily told a total stranger about our past is what bothered me the most.

Just as I inhaled to ask Coach why we were here at all, he proceeded. "You're the leader of this team, Riley. Of the entire team. It's a privilege, yes, but it's a responsibility before all else."

"I understand that, Coach. It's just..." I mulled over my words and ended up spilling the least remarkable ones. "It's just complicated with Martinez, Sir."

Coach nodded his understanding. "That should not affect you if you still have hopes to get drafted. Think of Messier and Gretzky. Or Lemieux and Jagr. Or Pronger and Niedermayer. And they are just off the top of my head, son. You won't be the first player who couldn't get along with a teammate. You wouldn't even be the first one to lose his career because of it. But it would be a shame, Riley."

That lit a fire under my ass and I lifted my chin in defiance. "I'm not going to lose my career over Cameron Martinez."

It was in that moment, when Coach's eyes glinted, that I realized he wanted to provoke this reaction out of me. He wanted to see the determination so that he could unload the worst task onto me. "Then you'll start training him off the ice. Get your heads aligned."

The words rang in my ears for a long while. Me? Training someone as stubborn as Cameron? "He's never going to sign up for that."

Coach's gaze didn't waver when he said, "He already has."

My shoulders dropped into a 'fuck me' slouch and I closed my eyes for a moment to steady my mind. "Fine," I sighed. "If that's what it takes."

Coach sucked his teeth. "Son, that's the least it takes. The price of greatness is steep." His tone was surprisingly soft and compassionate. "I'm afraid that's a lesson you have yet to learn."

And on that ominous note, I was excused and made my way to the team house. I picked the long way around campus unintentionally. It was only when my stomach growled and I realized how late it was that I understood just how badly I wanted to be away from Cameron.

Crossing paths on ice, even without exchanging a word, was enough to bombard my attention into smithereens. His mere presence at Northwood was a threat to my position and my future. His proximity irked me, tickled my stomach, and left me flustered. He made my mind skip over things and I couldn't afford that distraction. Not the least because he'd already shown his true colors three years ago and I would be smart to remember that. No amount of brooding looks and dark locks of hair falling over his brown eyes made him any less heartless.

He was just another one in the endless line of people who thought I was good, but not excellent. I had never been good enough; not for my parents and not for the only guy I'd ever truly fallen for. Mom and Dad had always wanted another doctor. And Cam... Fuck if I knew what he wanted, but it had never been me.

The only useful thing I could do was play like hell. My entire life depended on it.

But when I built up my determination and walked into the team house, the last person on the planet I wanted to see shot up to his feet. Cameron had been sitting in an armchair in the open common area of the ground floor, a duffel bag next to his feet. Upon seeing me, he grabbed it and made two steps forward. "Let's get this over with."

"The fuck?" I rasped.

He stared at me like I was speaking in tongues. "Workout, Riley. Let's get it done."

"I literally just walked in," I spat.

"Don't take your shoes off," he replied, his black eyebrows flat over his eyes and his cheeks flushed. He'd gotten ready in a rush, I could tell.

I sighed. This was one of those times where picking your battles came in handy. Except doing what Cameron demanded left a bitter taste in my mouth. "You're such an asshole," I muttered to myself and passed him to get my gym stuff from my room.

I returned a few minutes later to find Cameron

standing by the front door. The brick, wood, and leather upholstery of the interior of our team house created a dim atmosphere that emphasized the darkness in Cameron's features. The sharp, high cheekbones and the straight nose cast shadows on his face. His resting expression was that of someone gravely impatient.

I wasn't wrong. The fucker was burning up with impatience. "Can we go already?" he asked, probably fighting the urge to tap his goddamn foot.

"Yes. Fucking yes." I marched past him and out of the house. I didn't need to look over my shoulder to know he was rushing to catch up with me.

"This isn't going to work if you're perpetually pissed, Brooks," he said.

I snorted and gave no reply. For once, I wouldn't rise to the bait. Within moments, he was walking slightly ahead of me and a late summer breeze lifted a wave of his scent, then shoved it up my nostrils. Smoky sandalwood and some kind of citrus in strong contrast. It was electric and dangerous, pushing itself into my memory and sparking images of him from years ago. Though it wasn't the same scent I had once known him for, it was close enough that I remembered every curve of his body when it towered over me and took all the earthly pleasures for our time alone.

My throat closed and I struggled for breath, making it imperative that Cameron stayed totally unaware. It didn't help at all that he was still fond of sleeveless T-shirts that left his entire arms bare and his armpits in plain view for all who cared to peek.

I didn't care to peek, but it was just there, right in front of me, dammit. And it was distracting as fuck, so I hurried to walk in front of him.

We reached the gym that was just behind the student center. Inside, there were a few girls and guys, ears plugged with headphones. The start of the semester was still three weeks away, so only the jocks and the nerds were around.

I preferred a bigger crowd. Working out in an empty gym felt like being in a haunted house, but instead of ghosts, you had really crappy music blasting out of the speakers. However, right now, a haunted gym would be better than what I had on my hands.

Cameron and I went into the locker room, nearly tumbling over one another at the door when he tried to push in front of me. "Let me pass, dammit," I grunted and headed for the far corner of the locker room. Cameron lingered closer to the door, staying at the opposite end.

Good.

I'd had enough of him undressing three inches away from me this entire week. It was like the universe was desperately trying to make us cross paths. But the universe wasn't counting on how stubborn I could be. Changing into a T-shirt and shorts was quick, methodic, and without any room for looking around. With my fists clenched and lips pursed, I paced back to the door and muttered an invitation to Cameron, who followed silently.

If there was one thing we could agree on, it was that the lack of spoken words made us get along swimmingly. The moment he opened his mouth, my temper flared; and it wasn't any different the other way around. But there was another, just as evident, truth of the universe. Cameron couldn't keep his mouth shut. "Time to align our heads, I suppose," he said in a low growl as we climbed adjacent treadmills. He checked something on his smart watch, made it beep once, then glanced over the treadmill's control board.

"He told you the same thing," I noticed. It bugged me that Coach had talked to Cameron before approaching me. "Why did you agree to this?"

Cameron was already setting a quick walking pace on his treadmill and I hurried to do mine. Glancing at his three and a half miles per hour, I set mine at three-point-eight. That wasn't ideal since my legs were shorter than his; now, Cameron looked like he was walking, and I was skipping along next to him.

He shrugged. "Maybe because I'm here to play hockey, Riley."

"And I'm not?" I demanded.

The contemptuous snort that erupted from him was designed to make my temper flare up. "Honestly? You seem preoccupied with this stupid animosity."

He would be preoccupied with it, too, if he'd ever cared about anything that had existed between us. The fact that he so casually dismissed it only helped to entrench me in my position. And my position was, 'Fuck. Him.'

"Can you maybe focus on what really matters here?" he asked, punching up his pace by half a mile per hour.

I raised mine a mere heartbeat later, sliding into a comfortable jog. "I am focused. I'm focused on bringing this team to the top. I'm focused on the championship. I'm focused on carving my way to the NHL no matter what it takes." My breaths grew short.

I spotted him glancing at my dashboard and bringing up his own pace. That was enough to force me to steady my breathing and take lungfuls of air. If he wanted to play the game of endurance, he would definitely lose. After all, I was the one who had to endure life after he'd abandoned me. My pain tolerance was above average.

Not that I would ever tell him how much it fucking hurt to lose him. Of all the people in the world, Cameron Martinez deserved that knowledge the least. By right, I shouldn't even be remembering it, but this cruel twist of fate that had brought him back in my vicinity meant I was reminded of it every waking moment.

It wasn't fucking fair.

For the next few minutes, we kept outrunning one another in a pathetic duel of wills. The fucker seemed desperate to run faster than me, but I wasn't just going to lie down and take it.

Sure enough, I ran like there was an ugly past chasing me. Sweat covered my brow and soaked my back, but that was nothing new to me. With controlled breathing and proper posture, I could do this all day.

Cameron pressed his dashboard and began speeding up, but a sudden, loud rhythm of four quick beeps made me look at him. His face twisted in annoyance.

"The hell? Are you dying?" I panted, embarrassed that I couldn't force my voice to sound any more normal.

He began lowering his speed. Although I would rather drop dead than admit it, I was glad to lower mine, too.

"Ah, abnormal heart rate," he huffed with an eye roll, tapping his smartwatch that had raised the alarm.

I scoffed. "Truly, the definition of smart."

Cameron rolled his eyes, then went into cooldown on his workout. I matched it, bringing my pace back to a nice run, then to a speedy walk a few minutes later. He looked like he wanted to say something, but he thankfully kept it to himself for the remainder of our warmups.

The same crap continued happening when we got off our treadmills and picked up dumbbells. Mr. Successful just had to go with a few more pounds even though it made his face twist and contort with exertion. And me? I had to match him, at least. I was the captain, so I was supposed to show strength. Especially to someone who, by default, didn't respect me.

My arms felt like jelly by the end of the fourth set. I saw no way to get our heads aligned this way, but I wasn't exactly planning on saying that to Coach Murray's face.

It was close to the end of our training that Cameron was leaning against a wall and his smart watch lit up. The short sound was awfully familiar; a trill that practically ended before it had started. My eyes skipped down his arm, glossy with perspiration, and caught the icon on the display just as Cameron silenced it.

"Tsk." That was all I said.

"What?" he demanded, pushing himself away from the wall. He came over to me to do his bench press set, adding twenty pounds of weights and waiting for me to answer.

"Nothing," I said.

"No. It's something. What is it?" he asked. His tone was clipped and snappy and his eyes narrow.

I inhaled and held my breath for a moment or two. "It's just… Who the hell needs a Grindr notification on their watch? Can't it wait?"

Cameron rested his hands on his hips and swayed his shoulders as he stepped up to me. Those couple of inches he had on me really mattered in moments like these. He was looking down on me and I was the one having to lift my chin and gaze. "And it doesn't bother you to think I might be fucking around?"

"Hmpf." I had a sudden urge to retreat. *Whatever you do, don't picture him fucking anyone*. "As if I care what you do off ice."

"Apparently, you do. Why else would it bother you that I have Grindr on my watch?" His expression was so smug that I wanted to wipe it off his face somehow. A few things came to mind, but I pushed them all aside.

"It's just rude," I said. "We're here to align our heads and you're busy with some fuckboy."

"Oh and you did so well aligning. All you've done was one-up me at every turn." The fucker slow-clapped. "What camaraderie. Well done, Riley. True team building right here."

I slapped his hands away with a lazy swat, but he wiggled one around and grabbed my wrist. "Get off," I barked.

"Listen to me," he said, venom in his voice finally on full display. It had only taken him five days to show his true face again. I considered myself lucky that I hadn't fallen for the quiet, brooding persona he showed everyone. "What I do in the privacy of my room is none of your business, Brooks. I'm a grown ass man with a life that isn't your concern. And just because you used to know me and we fucked, like, five times, that doesn't give you any right over my affairs. Now, grow the fuck up and let's get this thing done so we can go back to our separate lives until Monday. Okay?"

And that patronizing 'okay' at the end really rubbed me the wrong way. I spun my arm around and he lost his grip on my wrist, but I caught his. "It wasn't five times. We fucked every Sunday for months. Get your facts straight, asshole. And I'm not intruding on your shit, but excuse me if it's not a hoot to hang out with my ex while he's on Grindr."

The moment my words were out, I regretted the fuck out of them. How I wished to inhale really deep and suck them all back in. Instead, I bit my lip, intentionally hurting myself just to distract my brain from the mountain of embarrassment.

He picked up on it. And you could trust the fucker to go down the trail with the most pain. "Ex? What the hell are you talking about, Brooks? We never dated."

"I misspoke," I muttered and released him, then stepped back. "Just do your set."

He stared at me for a while longer, then added five more pounds of weights and dropped onto the bench. He did his set, then got up to let me do mine. And I would rather be damned than take off any of the weight. I was just as strong as he was.

Though it was a real struggle, I did three sets. The third one nearly killed me, but I huffed and puffed and got the bar up.

Cameron did his fourth and crossed his arms on his chest when I went for my final one. "You can take some of the weight off."

"Oh, can I?" I mocked. "Thanks, Doctor Gym."

"Fuck you." He spun on his heels while scoffing the words out.

In the meantime, I took a deep breath and prepared to suffer. Just ten reps. That was all I had to do before I could go home without tucking my tail between my legs. Ten little reps. I could do this.

The moment I freed the bar and lowered it to my chest, I knew I fucked up. My arms weren't even burning.

They were completely numb at this point. The iron bar was touching my chest and I began to exhale, which was the worst thing I could have done. Trying to push the bar off my chest, I saw only two ways forward. I would either have to tilt the bar and drop the weight on one side. Or, ideally, I would let the thing suffocate me and never suffer Cameron's gloating for this disaster.

"For fuck's sake," he muttered somewhere far away. My vision was narrowing as I pushed all my cells to burn the last of their energy to no avail.

A shadow dropped over my face and Cameron towered from somewhere above my head. He spread his legs and his loose shorts revealed a few inches of his thighs from my perspective and he grabbed the bar with both hands, then lifted it off of me.

When Cameron tugged the bar back to the safety of the bench, I growled, "No," and yanked it down. He could assist me if he insisted, but I wasn't leaving with fewer reps.

He groaned and squeezed another curse, then obliged. With one hand, he provided just enough extra strength that I could get the initial lift off my chest. My breathing was all wonky, but that was equally because his crotch was ten inches away from my face as it was because of the effort it took to lift the weight.

I did my ten reps, pretending that I hadn't been looking at the smooth skin of his thighs whenever his shorts flapped loosely or the bulge that needed no introduction. Half of me was certain he was doing this on purpose, just to feel superior and wanted. Why else would he be practically squatting over my face? And why else would he want Grindr to notify him while he wasn't near his phone to respond? It was just his vanity.

And yet, I stared.

With my throat constricting and my stomach hollowing, I stared. I looked at him until I finished the set and felt something stir deep in me, descending to my groin and shooting up my spine at once.

When I was done, I jumped up to my feet and spent only one lingering moment looking into his eyes. My breathing sped up and I wondered if I owed him a thanks for help. In the end, I didn't have enough time to decide. Cameron bent down and grabbed his water bottle, then proceeded to leave the room.

It was better that way, I decided. Thanking him would just make this dynamic extra weird. Besides, what else was the point of having him here?

I found my bottled water and drained it, then headed to the locker room. By now, Cameron was already showering, so I was safe to undress and choose the furthest shower from him. But, as I did just that, and as water soaked me from above, I needed to squeeze my eyes shut and search for ways to carve the images of his muscular thighs out of my memory.

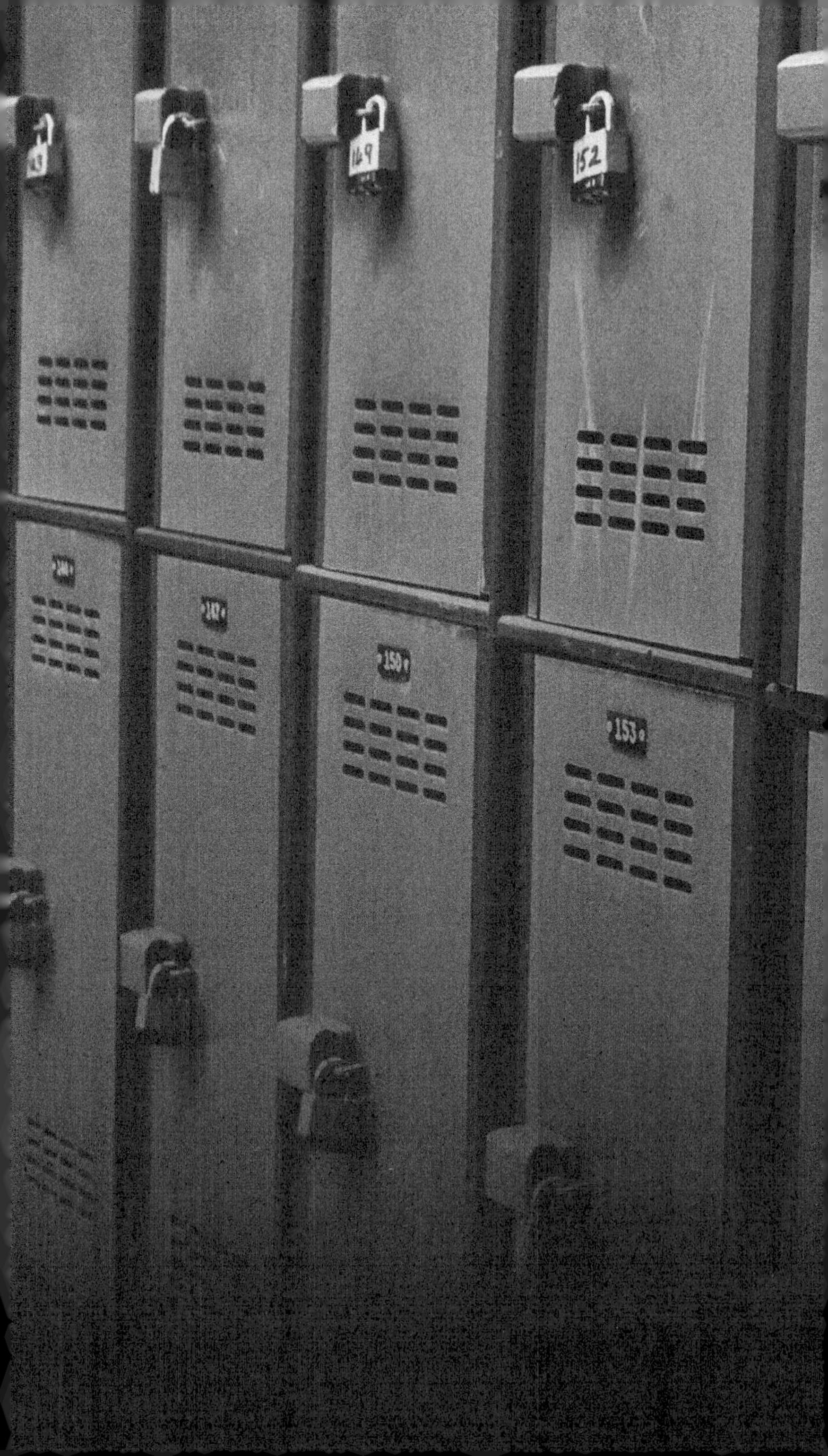
149
152
150
153

FOUR

Cameron

"You're awfully quiet," Beckett mused as we headed down the narrow lane between housing facilities. Just around the corner was a neocolonial frat house where a mass of students was shifting in and out, loud music blasting out the windows. This was the last weekend before the semester started and people needed to get the summer out of their systems.

"Hm?" I reined in my thoughts and glanced at Beckett.

He snickered. "Yeah, I'll rest my case."

"Sorry. I was miles away." I scratched the back of my head and let him pass first into the frat house. Lights were subdued inside and people were already sauntering by the look of it. It wasn't very likely I would enjoy myself tonight. Even less likely were the odds of ending this goddamn dry spell. Grindr had been of no use. Nobody tickled my interest in the slightest since I had arrived here.

Worse still, the entire idea of hitting someone up, determining a place and time, doing the deed, wiping off, and heading back bored me to death. My fist achieved the same goal just as well, but that wasn't what I was missing.

And whatever it was that I missed, I wouldn't find it at a frat party.

I'd done my fair share of parties back in Santa Barbara, so the prospect of chugging from a keg hardly excited me. But the whole team was here and I wasn't just going to let Riley think he won some silly dick measuring competition by appearing asocial.

Not that I cared what he thought.

Okay, maybe I cared a little. It was just frustrating that he was constantly looking to score a point against me. It was like he couldn't see I wasn't competing with him. *Except, you kinda are*, my voice of reason whispered.

The full truth of it was that I simply couldn't let the fucker get away with it. I was compelled to protect myself when he got too cocky. Whether he was carrying some seriously heavy baggage from our history or he was just so competitive, I didn't know. And I had no plans on finding out.

But avoiding Riley Brooks was impossible. Just as I followed Beckett into the house, I lifted my gaze to the upper floor's gallery, and held my breath. Blond, blue-eyed, deep-dimpled, and stiff as a tree trunk, Riley stood with his hands on the railing, watching the mingling crowd below. The smile on his face was a reply to something Caden Jones was saying and Riley began to turn his head to reply, but his gaze caught mine and he froze. It was like a flicker of something went out of his eyes.

My stomach felt empty, my chest hollow. He stared at me, his features hardening.

I decided that my wisest course of action was to ignore the fuck out of him. The less we went head to head, the fewer chances there were of saying something wrong.

"I see what's distracting you," Beckett said with mock seriousness.

"Him? Hmpf." It was a poor disguise because my voice cracked at the suggestion.

Beckett threw his arm over my shoulders and shook his head. "Don't get me wrong, I'm not complaining. When you guys are gone, I have two more years to build my path forward. I'm happy to eat popcorn and watch you two nuke each other's careers on ice this entire year."

I deadpanned. "But?"

His grin broadened. "But is that really what you want? This stupid feud is hurting your chances to get drafted."

"Why exactly are you telling me that?" I asked expressionlessly. "He's the one feuding."

My sole ally on this campus nodded a reluctant nod. "I'm not head-over-heels for Captain Brooks," he admitted. "But even I can tell you're not so innocent, Martinez."

"Your wisdom is much appreciated, Partridge," I said, mocking his tone.

Beckett's eyes turned lust-glazed when he spotted two girls on the other side of the large common area, so I released him into the wild. I wouldn't be seeing him tonight, I was sure. If this month of prep at Northwood had taught me anything, it was that Beckett followed his dick's ideas to a dot.

I grabbed a can of cold beer from a stoned senior and glanced around the house. Riley had disappeared from the gallery, so I went up to assume his place of the brooding overseer of things. Sipping every now and then,

I leaned over the wooden railing and watched the party heat up. As people relaxed and music picked up its beat, I said goodbye to the last hopes of scoring something more than a bathroom quickie with the lights off. I was sober and, by the look of it, the only one in that state. And maybe I was an emotionless asshole, but I wasn't exactly looking to lead some poor drunk guy on and have him puke all around.

I sighed to myself and scanned the room down below. People danced, which was nothing noteworthy, until I spotted him. He'd left here to get a drink and had no intentions of returning, it seemed. In fact, Riley was fully immersed in conversation with some guy I didn't know. They were standing by the windows where a desperately thirsty plant was enduring the fraternity's neglect. Riley laughed and even though he was too far in a loud environment, I knew he snorted mid-laugh. I'd heard him do it in the locker room and I remembered it more than a little from high school. I counted down from three and saw his cheeks turn a shade redder.

A long time ago, he had been blushing like that because of me. But that had never been real. Those had been the days of boyish fantasies and long Sunday mornings. That hadn't been real life. The reality had always existed outside his bedroom door. Couldn't he see that? Hadn't he known?

Someone bumped into me in the gallery and it jerked me from my thoughts. My attention drifted from Riley's reddening cheeks to his companion. He seemed about the same age as us, tall, dark haired and dark eyed. He was bulkier than Riley and wore a confident expression. I almost looked away and told myself not to care, but the guy leaned in and whispered something into Riley's ear while lifting his dark gaze right at me. He seemed to have stumbled over his words, eyes glued to my glowering expression.

It was too late to look aside now. I would only come across as a creep. Instead, I let my frown deepen and forced the guy to look away. But as he did, he said something else to Riley, who spun so quickly that I didn't have a moment's warning.

Shit.

His blue eyes pierced me, draining oxygen from my lungs. He let his cold gaze linger on me until I felt frostbites. In the mess that unfolded in my head, I noticed Riley turning away and the guy touching his elbow.

I tried to lose myself in the crowd that dotted the gallery, but as I went deeper into the mass, the harder it was to move any further. Someone was carrying six cups of beer and tripping over his own feet. A girl was rushing past me in visible need of a bathroom after a few too many drinks. Three guys I'd never seen before were making out against a bedroom door, seeming more confused with the amount of limbs between them than aroused. As I rolled my eyes at the utter chaos, someone grabbed my shoulder and spun me around.

I sucked in a breath of air and frowned at Riley when he brought his face close to mine. "What's your problem?"

"What? Get off me," I grunted and pushed his hand off my shoulder.

"No," he snapped and took my wrist in his hand, squeezing threateningly before releasing me. "Tell me."

"I don't know what you're talking about." I retreated two steps back. That was a mistake because I was pressing against the railing with my ass and had a furious guy rising on his toes and bringing his nose dangerously close to mine.

"Drop the act, *Cameron*," he said, mocking me for wanting to use my full name. "I'm sick of your mixed messages. Why were you staring at Vaughn? And, while we're at it, why did you tell our entire history to the biggest gossip on campus?"

I pressed Riley's hard pecs with the tips of my fingers, pushing him lightly away so I could straighten my back. "I didn't know Beckett was a gossip."

"And you didn't think to check before talking about our — what did you call it? — situation-ship in high school?" He cocked his head to one side and glared. "Is that what you tell everyone the moment you meet them?"

"Don't be ridiculous," I said, rolling my eyes.

"How am I ridiculous? Everyone knows we had a thing and I can't talk to a guy without your brooding face scaring him off." He pushed a few inches closer to me. It didn't seem to bother him that he needed to look up when scolding me.

What bothered him was the laugh I barked out. "If that's what it takes to scare a guy off, you're better on your own."

Riley's fury escalated when I said that. And, upon reflection, I could totally see why. "That's none of your fucking business," he spat, his lips inches away from mine. It tightened my chest and made my body tingle with an odd mix of excitement and fear. Not that I was afraid of Riley. He could bark all he liked. But I couldn't shake this feeling off. I'd had it so many times in the month we had spent clashing on ice, at the gym, and in the locker room. "Maybe I should decide who's worth my time and who isn't." He gave me such a pointed look that there was no mistaking his meaning. I wasn't worth his time.

And yet, here he was, inching closer into me. I straightened, practically threatening him with physical contact if he didn't step back. He did, but only enough so we wouldn't touch. "Riley, I wasn't trying to scare your boy toy away," I said flatly. "It would be a very pathetic thing to do." And yet, the nerve of that guy to just put his hands all over Riley bugged me more than words could say.

"I wouldn't put it past you," he muttered.

I narrowed my eyes, deciding not to give him the pleasure of knowing I might have had a zing of jealousy. A long time ago, he had been mine, even if that pipe dream never could have lasted. "That's rich coming from someone who got all flustered over my Grindr message."

Riley's cheeks reddened. "I didn't... That's not..."

A moment of confusion was all I needed to round on him and swap our positions. It had been too long since the last time I was in control. Three years of distance and a month of me keeping my head low gave Riley some ridiculous fancies about this power dynamic. Pressed against the railing and with nowhere to go, he jutted his chin out in defiance that did little to soften me. I leaned in, fearlessly allowing my body to press against his even though his heat on me was the last thing I needed. "You're forgetting yourself, Brooks," I growled into his ear. "Maybe you have had your skates licked too much since your captaincy, but don't expect me to follow along. I'm not someone you can boss around, Riley. Or did you forget that?"

The heat that radiated off his body seemed to rise by ten degrees in the next instant. He was still. As I pulled back from his ear, I glanced down and noticed the goosebumps along his neck. His blue eyes were wide, black eyebrows high on his brow in surprise. He licked those red lips quickly and recuperated enough to frown at me. "We're not those boys anymore," he huffed. "As you keep reminding me."

For the briefest of moments, it felt like firecrackers went off in my chest. I didn't want to dive into the useless talk of why things had gone this way or that way. None of that mattered. The facts were as plain as they could be. I'd broken off whatever it had been that we'd had and Riley was far more butt-hurt about it. Had I not done it, he would have dumped me sooner or later. Or we would have turned into a horribly codependent couple. And that would have been worse than what had actually happened.

But right now, as we entered an impromptu staring contest, jitters filled me. The memory of those Sundays blazed before my eyes. Riley's skinny frame that made him the butt of all the jokes on our high school team and the fierce desire to do anything and everything in the two hours of privacy we'd had each week; the fire that burned in him to this day had once been directed to the sweetest, most exciting acts of pleasure. And, as I glared at him now, I could see that it had never truly gone out. He was just as feisty, but not nearly as skinny as he had been in high school.

Where the years had worn me down, they'd only shaped him into someone far more cocky. And, admittedly, handsome. The momentary temptation to seek common ground with my oldest friend and first flame just because there existed such a bright passion somewhere behind his cold glare was hard to push aside.

I held my breath just so I wouldn't wheeze before him. It took me a moment to find my voice again and pitch it low. And there, I went in for the kill. "You're right. We're not those boys anymore. You'd better keep that in mind. If I could break your heart so easily at eighteen, what do you think I'm capable of after three years of booze and sex and deprivation?"

His expression melted into some blend of horror and hatred. He detested everything about me as plain as day. And it was just simpler that way. But he managed to squeeze out a few more words. "For you to hurt me, I'd need to give a fuck, Cam. But you've taught me how to not care."

"Good."

I turned on my heels and marched out of the frat house. The storm of emotions that warred in me ranged from self-pity to hateful competition. But what I tried and failed to ignore was the sliver of excitement. I hadn't been this close to him in years. I hadn't had my lips so near his earlobe since high school. I hadn't felt his wavy blond hair brushing against my cheek since the morning I last had him in my arms.

We were probably the wrongest choice for one another. I had resented him, to a degree, my entire life, even at our closest. He hated me for putting myself first for once in my shitty existence. If there was such a thing as self-destruction by lust, he would be mine. Just the scent of his sea breeze cologne made my cock stir. And if I allowed myself to think of the things I'd wished to do when he was at his snappiest, I would soon find myself panting for air. He irked me in ways nobody ever had or would. The defiance in those eyes and the way his nostrils flared made me want to put him in his place any way I could.

And I knew one way of subduing Riley Brooks. But that way was as off limits as it could get.

At the empty team house, I slammed and locked my door, undressed, and treated myself to a cold shower. My head was spinning with conflicting thoughts that attacked one another, but one thing was constant. Riley Brooks had inadvertently made me hard and the cold water wasn't cutting it.

Either this dry spell had left me far more desperate than I'd realized, or it was muscle memory reacting to his proximity. I only knew I needed to tread very carefully from now on.

But that was a lie.

I knew one other thing that terrified me. It wasn't just sex I was lacking. That much I could get with a few taps on my phone. It was the familiarity. It was the companionship. It was the sense of longing for a place I'd never known. And Riley ticked those boxes just by being who he was.

I'm not doing it, I told myself firmly. *I'm not considering it. He doesn't even want to be near me and the only thing that can come out of all this baggage and resentment is heartbreak.*

I kept telling myself these things all the while closing my eyes and pulling an old memory from the depths of my mind. A Sunday morning. His family wore their best clothes for the mass. It was spring. The fact that Easter was only one week away made it so much more sinful to sneak behind their righteous backs. Riley was at his wildest so far and he had me every way a human body would allow, doing goddamn splits on the bed while moaning the roof off the house.

Sliding back into those days was so much easier than I'd expected. It was all still intact in my consciousness. His scents and sounds, the feel of his fingertips dragging along my torso, and the pain when he grabbed fistfuls of my hair as he neared his orgasm. I'd preserved it all in my head for years.

Afterwards, as I lay in my soulless dorm room, guilt wrecked me. The emptiness of the last three years of my life threatened to engulf me and carry me far from the coast. The longing for something more hadn't faded even for an iota.I grabbed the pillow and pressed it over my face, then growled into it to no relief.

Frustrated out of my mind, I got up, put some clothes on, and headed to the basement. Everyone was at the party except me, so I browsed the common area with a can of cold beer in my hand until I came upon another ancient memory. On the far side of the basement, near the soccer table, up against the red brick wall, was a gaming console I had spent hours enjoying, side by side with Riley, who had always been glowing after soaring through heaven and hell with me.

He still had it. Here, in the common room, was his old *PlayStation*.

I chugged the beer and decided I didn't care if it pissed him off that I touched something of his. It was in the common room. And I was the common folk of the house. Losing myself in *The Fallen Order* for a few hours suddenly seemed like the brightest prospect a wreck like me had.

And, for the first time in longer than I cared to remember, I actually, truly smiled.

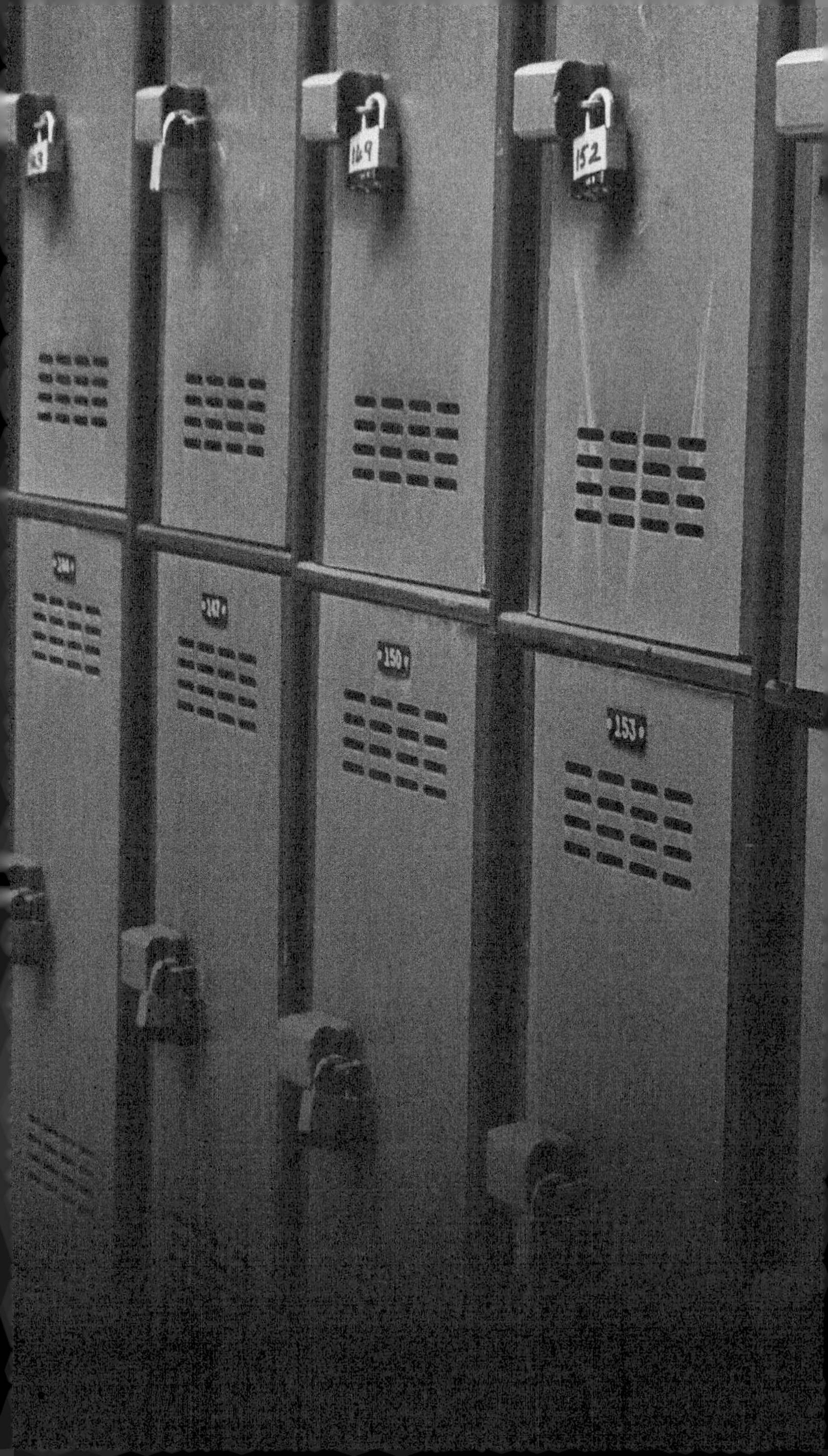
149
152
150
153

FIVE

Riley

It felt like the first week of the semester slapped me across my face early on Monday and continued slapping me all the way until Friday. My head was spinning and my ears were ringing with the amount of work I was assigned. Normally, I had no problems haunting the team house and mulling over my notes most hours of most days, but with Cameron having a similar idea, we bumped into one another way too many times. And he was a distraction I couldn't afford in my final year.

I hadn't forgiven him for scaring Vaughn off last weekend. In fact, the nerve of that move bugged me so much that I found myself scanning the hallways for any sign of Cameron attempting to flirt with someone, be it at the house or in some of the faculty buildings we shared.

The odd thing about that was how little I discovered. The more I looked, the less I found. Cameron was in every night and nobody was coming over. Other guys on the team were bringing enough girls over that it warranted a revolving door, even if they thought they were being sneaky about it.

I didn't have a plan on what to do if I discovered him with some guy. Would I stare like he had at the party? Would I pretend I hadn't seen anything? It didn't matter in the end, because Cameron haunted the hallways with that sulky expression and few people interacted with him. Beckett was there whenever he wasn't flirting with every girl that was so unlucky to cross his path, but Beckett was just sniffing out trouble for his schemes. Sawyer, who outmatched Cameron in quiet brooding, sometimes sat in the same room as Cam, but no words were spoken beyond a passing 'Sup, dude.' And Caden, loyal to a fault, avoided my arch nemesis like it had been his heart Cameron had broken.

All in all, Cameron led a quiet life whenever I wasn't in his immediate vicinity.

On Friday evening, after two hard sessions of on-ice drills this week, we filled the locker room in prep for a scrimmage. Two weeks from now, we would kick off this season with a game against the Breakers and I was dead set to win the first match.

I stripped down to my underwear and began to armor myself like always. Ignoring Cameron, who was doing the same two feet to my right, would have been so much easier had he not spilled a gallon of his cologne all over himself. His unruly dark hair kept falling over his brow as he peeled off his pants and my breath hitched. He lifted his gaze through the messy locks and pinned me with his eyes. "Can you stop doing that, Brooks?" He stepped out of his pants and straightened, then brushed the rebellious locks aside with one hand. "You've been staring for a week."

He was courteous enough to keep his voice low under the chatter of the locker room where the excitement and anxiety were growing with each passing second. "I haven't," I protested.

Cameron stepped toward me. "If you're so desperate to see it…"

He didn't get a chance to finish that sentence. He'd leaned into my space an inch too close and I pushed him back. He staggered, a proper shock rippling on his face, and laughed darkly.

"What do you want, then?" he asked.

If only he wasn't in his fucking underwear. I directed all my effort at looking at his face. If I dropped my gaze now, I would be a dead man. "You're imagining things, Martinez," I spat. "I wouldn't look at you if you were the last guy on the planet."

"Not even to save the species?" Beckett murmured, his smirk stretching.

"We can't fucking reproduce, Partridge," I snapped, tempted to pinch the bridge of my nose and sigh.

Beckett shrugged. "You can try."

Cameron snorted in amusement, but I glared at them both. "Enough."

"Not to be crass," Beckett said while setting his shoulder pads in place and picking up his helmet a heartbeat later. He was fully dressed while Cameron and I still stood in our underwear. "But you two look like you should hash it out somewhere private."

"Partridge, I swear to God," I huffed, wincing at my choice of words. It was a remnant from my home and not using His name in vain.

"Sorry, Cap," Beckett said innocently, his shrug accepted with the pads on his broad shoulders. "We're all dressed and you two look like you're not even done undressing."

"Dude," Cameron sighed at Beckett, but got a slap on the shoulder and a friendly shake. Beckett made his way out of the locker room, madly proud of himself by the way his shoulders swayed.

"See what you did?" I asked quietly.

Cameron's expression turned to hurt quicker than I'd expected. "I didn't do anything."

"No. Of course. You just spilled our entire story like it's got nothing to do with you." The words spilled fast and I yanked my jersey out of the locker, pulled it over my head, and continued gearing up with quick, vicious moves.

Cameron stood still, looking at me without his signature look of superiority. His muscles bunched as he bent down to put his socks on, but I directed my gaze elsewhere. Looking at him hurt way too fucking much. It shouldn't have, but it did. Underneath all the contempt I had for my high school fling, this runaway guy had been my entire world once. And watching him treat our history like it had been nothing stung more than I wished to admit.

"Riley, I didn't…" he began in a whisper.

I rounded on him, fully dressed against his bare torso, and pinned him against the locker. "Don't talk to me, Cameron. Whenever you open your mouth, you make it worse."

He winced and looked away, which I considered my victory for once. As I stepped back, he rasped, "You're wrong."

I snorted and marched out of the locker room with my skates in my hands, unwilling to spend another minute alone with him. And as I did, I decided not to wonder what it was I was wrong about. That he didn't make things worse by talking? That he hadn't spilled our story carelessly? That he wasn't treating us like acquaintances? Take a guess. I was right about all of them.

I put my skates on and joined the rest of my team out on the ice. Coach Murray was already checking the time and I made a point of apologizing for my tardiness. Then, we waited for Cam, who took an extra few minutes to get ready.

When we all lined up, Coach Murray scanned us with his steely eyes and nodded impatiently. "Let's keep it punctual, guys, or we'll have locker room drills next week."

A ripple of low laughter passed through most of the team, but Coach was too busy outlining strategies to let it settle. Today, we were scrimmaging and sparing no quarters. And of course Cameron and I played center for the opposing teams.

Coach was slapping his hands impatiently as we spilled around the rink on our skates. "Show me what you've got, boys," Coach chimed.

And show him we did. The ice was a blur beneath my skates as I weaved through the frozen battlefield. The sound of sharp blades scraping against the ice reverberated through the arena, drowning out the cheers of the spectators. I gripped my stick tightly, feeling the familiar weight in my hands as I charged forward, eyes fixed on the goal.

The first twenty minutes of the scrimmage were a whirlwind of speed and intensity. Every stride, every pass, every shot carried the weight of years of competition. As I raced down the ice, the cold air stung my cheeks, igniting a fire within me. I dodged an opposing defenseman, cutting through their line of defense. The puck danced with my stick, waiting for the perfect moment to strike. With a flick of my wrist, it soared towards the net, only to be met by the goalie's outstretched pad.

Cameron, relentless as ever, retaliated with a thundering slap shot that sent the puck sailing towards our goal. Sawyer, playing for my team today, was a wall of determination, and deflected the puck with a lightning-fast glove save.

Back and forth we battled, the ice becoming our arena of determination. Bodies crashed against the boards, sticks clashed with a symphony of resounding thuds. Every pass, every check, carried the weight of the game. As the first twenty minutes drew to a close, beads of sweat mingled with the cold air, freezing on my brow. I glanced at the scoreboard, the numbers deadlocked. Neither team willing to surrender an inch.

Cameron gloated for another twenty minutes, but by the last round we were all exhausted. Coach Murray wanted us to battle, so we battled. I gave it my all, partially inspired by the flickering image of the NHL drafting and partially by the desire to wipe the smug smile off Cameron's face. That he would be so casual about months of intimacy and treat me like nothing more than a long-ago hookup reached deep into my heart and touched the very familiar feeling of worthlessness. Not only was I planning to chase this puck for the rest of my working days and not only was I rendered to the last place on Cameron's list of people who mattered, but deep within me, like a ball of darkness, the fact that had defined my entire life unraveled. A gay son to people who attended Sunday mass their entire lives. A gay brother to a man who believed in prayer just as much as he believed in the medicine he practiced every day. A gay hockey player with a head full of silly dreams of the NHL.

What a twisted freaking joke.

It filled me with anger as we warred for the final twenty minutes and I wanted to let the fire spread out from inside me. This anger was almost like a blanket of comfort. Since the day Cameron had shown me how tender a human heart was, I knew how to grab this anger and wrap myself in it.

I spotted him as he snatched the puck from Caden and glided toward us. Determination fueled my stride as I tracked him relentlessly, my eyes fixed on his every move. Anger bubbled and welled within me. With a burst of speed, I closed the gap, feeling the adrenaline surge through my veins. Then, with a perfectly timed hit, I delivered a bone-crushing check, sending him crashing into the boards. The impact reverberated through the arena, drowning out all other sound. In that moment, a mix of satisfaction and fierce rivalry coursed through me, fueling my desire to dominate the game.

"What the fuck?" Cameron staggered, his eyes wide with surprise and frustration. A mix of anger and determination flashed across his face as he quickly regained his composure. I could see the fire burning in his eyes, his competitive spirit refusing to be extinguished. With a swift push, he propelled himself back into the game, his resolve unshaken. It was a fleeting moment, but I sensed the simmering intensity, the unspoken vow to retaliate. But there was more to it.

The hurt look on his face had nothing to do with being crushed against the boards. Those eyes were flashing with anger that wasn't directed at his opponent. I was soon filled with guilt that I bruised him so harshly for so little. And though the instant passed before I could bat my eyelashes, it left a bitter coating in my mouth.

I spotted Coach Murray glaring at me after the incident. I hadn't body checked him too harshly to get my ass sent to the sin bin, but we both knew I'd done it not because I had to, but because I saw an opportunity. He knew what I'd done.

Even so, as we skated after the puck, I could almost feel the pressure of my body against his, trapping his against the boards. I'd shouldered him, but my need to assert dominance over Cameron Martinez was stronger than my reason, so I had turned and pushed him with the entirety of my torso. Even under all the protective gear that bulked up our bodies, I could feel *him*. My vicious mind supplied the memories right away; Cam, topless and sweaty, sitting at the edge of my bed, playing games silently while I watched his broad back and sweat-matted hair, feeling the tingling aftermath of our passion.

The scrimmage was yet another disaster in a long list of failures of the season. Coach was shaking his head at every turn and we wrapped up the scrimmage with Cameron's team narrowly winning to my deep chagrin.

It wasn't surprising that, after we all showered and dressed, everyone filed out except Cameron and me. Coach had marched into the locker room to invite us both to stay. Caden, as loyal as ever, had raised his hackles and offered to wait for me, but I sent him away. This was my shit to deal with.

Cameron and I shouldered one another at the office door with me taking the satisfaction in winning this round and walking in first. Coach Murray, however, seemed utterly defeated.

I stood shoulder to shoulder with the guy that had once consumed my dreams. We looked at our feet as much as we looked at Coach Murray until he spoke. Then, our gazes locked onto his mustache and we both shuffled uncomfortably. "I have never seen this level of competitiveness," Coach said in the beginning.

Something in me flared with hope. "But that's good, right?" I asked before I could stop myself. "Competition makes us better."

By the glare Coach Murray directed at me, I knew I had said something profoundly stupid. Heat blossomed in my cheeks when Cameron muttered: "Stop talking."

Coach set his hands on his desk and got up. "In my twenty years of doing this, I have never seen a pair happier to prove that adage wrong. No, Brooks. You are most definitely not making each other better." The restrained anger in his voice was the closest I'd ever heard Coach Murray to actual rage. He was a calm, composed man who dealt in quiet disappointment rather than outbursts of shouting and insults. Even now, his demeanor was that of a father who couldn't believe what his son had done. There was protectiveness in there, but it was buried deep beneath the disappointment.

It shamed me.

"You two cotton-heads are so preoccupied with this childish rivalry that you are completely forgetting why you are here in the first place. Today's scrimmage was a travesty and I will sooner take you both off the team than let you bring everyone down with your games when we face the Breakers. Am I making myself clear?" The clipped words cut me deep. I was the goddamn captain of this team. He couldn't do this to me.

But I also knew the flip side. I couldn't blame

Cameron for my shitty performance. Yes, the fucker got under my skin and distracted me, but it was my own fucking fault that I'd let myself be distracted. Every muscle in my body tensed as I listened to the coach. I widened my stance and pulled my shoulders back, taking it like a grown up. My chin lifted just as Cameron jerked his head up.

Coach tapped the wooden surface of his desk with a knuckle, buying himself a moment of silence and pulling both our attention to him. "You have two weeks to straighten up, boys. Otherwise, one will have to go." I held my breath and wondered if that meant Cameron's ass was on the line. But Coach read my mind and pinned me with a stare. "And Brooks, just because I named you the captain, it doesn't make you safe. I'll make my decision rationally and consider what's best for the team."

My heart pounded twice its normal rate. If I wore one of those stupid watches like Cameron, it would be blaring right about now. "Coach, please..."

"I think I've made myself clear." Coach's stare hardened.

I wish I could have been the one thinking rationally at that moment. I wish I could say I had thought of making the next move. But it wasn't me. I was a mess of jumbled thoughts. My entire life, I had been focused on hockey because everything else was like grasping for a beam of sunshine that penetrated a forest canopy. This had been my only constant. As soon as I realized that being gay would cost me my family — as it had in its own way — and that falling in love was a risky endeavor bound to result in heartbreak, I had hardened myself and remained focused on the game. And now, as Coach Murray dangled the possibility of taking my future away, my mind was spinning.

But Cameron was composed enough to do the right thing and I hated myself for it much more than I hated him. It should have been me who asked the question. He swallowed, nodded, and lifted his head a little. "How can we do better?"

Coach Murray was silent for a beat. It was almost like he was taken aback by the rightness of Cameron's thinking.

I bit the inside of my cheek, anger at my own messy emotions dominating. I hated that I depended on Cameron Martinez to get out of this mess. And right now, he was all that stood between one of us dropping out.

Coach considered this question carefully, then nodded to himself. "Are you conditioning together?" he asked first.

We gave half-hearted nods. It hadn't exactly been great. We had been going to the gym around the same time and we had been acknowledging one another's presence. But that had been it.

"That's a 'no.' Very well. You will start tomorrow. Fitness and conditioning five times a week. On-ice practice with the rest of the team as scheduled. And..." Coach hesitated and glanced at his computer screen, then stepped back from his desk and crossed his arms on his chest. "Tomorrow, seven am sharp, I'll have you both in full gear, on ice, learning basics."

A frown contorted my face, but I bit my tongue and remained silent just like Cameron.

"Basics," Coach repeated. "You'll pretend you've

never seen a puck in your entire life. Heller will guide you through the first session."

I opened my mouth to say something, but I realized it was going to be a protest so I shut it closed again. With a nod, I swallowed the welling words and glanced at Cameron. He was expressionless and so subdued that I wondered what the hell had happened to him.

This was far from the guy I had once known. This guy was just taking it like a champ, culled and on the verge of surrender.

And, as Coach Murray dismissed us, I fell in line behind Cameron, inhaling a lungful of air and his spicy, smoky scent. We didn't speak a word, but I stared at the back of his head and realized that we had both changed since the old days.

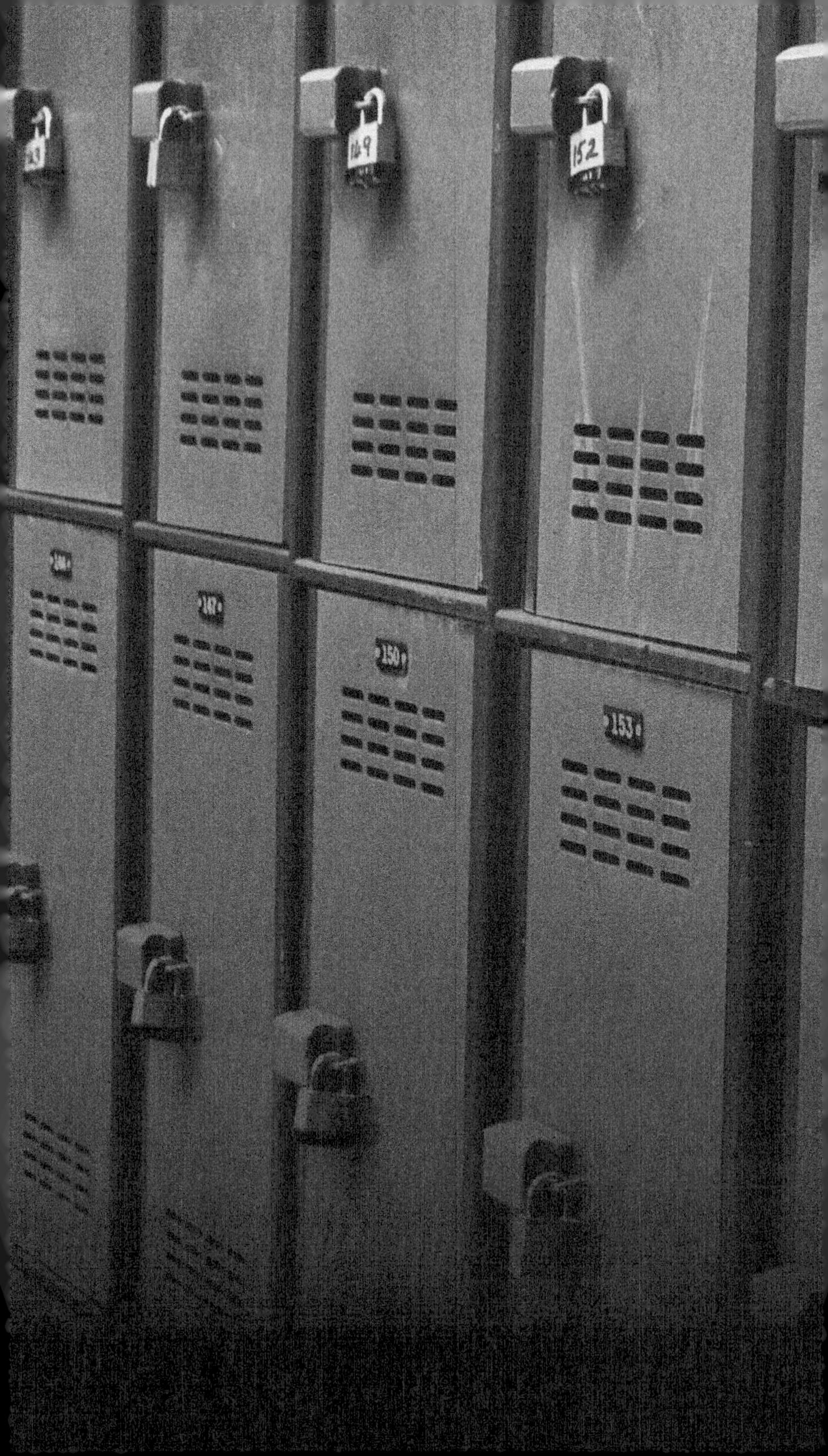
169
152
150
153

SIX

Cameron

I CLUTCHED MY STICK AND STOOD STILL, INCHES away from Riley, as the cool air bit my nostrils. Assistant Coach Brent Heller walked in with a lopsided grin at exactly seven in the morning.

For the past four minutes, Riley and I had been standing in total silence. In fact, all he had said since we crossed paths at the team house was: "This is bullshit." I couldn't agree more, but I knew to keep that to myself.

"Morning, guys," Brent said. He was a handful of years our senior and normally played the part of a mediator between the team and Coach Murray. He was the good cop when Coach Murray's patience thinned. Which, in just over a month of being on this team, we had managed to do many times.

The talk among the teammates last night had been that Coach Murray was at the end of his wits with us. Nobody had seen him agitated this often and this much in the past. The fact that it correlated with my arrival meant I had to be extra careful to prove there was no causation. Just because Riley decided to make everything hard because he was pissed at my presence, I wasn't actually the cause of this mess.

Not directly, at least.

He needed to grow the hell up and I needed to get him out of my head. It was easier said than done when he pouted like a brat and I had the strongest urge to spank him into obedience.

My cheeks heated and I prayed to all the gods listening that it could pass as being cold this early in the day.

We greeted Heller and waited for instructions. This ridiculous exercise was going to suck balls twice as hard now that I'd considered spanking Riley.

I pursed my lips and breathed slower to get my pulse down.

"Right," Heller said into the open folder. "Seems like easy drills to me." He looked up at us and tossed the folder on one of the seats nearby. As he crossed his arms on his chest, his blue eyes catching a mischievous glint, he gestured at the puck with his head. "Can anyone tell me what that is?"

I snorted and Riley visibly tensed.

"Alright. Enough fooling around. Let's start from the top," Heller said, chuckling to himself. "Coach Murray wants you guys to practice the very basics, so that's what we'll do. I'd love to know what you've done to earn that fate, but we can leave that for later. I'd also love to know what I've done to be tasked with this when I have a pregnant wife at home to take care of, but that, too, can wait. As for right now, Brooks, you'll be our goalie, and Martinez, you'll be learning how to lead the puck. Nothing fancy, alright? Just...lead the thing and try to score. Alright? Alright." He clapped his hands, signaling us to get in our positions.

Exhaling in annoyance, Riley skated over to one of the goal posts and I dragged myself and the puck to the middle of the rink.

"Do I need to explain any of the rules?" Heller asked.

"No," Riley and I replied in unison.

"Let's go, then," Heller said, his impatience rising. I felt sorry for the guy. He was supposed to be off and there was no way he didn't blame the two of us for being dragged to campus when his wife benefited from his company more.

I held my breath, then began to play as instructed. I didn't understand what the point of this exercise was, but I could do my part and make sure Heller was free sooner rather than later. Slowly, almost clumsily, I led the puck across the ice, my blades cutting against the frosty surface and the cold biting my cheeks and eyes.

Riley, who was as baffled as me at the mystery of our purpose here, stood at the goal post and glared at me. Obviously, my meager attempt at scoring was exaggeratedly clumsy. He defended his goal with two swift moves of his skates and a predictable switch of his stick. In an instant, Riley had the puck and began showing off as he led it away from me, across the rink, and to the other goal post. He was spinning skillfully, seemingly lost in some mixture of ballet and battle, until Heller blew his whistle.

"Nothing fancy, Brooks," he shouted from against the boards. "Beginner lessons, remember?"

Riley mock saluted Heller and finished his maneuver by scoring into an empty, undefended goal post.

"Well done, Riley," I called across the ice, slow-clapping with my gloves on. "You really showed me how it's done."

He spread his arms wide in defense. "What's the point of this?"

Heller answered the question before my silence could reveal I knew as little as Riley. "The point is to get you two to work together, Brooks. And if you can't show Coach Murray that you're able to set your differences aside for the duration of practice, it's not gonna be nice. Let's try this again, alright? Martinez, you're the goalie. Brooks, keep it simple."

Brooks did not keep it simple. He tried to, but the moment he lifted his gaze off the puck and met mine, he did the old bait and switch, trying to fool me. I wasn't going to rise to the bait. I wasn't going to fall for his taunting. We were here for the exact opposite reason. And yet, as he shared a smug smirk, the space between my eyebrows creased and I found myself skating out.

He had been needlessly harsh yesterday. And sure, the rules allowed as much, but he had gone into me for a reason, rather than simply snatching the puck from me like he could have.

And for all my forced calm, I hated being in this position. So, when I found myself nearly clashing into Riley, we began a fierce battle for the puck. I stole it, but he was as swift as ever in catching up with me and kicking it aside when he couldn't control it.

The whistle blew furiously, but we didn't pay attention to Heller until the second time. "Stop. Guys, stop this. I...I gotta..."

Riley and I slowed down and Riley gave a little twirl on ice just to spice up his performance, then faced Heller.

"Guys, that's all wrong," he said hastily. "You're not

listening." He was holding his phone and backing away. "I gotta take this. Just wait there and stop flaunting." Heller spun away and disappeared while Riley and I caught our breaths.

"What's the matter with you?" I asked in a low growl, taking my helmet off.

"Jesus, Cameron. This is ridiculous. Can we agree on that?" he asked.

My silence was all the confirmation he needed. He tore off his helmet and revealed his heated cheeks. His blond hair was matted and darker now that sweat had dampened it. His cold gaze was like fury and it rubbed me the wrong way. I pressed my stick against the ice and slid toward him until we were barely a couple of inches apart. "You're risking both our careers just because you're a brat, Riley."

"Screw you, Cameron." He pouted and my vision narrowed, a dark vignette framing it and Riley glowing in the center. I wanted to grab him, and shake him.

"You're effectively screwing me already, Riley." I leaned in until I could feel the heat of his face on mine. "And if you want to tank your future because of this, be my guest, but I won't be dragged down with you." I glared at him as he opened his mouth to speak, then continued. "I know you don't actually want to destroy yourself, Brooks. So get off your high horse and play, dammit. Can you do that much?"

He chewed his lower lip as his face hardened. This moment of silence felt like an awkward eternity. A brief tremor passed around the corners of his mouth and he frowned. "How is this so easy for you, Cam?"

I clenched my jaw. He was relentless. "Why is it so hard for you?" I asked coldly.

An air of determination passed over him as I relaxed a little and pulled back from him. "I don't know," he said in a flat tone.

He truly wasn't over it all. He hadn't forgiven me, but he'd never given me a chance to explain, either. I opened my mouth, although I had no clue where I was heading with this, and inhaled to speak.

"Sorry, guys, I'm going to have to leave you to practice on your own," Heller said, rushing back in. "It's my wife. We're having a baby." His voice was ecstatic and Riley and I managed to exchange a confused look before spilling awkward congratulations and wishing them well. Heller barely noticed us as he collected his things from the bench and dangled the keys before us. "Murray said to leave these with you. Lock up when you're done. Or he will. Not sure what he said. Sorry. Gotta go." Frantically, Heller picked up the folder and his backpack, then ran out.

Riley and I stood still, dumbfounded, and let the realization sink in. Coach Murray still expected us to do these drills.

I exhaled and yanked the helmet back on my head.

"What are you doing?" Riley cocked his head to one side.

I spread my arms and shrugged guilelessly. "Let's just play."

"Play? I, um..." He moved the helmet around in his hands, then gave in. "What the hell," he sighed and pulled the helmet on. We left the puck in the middle of the rink and skated in opposite directions. What followed next was forty-five minutes of blood-thirsty battling, skirmishes, and body checks.

For a short while, as sweat, fire, and ice mixed and

merged, I forgot who he was. Hell, I forgot who I was. I forgot the way I had felt for the past three years. I forgot the hopes that had led me back to Michigan. I forgot the bitter disappointment when none of the things I'd expected came to pass. The only thing that mattered, for a little while, was the rubber disk sliding between Riley and me.

We weren't keeping a score, for once. We had tried, in the first few minutes, but we soon lost count. And so, we let a short while pass. We let this thing play out and we struggled to outdo the other, but there was something so profoundly different that I was certain Riley felt it too.

It was fun.

It was pure, swaggering fun as we whirled and skated and slammed each other against the boards. There was no anger in me when I hard checked him. In fact, pinning him against the boards and getting our helmets to bump against one another only gave me a glimpse of a time long gone. Way back in our senior year of high school, when the first feelings of attraction and excitement had emerged, I had been craving these moments like a starving man. I had been dying for body checks like these just to feel Riley Brooks on me.

The excitement and fun of the game returned to me in this silly little exercise. And when we were heaving for air and dripping with sweat that would soon freeze on our faces, I took my helmet off and grinned from across the rink.

I didn't know what the hell I expected. The bubble in which we had existed for the better part of the last hour burst as soon as the game was over. Riley spotted me, but turned away and headed for the locker room instead.

I skated quickly to the other end of the rink and took

my skates off as soon as I could. In the locker room, still adjusting to standing on my own two feet, I found Riley partially undressed. The eerie silence of this place felt like reality was slightly altered. Normally, this place was brimming with guys who had a lot to say. Now, there was nothing. Just the tearing of velcro filled the locker room with a rapturing sound.

As quickly as we had fallen into the good old fun of hockey, we had fallen back into the awkward, agitated silence just as fast. Riley stripped down to his underwear and grabbed a towel from his locker, then walked away.

I told myself there was no reason for me to care. We'd shared an hour on ice that wasn't as hate-filled as all the other moments we had had to endure this month. It wasn't groundbreaking.

Bit by bit, I removed my gear and clothes, then took my own towel and went into the shower. Riley's cabin was releasing steam like the *Orient Express* at full speed and my heart tripped in the moment when I considered my earlier thoughts. He was probably just sulking in there, his eyebrows flat over his eyes and his lips thrust out. But he was also naked.

I shut myself in the stall a couple doors away from him and turned on the shower. It splashed against my skin, chasing away the cold of the rink but failing to push aside my sinful thoughts of Riley.

I told myself it was just the odd feeling of an empty shower room after practice. I told myself it was just the remnants of days gone. But I knew I was fooling myself. He'd asked me how it was so easy for me and I had given him a non-answer.

I soaped myself up, then rinsed, and by the time I was done, Riley was wrapping up, too. I quickly dabbed myself with the towel, then wrapped it around my waist. It was tight and long, reaching below my knees.

We got out of our stalls at the same time, Riley lost in a thick cloud of steam. He was pink with heat and his hair was almost brown. He glanced at me, then made a point of not looking at me again as he walked out of the shower, but that brief moment had been enough. He hadn't caught my eyes; instead, he'd scanned my torso. And it was enough to make my heart clench. It was enough to make me want to reach out to the hellfire that his feelings for me had become. I didn't mind my flesh and bones melting if only I could graze his body with my fingers one more time.

I closed my eyes and fought these wild ideas back. But when I walked out, Riley was standing dull and almost lost in the locker room, his towel wrapped tightly around his waist, too. He hadn't started changing yet.

I swallowed and walked up to my locker. It was just an excuse because they were next to each other. I was actually walking up to Riley and I opened my mouth before I could think this through. "It's not easy."

Riley turned to me. "Huh?"

"None of this is easy." My voice was raw when I spoke. I patted the back of my neck where a drop of water trickled from my hair. "But I'm out of options, Riley. This is the only thing left to me. I would've spared us both the pain if I could, but I had to come back or drown." My voice cracked at the last part. I had never said these words aloud and I hadn't planned on telling them to Riley of all people. But California had done a number on me and I was struggling to claw my way out of the abyss. "I knew you were here, Riley. I knew it would be hard to face you. Hell, man, I was terrified until I saw how much you hated me. That..." My words faded and I looked down. His hatred made it ever so slightly easier. "It freed me of my guilt," I said quietly.

Whatever I thought I was saying wasn't what Riley heard. His face twisted in an expression of contempt and he closed the distance between us. "So just because I'm not rushing to forgive you, you get to act all superior?"

"Christ, Riley, that's not what I'm saying," I snapped, annoyance overtaking all the other feelings. "You're acting like a brat again."

"Freeing you of your guilt, huh?" He bared his teeth. "I can't fucking believe you, Cam."

The aggressive expression combined with the sudden move he made toward me had my body reacting before I knew what I was doing. My palms pressed his bare chest a moment before he collided with me and I pushed him back against the locker. "Calm the fuck down," I hissed, pinning him against the locker. His angry look melted into a surprised one as I pressed the length of my forearm across his chest and held him in place. "I'm trying to tell you that this is just as hard for me as it is for you, asshole. If I had any other option but picking at these wounds, I would gladly be someplace else. But I don't." To emphasize, I added pressure on his chest in jerky moves just as I snapped the words at him. "Do you think I'm enjoying this? That I like taunting you with my presence? Today was good, Riley. It was fucking good. Can we just take one good day and not fucking ruin it? Just for the fun of it?"

He was calm, if surprised, when he lifted his arm and wrapped a hand around my wrist. "Is this what you call a good day?"

I stepped back, pulling my arm off his chest, but his hand remained firmly in place. "Sorry," I huffed.

"It's too late to be sorry, Cam," he said and gazed at me.

What did that even mean? Was he talking about this or about the way I'd walked away from him? These thoughts swirled through my head for one endless moment until I realized that his hand was still wrapped around my wrist. We were still touching.

My heart picked up the pace and I licked my lips while Riley's chest rose and fell with each breath. The thundering heartbeats flooded my ears soon and I realized that I could see Riley's pulse on his neck. And though he was still glaring at me, his expression was softening.

Riley wasn't releasing me even though he wasn't gripping me as tightly. His gaze dropped to my torso and returned to my eyes. He waited. He expected me to…do something. And every shred of my being was tearing itself apart because this was a dangerous crossroad. Oh, I'd found myself here many times in my fantasies. I'd imagined this very thing more times than I cared to admit.

But I hadn't expected to ever truly have a chance to make this choice.

It was like sirens were going off inside my head. And the couple of inches of space I crossed in the next moment felt like I was traversing galaxies. I felt like I was leaning in, but I wondered if there was any change in our physical distance. The only thing I was sure of was that Riley wasn't pulling away. He held onto me and his cheeks were turning a darker shade of pink.

It had always been easy to make him blush.

I held my breath and gently closed my eyes as the world around me tilted to one side. Was this really happening? Fright and thrill spread through me in equal measure as I felt myself leaning into it.

Perhaps the heightened senses made it a million times worse, but when the heavy door of the locker room banged on its opening, I jumped a step back and my eyes shot open. Riley, just as frightened, looked away, his cheeks blooming with redness.

Coach Murray hurried in. "There you are," he said with audible relief before examining the scene.

Frustration spread through me like wildfire. I clenched my fists and swallowed the scream that welled in me. "Coach," I said in an airy, frail voice.

Riley was too stunned to speak. He glanced at me, then quickly pulled his gaze away, turning to his locker and pretending to be busy.

"I was looking for you," Coach Murray explained. "I'm sorry about the..." He waved his hands and left the rest unsaid, then nodded. "How were the drills?"

"Good," I said for both of us. "You were right." I was rambling. "That's just what we needed."

Coach Murray was nodding, pleased but distracted. "I'll lock up when you boys are finished. And let's do this again on Tuesday. Seven pm? Yes, let's do that. I'll coach you myself." Riley murmured a question about Heller's wife and Coach Murray nodded in earnest. "She's in the hospital. Brent's there. Still waiting."

Coach left us to it like he'd said but I wished I could somehow grab his sleeve and keep him here. When the door shut behind him, the awkward silence filled the locker room and my skull evenly. I stepped to my locker and began digging through my stuff until I found clean underwear. There was no way in hell I was taking this towel off with Riley next to me. Not after we'd almost kissed.

But it seemed like Riley was having the same thoughts because he bent down and stepped into his underwear with the towel still around his waist.

I did the same thing, then finished dressing in silence. As we left the rink, Riley muttered: "See you."

I didn't get to say it back because he took the opposite turn of where we would normally go to get to the team house. He disappeared in the golden rays of the morning sun and I remained outside the rink, wallowing in mixed feelings and an unbearable amount of frustration.

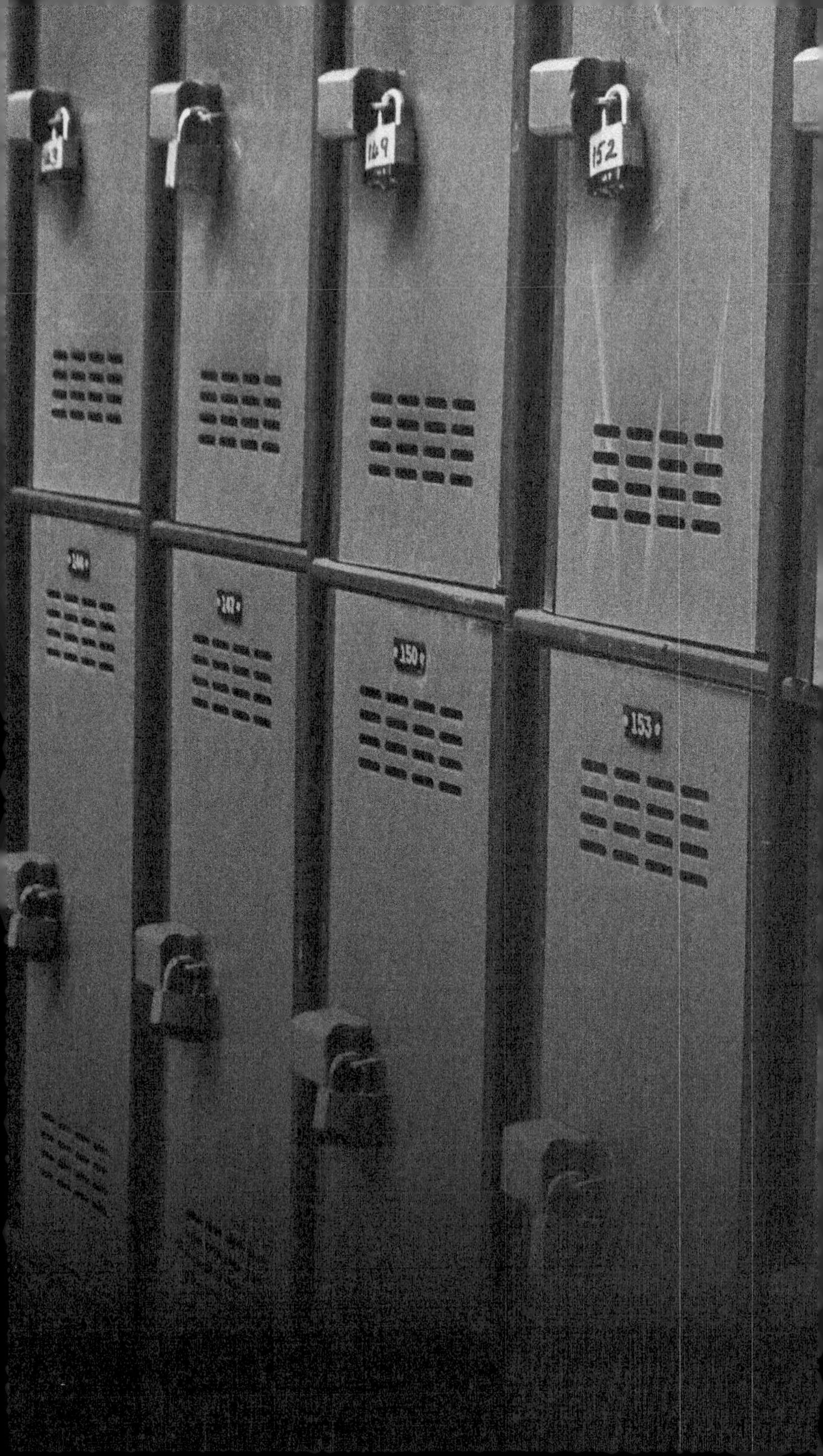
149
152
150
153

SEVEN

Riley

The house was oddly quiet on Sunday morning. Last night, there had been another wild party at Alpha Kappa Phi and I figured everyone was nursing a hangover today. I made myself a couple sandwiches in the kitchen, spotting Sawyer and Tyler napping in armchairs on the far side of the common room, arms thrown over their eyes to protect them from the early sunlight.

I made my way downstairs with the plate in one hand, chewing my lip and grasping meandering thoughts. My mood was funky as best, not least of all because he had started haunting my dreams, now, too. The night had been full of tossing and turning until I'd given it up.

As if skating back into my life hadn't been painful enough, Cameron had torn the stitches that held my heart together with one brilliant moment of truce. I'd been so stunned that I decided not to act at all. I hadn't a clue as to what the right reaction would be. Should I have pushed him away? Should I have leaned in?

Should I stop wondering because nothing had happened in the end?

That was the only question I could answer. Hell yes. I had to clear my head of Cameron and this stupid tightness in my chest. Even if Coach hadn't walked in and stopped us from making that horrible mistake, what was there to hope for? That we would kiss and...what? Live happily ever after? Bullshit. Cameron Martinez had maybe reined his temper in, but I hadn't halved my IQ just yet. I'd been fooled once and it had been one time too many.

I sank into the sofa cushions and crossed my legs over the small coffee table in the basement. As I finished the first of the two sandwiches, I shifted restlessly, sitting on something hard. I dug under the pillow and snatched the wireless joystick that had been buried there.

Lacking any other entertainment, I fired my *PlayStation* up and let *Fallen Order* load on screen while I finished the other sandwich. My mind returned to the conundrum of Cameron's wet lips, his chiseled features, his torso still glistening after the shower, and the fact that we had been wearing nothing more than towels when something possessed him to offer me a kiss.

I would be a liar if I said that being slammed against the locker hadn't woken something deeply primal inside of me. Something was severely messed up with me, I was sure, but that didn't alter the facts. When Cameron pressed his arm across my chest and pinned me against the cold metal of the locker, I felt it in my stomach, my spine, my cock. It made me fluttery with desire and fiery with rebellion. Every shred of me wanted to fight back just so I could provoke his wrath.

Cameron was incapable of letting go no matter what he pretended to be like. He was smart enough and quiet enough to appear subdued, but he never stopped watching and he never stopped trying to outmatch me. I was just explosive enough to cut to the chase.

And when I did, he wanted to put me in my place, so to speak.

I lifted the controller and checked the recent game saves, almost choking on the last mouthful of my sandwich. *Palpie_The_Man* had saved a game just last night. Palpie, as in Palpatine. This was Cameron's gameplay. I would have bet my ass on it.

My throat narrowed so quickly at the dusty memory of the long Sunday mornings from our senior year. Whenever the doorbell rang, and my heart leaped, I would pretend I hadn't been pacing my room in expectation for minutes and minutes. I would open the door and find him leaning against the doorframe, darkness enveloping him, and locks of his hair falling over his brow and hiding his reddened eyes.

I never asked.

I had learned that lesson early on. Asking only made him agitated. It was better to say nothing and let him in, embrace him, and help him take his mind off of it.

Every Sunday, I extended my arm and waited until he took my hand, then pulled him inside and shut the door behind us. He rounded on me before we reached my bedroom and I laughed, tripping over my own feet. His arms would wrap around me and he would pin me against the wardrobe in my room, stare into my eyes with unrestrained lust, and purr the sexiest words I'd ever heard. "Have you been bad, Riley?"

Even now, I shuddered at the color of his husky voice. We'd known the meaning of his question. It had belonged to a language of our own.

"Have you played with yourself without me, Riley?" he was really asking.

And he could tell when I lied because I had the uncontrollable and freakishly annoying habit of turning red. But I also had a habit of doing the opposite of what I was told because I learned early on that there was so much fun when you toyed with dishonesty. So, I would deliberately lie and blush, just like I'd deliberately touched myself so I would earn the punishment.

"You know what that means," he would purr and I would melt away. In a heartbeat, I would discover that my ass was bare. He never knew this, but I'd intentionally untied the drawstring so he could undress me quicker. And when he did, finding myself bent over his lap was just a matter of seconds.

I loaded Cameron's gameplay just to make sure. None of my teammates cared much about *Star Wars* or the sheer immensity of this game's world. There was only one person other than me who played it as thoroughly and immaculately.

I didn't touch his actual game. Instead, I opened his character Cal's inventory. It stretched my lips into an unwilling smile to see that he had collected every single poncho along the way as well as all of the skins for his companion droid, BD-1.

"Is that my save?" His husky voice startled me and I threw the controller to my right, yelping as my heart skipped a beat.

"Jesus. Fuck." I spun on the sofa and glared at Cameron. He wore a pair of black, cotton shorts and a dark gray T-shirt that revealed his muscular arms. The worst of all was the smug smirk at scaring me. "Maybe knock the next time."

"I live here," he pointed out lazily, tightening his smart watch around his wrist. "Anyway, are you messing with my inventory?" The white running sneakers with blue stripes drew my attention. He was getting ready to go out. In all my mornings of running, I'd never once encountered Cameron. What the hell was up?

"It's my console," I said, sticking to one battle at a time.

"In the common room." His words carried little emotion, leaving me to wonder where he was taking this.

Touché, I thought. "It never occurred to you that maybe I wouldn't want you to mess with my stuff?" I asked, getting up from the sofa and taking a couple paces toward him.

He leaned against the soccer table and crossed his arms. "It occurred to me."

"And you still touched my console," I concluded. *Fuck*. The cocky way he made himself the center of everything really should have angered me more than it turned me on.

Cameron cocked his head. "Are you mad?"

Was I? Not at Cameron playing our old favorite, no. I was irked by his attitude far more. And yet, I was drawn to it.

In all these weeks of orbiting each other, lurking, stealing glances, and going head to head, we had never truly had an exchange like this. He had never allowed himself to be the way he had once been. Oh, he'd been close, at that party last week. He'd husked out a few words of warning that had sent chills down my spine and made my cock hard.

"No," Cameron answered for himself. "You're not mad."

I shook my head. "You could have asked."

"Then you'd definitely say no." He laughed mirthlessly and pushed himself away from the soccer table, crossing the distance between us like he had something to prove. "I might play some right now."

"Aren't you on your way out?" I asked, pointing at his attire as he passed by me, leaving me lost in a cloud of smoke and sandalwood.

Double fuck.

"Outside won't go anywhere," he said, not really paying attention to me at all, now. He lifted the controller and glanced at me over his shoulder as if daring me to stop him. "And you might lock this thing up by the time I'm back."

I was silent, watching him as he turned back to the flat screen TV mounted to the wood paneling on the wall. I stared at the California tan he brought back to Michigan, the smooth skin of his arms and the back of his neck. I looked over the cowlick at the top of his head.

He must have felt the weight of my gaze on him because he never left the inventory in the game. He was just holding the controller and staring at the screen like it was the most interesting thing in the world.

A time later, he lowered his gaze from the screen and mulled over his words, then slouched. "What is it?"

"Yesterday," I said, my voice so frail it sounded more like air than speech.

"What about it?" Impatience touched his tone and made all my nerve endings buzz. He dropped the controller and checked his smart watch for nothing, buying himself time. When he was out of it, he got up and faced me. "What do you want to know, Riley?"

"We almost kissed, didn't we?" Heat rose to my

cheeks as I bared myself so fully to the person who had a habit of hurting me. I aced all my courses and had an entire year of captaining experience; how was I so stupid?

"Did we?" he asked, his tone genuine.

I wasn't sure which of us was moving toward the other. Perhaps we had moved at the same time. Regardless, we were standing much closer now than a heartbeat ago. "If Coach hadn't entered, what would have happened, Cam?"

Cameron looked up, lips parting as he inhaled, then exhaled. His minty breath tickled my nostrils before he returned his gaze to my eyes. "I don't know. I didn't have a plan." His words seemed carefully constructed and somehow dragged out of his throat. When he inhaled again, his shoulders pulled back and his chest rose.

I licked my lips, finding myself moving closer to him, and lacking a plan. "I don't believe you," I said.

A snort. Of course.

"You still don't trust anyone around you, Cam," I said.

"And I'm supposed to trust you? After you've marked me as your arch-nemesis?" The sarcasm was thick in his tone as he lifted his foot and dropped it near mine. "After you and Caden made half the team look at me like I'm a foreign spy."

I'd gone into this conversation far more softly than I was feeling, now. Every word he said hardened my resolve that yesterday could have been a horrible disaster had Coach not walked in. And yet, each sandalwood spiced breath I drew affirmed Cameron's monolithic presence in my life. "You can't blame me if people choose sides."

"I can do whatever the hell I want, Riley," he growled. "And I blame you for making sides."

"You obviously have no clue what my life was like after you left," I hissed at him, lifting my head just enough to level our noses.

"And you have no clue why I left," he said. "You've always liked playing the victim. Even then, it was your favorite role. Not that I'm kink-shaming. It's mad fun turning your ass red..."

I grabbed his T-shirt so abruptly that it cut off the rest of his words. My body slammed into his, stomach against stomach, hips on hips. I felt him press against me and draw back, amusement in his eyes flaring in effort to disguise what I had just felt. He was hard.

It made my heart thunder, my ears ring, and my cock thicken as I desperately searched for a way to de-escalate this. But I was holding his shirt in my fists, glaring at him, deadlocked in this precarious place. There was a hair's width between my wish to slap the smirk off his face or kiss it.

We breathed deeply, quickly, as Cameron slowly put his hands around my wrists and freed his T-shirt from my iron hold. We swapped our places from yesterday, but I still felt just as submissive to his temper.

Every muscle in my body was tense. My soul split through the middle, two sides battling fiercely. He held my wrists as I licked my lips, part of me desperate to have one more taste of him. That part was winning the fight my heart waged against my brain. I didn't need a PhD to see this was a mistake. But ten PhDs wouldn't have shed light on a way to avoid it.

"What are we doing?" he whispered, leaning in as slowly and insecurely as I was.

I inhaled to tell him, although I didn't know how to put any of this into words. Somewhere in the deepest corners of my consciousness, his question bought milliseconds of spare time that forced me to think it through. I couldn't do this.

I shouldn't.

Our past was way too complicated. We were on the same team. We lived in the same house. An entire year was still ahead of us. This was wrong no matter how good it felt.

I had to stop.

In less time than it took a butterfly to bat its wings, I slouched and stepped back. The disappointment was instant, filling the space between us. But, a fraction of a moment later, an alarm blared from his wrist watch.

We both looked at it.

Abnormal Heart Rate Detected.

Though it felt like a lifetime of weighing pros and cons, the next move had been written by the Fates and forged in a star an eternity ago. Cameron let go of my wrists and hurried to conceal what his watch had betrayed, but he didn't get a chance.

My hands closed around his face. His eyes widened in a split moment that allowed him to react. Before either had a chance to change his mind, I let my wildest self take control of my body.

I leaped.

If there was any expectation of familiarity, it faded out of my mind as soon as my lips pressed against his. This was nothing like it had been years ago. Time and experience had taught us a trick or two; no teeth scraped and noses didn't slam against each other. Instead, I was submerged in the ecstasy that came with such intimacy.

His lips were softer than I'd imagined. Had I been imagining this? Somewhere in the back of my mind, I had, this entire time. Every bark and snap of my jaw had been a symptom of the longing that his arrival had filled me with.

I sucked his lower lip between my teeth and leaned into him, still holding his face like there was a risk of him escaping. But his startled pose was soon melting into one of embrace. He didn't flail. Instead, his hands rested on my upper arms and he thrust one leg between mine, preparing himself to take control.

I wasn't going to make it easy.

His minty breath filled me with kinky aspirations. My heart stumbled over and over as I bobbed my head from one side to the other, sliding my tongue between his lips and tasting him like I hadn't in forever.

Cameron's throat released the gentlest of moans. My hands dropped from his face to his slender neck, then down to the collar of his T-shirt. I closed my fists around it, pulling him closer to me until our bodies were pressed so close it felt like I was about to tackle him.

It was as if Cameron needed a good, long moment for his body to catch up. His arms wrapped around me with viper swiftness, sliding down to the small of my back. The way he yanked me pressed our hips together, his crotch rubbing against mine. He was as hard as marble, his cock bulging out of his cotton shorts, stretching the fabric of his underwear. Mine throbbed hard at every touch, the pulse soaring through my body, pouring out of my fists as I tugged Cam's T-shirt like I would soon rip it apart.

He spun us around until I bumped against the side of the sofa.

Cam's hands moved lower, following the curve of my

ass, until he cupped my cheeks and revealed all of his intentions. His teeth sank into my lower lip, pain almost dragging a whimper out of me.

I released his T-shirt, one fist sweeping around him and snatching locks of hair on the back of his head. I pulled him back, parting our lips and watching him growl. "You've made my life a misery, Cam," I accused and watched the flicker of something dangerous burst to life in his eyes.

"Shut up, Riley," he said, his voice huskier than ever. He squeezed my cheeks firmly, pinning me with his hard, fiery gaze. His lips hovered over mine as he slipped from my hold and leaned in.

"What if I don't?" I whispered.

In reply, he moved one hand around my waist and lowered it between us, pressing his open palm against my painfully hard cock and forcing a choked whimper out of me. "You haven't changed a bit. Not truly."

I couldn't tell if he was praising me for being constant or scolding me for never growing up. Whatever his meaning, I didn't get to bite back. He pressed his lips against mine, shutting me up for good, and exploring my mouth with his tongue. It reached deep into me, sending a painful twitch to my cock that stretched Cameron's lips into an amused smirk.

Every cell in my body combusted when Cameron moved his other hand to the middle of my butt, reached low under my cheeks, and dragged his fingers over the center. His left hand, firmly on my cock, closed tighter. I thrust my hips forward, rubbing myself through his hand, trapped in the excruciating pressure of my tight underwear and sweatpants.

Cameron pulled his head back just enough to speak

over my thirsty, open mouth. "You have been asking for this since I came, Riley."

My cheeks burst aflame at his words. Part of me had to concede. The other part, the one which knew how this dangerous game was played, did the opposite. "I fucking wasn't," I snapped, slamming into him just to provoke his firmness.

His lips stretched into a sinister grin that suited his dark features perfectly. "Liar." And with that, he spun us around quicker than I could keep up with the movement. We crashed onto the sofa, Cameron sitting back with his arms coiled around my waist, dragging me off my feet and over his lap. When my head sank into the soft cushion, I found I was breathless. This grand and sweeping move brought back more memories than I could sort through. Bent over his lap, I moaned once and buried my face in the fold of my arm, narrowing my attention to Cameron's hand as it rubbed my firm ass. I suddenly wished I'd untied the drawstring like I used to, but he didn't seem to mind. "You knew," he whispered accusingly. "You knew we'd get to this, Riley."

I clawed at the cushions, incapable of speech. *Just do it*, I wanted to snap. Every breath I drew felt like the splitting of atoms inside my chest. My head was spinning as I squeezed my eyes shut and tensed for the first blow of his bare hand against my ass.

I had never admitted this to anyone since Cameron. Nobody knew how easy I was to leash and rein in. Nobody knew I had a total meltdown button but him.

Cameron's fingers hooked inside the waistband of my sweatpants, then yanked them over the thick curve of my ass, when hollowness opened in my chest and a flood of despair poured in. The footsteps stumbling down the wooden stairs outside the door made me want to scream my throat off. Tears of rage shot into my eyes as Cameron pushed me off his lap, handling me as easily as if I was a goddamn sack of potatoes. I found myself internally raging while sitting still next to him the moment Beckett marched into the basement.

Cameron already had the *PlayStation* controller in his hands, pouting and feigning great interest in *Fallen Order*. And I, with my ears ringing, couldn't get the image of ripping Beckett's head off out of my mind. A howl was building up in my throat when Beckett examined the basement.

"Did I interrupt a knife fight?" he drawled.

I unclogged my throat of the scream that was locked and loaded, inhaled, and steadily stood up. "I was just leaving." The murmur was barely audible. Cameron didn't react to it, pretending to be playing the game. The corners of his mouth twitched in frustration with which I was more than familiar.

I passed Beckett without looking at his dimples or his perfect haircut or his long eyelashes. If I met his gaze now, two things would happen in close succession. He would see through me and know what was up. And I would have to fucking kill him.

Holding a massive bubble of air in my lungs, I went upstairs, then marched outside, deaf to the chatter in the common room. The pounding of my heart drowned my ears. Heat radiated from my body until I wondered if I was literally glowing to all around me.

I shut the door on my way out and broke into a sprint as soon as I reached the paved path that connected our house to the rest of Northwood U's campus. It was my longest run since I could remember and I didn't stop even when sweat covered every inch of me and a burning in my muscles threatened to render me shit on the ice tomorrow.

As I ran, only two things floated through my mind on a loop.

First, we were cursed. It wasn't meant to be. It was a blessing in disguise that we kept being interrupted.

The other thought terrified me. Without a shred of doubt, I knew how badly I wanted him. Just a touch. Just a kiss. Just one firm slap of his palm against my bare ass. I needed him to drag me back to Earth from the clouds in which my head was lost. I needed him to hold me down and show me what it meant to belong to someone. Even if it was only for a night.

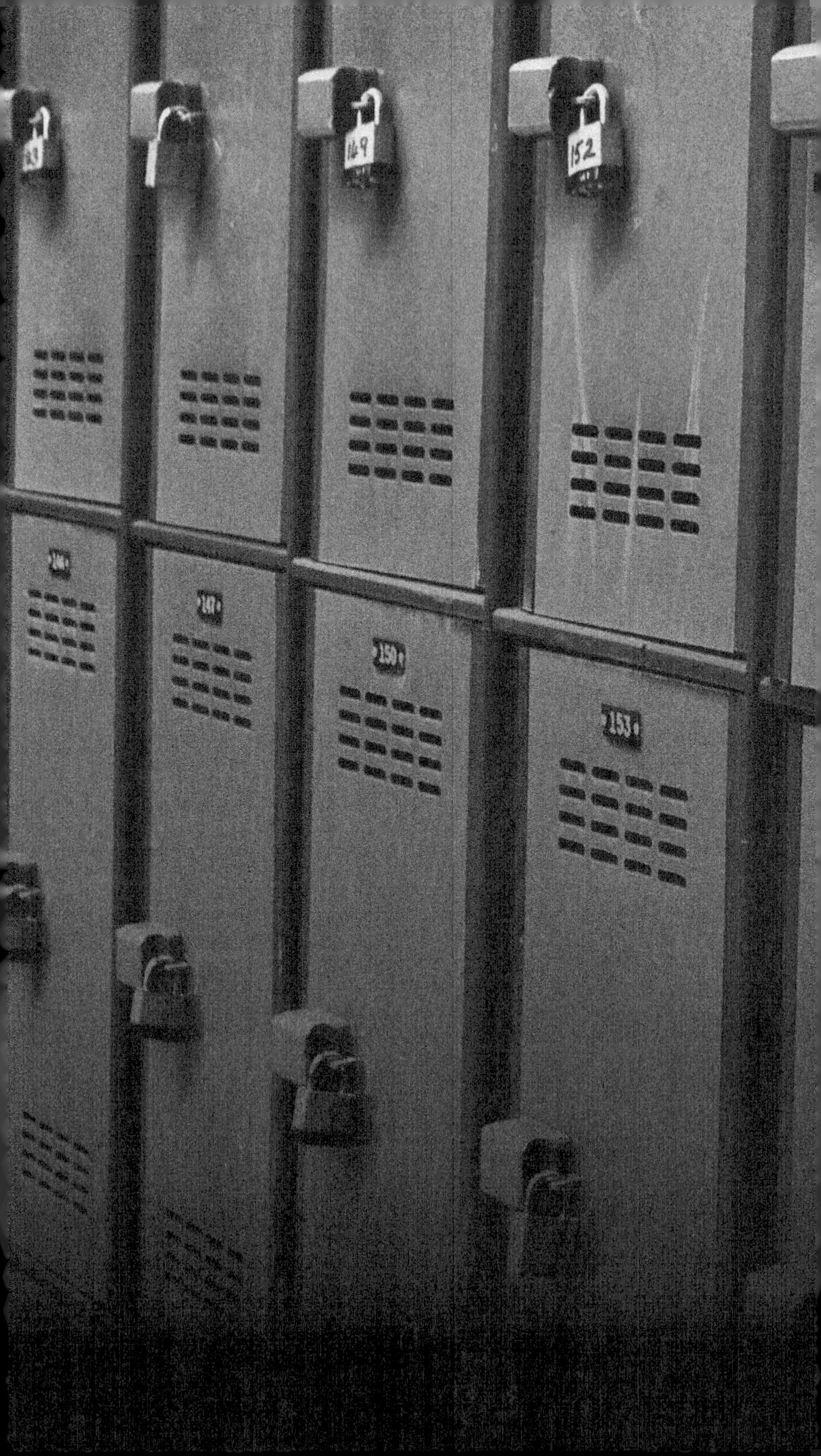
152
150
153

EIGHT

Cameron

GET YOUR GODDAMN HEAD STRAIGHT, Martinez, I snapped at myself as I watched the puck go sideways because my mind had been miles away. I skated ten more feet before stopping and twirling back only to bump into Partridge who was trying to correct my blunder.

"What the hell is up with you, dude?" Beckett asked, not unkindly.

I growled in return and shook my head, helmet weighing heavy today.

The sulking creature on the other side of the rink played as badly as I did, today. He dropped his stick in agitation once and nearly fell off his skates for no reason whatsoever. The few times our eyes met, he was close to snarling and I wondered what he was playing at. Maybe he was begging for me to tower over him and spank that bratty attitude out of him. Or maybe he was so fucking over this entire ordeal.

Whatever his reasons, Riley embarrassed himself today when he stared at me from across the rink, leading the puck between enemy lines, and slamming himself into the boards because his gaze lingered on me for a moment too long.

I fared no better. Sweat was freezing on my face all day and I'd fallen over Sebastian, sprawling on ice and biting my lip so hard I drew blood. It was far from my first split lip, but it was the first for these specific reasons.

Yesterday, I had gotten the closest to feeling alive in years. The electric current between Riley and me in those moments of heavy expectations coursed through my bones. It was like the static buildup that soared through the charts until it ignited a lightning bolt. Destructive as fuck, yes. But also awe inspiring and breathtaking at the same time.

I wanted to assert my dominance over our captain just as much as I wanted to feel the companionship of my first guy. I wanted to teach him a lesson in manners just like I wanted to feel every inch of his body under my lips.

God, I was a lost cause. We both were.

If one thing was certain in all this goddamn mess, it was that Riley didn't hate me enough not to give in. Whether his reason told him to run away or not, it hardly mattered. His body bowed to me. And his heart was in it.

But this knowledge made me clumsy like I'd never been on ice in my life. A waddling penguin had higher odds of scoring a point than either of us.

The blow of Coach Murray's whistle was both a blessing and a curse. "Martinez. Brooks. My office."

Riley tore his helmet off and glared at me like I'd caused his bumbling and stumbling today. I fucking hadn't. If I had that kind of power, I'd have used it a month ago.

We skated to the edge of the rink and let other guys

file out before we took our skates off and dragged our sorry asses to Coach Murray's office. The man was turning red, one of his eyes twitching. We hadn't even kicked this season off with a friendly match against the Blizzard Breakers and we were already a disaster.

"Never in my career has a player made me question my sanity the way you two seem to do every day," Coach Murray rasped, his voice metallic with anger, like a whetstone sharpening a knife's blade. He pointed his finger at Riley and I wanted to leap and stand between them. It took all my strength to stay still and not interfere. My turn was still coming. "I've given you the captaincy of this team because you were well liked and respected, Brooks. Those guys followed you all the way to the top and stood by you in the face of defeat."

Riley fidgeted, his breathing stopping abruptly.

"Coach," I said, my voice choking.

Coach Murray's finger snapped from Riley to me. "We offered you a full scholarship just to have you here, Martinez, because your skill on ice was wasted at SBU. One leading man with a band of rascals never even licked the door of the NHL. And now I discover that you've only been great in comparison."

His words felt like a very unskilled hand dragging a stitch from an unhealed wound. I stiffened in shock.

"The only thing I can think to explain it all is if I lost my touch. Have I misjudged the ones who I believed were this team's best players in three generations? Or am I seeing something wrong? I can't seem to make you two work together. And pitting you against each other to push the other off the team is failing, too. So, what do I do with you?"

I didn't dare open my mouth. If this was a hypothetical question, he wouldn't appreciate a smart-ass answer.

Silence dragged on for an eternity and soured everything else in the room.

Coach moved his gaze between the two of us like he was trying to see something that wasn't there. "Very well. Brooks, seeing as you are the captain of the team, you are going to bear the responsibilities for the discord of the entire team. The lack of focus, purpose, and camaraderie is solely on you. You will..."

"You can't do that." Silence dropped between us like an anvil. All eyes were on me before I realized these had been my words. My mouth dried and I worked it for a trace of saliva, but found none. Instead, I inhaled a shallow breath of air and avoided Riley's eyes. I stared at Coach Murray. "It's not his fault."

"Pray tell." Coach's words were clipped and he seemed to forget all about his anger with Riley. As far as I could see, Riley could have walked out this very instant and Coach Murray would still be slicing me to pieces with a look.

"I'm the cause of discord," I said.

"Shut up," Riley hissed under his breath.

"I am. And you both know it. Since I got here, it has all gone downhill." *Shut up*, I yelled at myself internally. "If you have to scratch one of us, it should be me." My voice softened by the end of that and I couldn't believe the stupid things that had come out of my mouth. In no universe was it my fault that Riley couldn't focus on captaining this team because I played alongside him.

Except, I kind of was.

No matter how often I told myself that high school crushes were just passing fancies, I never made myself completely believe it. Riley had never moved on. Not truly. And I had never felt as complete as I had yesterday, not since I'd run away. I'd thought I was sacrificing something small, something temporary, but it had been more akin to severing a limb. Or carving my heart out, if I were being sappy.

Even the impatient side eye he had given me this past month filled me with annoyance. Every eye roll and every contemptuous snort. Every time he insisted he could run as fast or lift as much. But in that annoyance, I felt myself drawn to this stubborn, heart-bruised, silly guy.

Nobody on this planet pushed my buttons quite like Riley. Which wasn't to say I would let him be full of himself, but I was going to try this risky mind game with the coach for both our sakes.

Come on, I thought. *Please work*.

Coach Murray narrowed his eyes at me, then looked at Riley. "Brooks, do you agree with Cameron's assessment?"

Riley dragged his gaze off Coach Murray to meet mine. There were sparks of anger bursting out of his eyes, but he blinked and shook his head. "You were right, Coach. I'm the captain. It's my job to ensure we get along."

Coach Murray measured us for a time, then gave a grave nod. "Very well. If I see anything less than exceptional on Wednesday, you will share the responsibility. You are dismissed."

We knew better than to argue or draw attention whatsoever. The way we left his office was easily the stealthiest on record. But it was only when we crossed the long hallway to the empty locker room that either of us felt safe enough to breathe again.

The locker room had a unique after-practice scent of sweat fading away to the overpowering body wash scents all the guys had used in the shower. There, we shut the door and began undressing in silence. By the time we stripped down to our waists, Riley couldn't hold his tongue any longer. "You just had to play the hero."

"What?" I demanded.

"He was almost done, Cam. You didn't have to meddle like some sulky Prince Charming." Riley looked right into my eyes, his face still glowing from the exertion on ice and the following embarrassment.

"I was trying to save your ass, you ungrateful little shit," I snapped, my mind narrowing to annoyance as I rounded on him.

"I didn't need you to save my ass." He fought back for the sake of pride and that rubbed me the wrong way. My frustration was spilling and spreading, but I knew where it was coming from. And it wasn't Riley's stubbornness.

"He was about to scratch you and I intervened," I said. "You're welcome."

"Now both our asses are on the line," he hissed, tossing his jersey into the locker and shutting the door while still wearing the bottom half of his attire. "Do you seriously think we can just magic our way out of this, Cam? That we can just start playing well together by Wednesday?" He scoffed and gave a jerky shake of his head, his chest rising as he inhaled. "We're screwed."

"We're not." I wasn't admitting defeat now. "I bought us time."

"Great. Now all we have to do is figure out how to learn to play together." The sarcasm cut me deeper than it should have.

I narrowed my eyes and leaned closer to him. "No. We

just need to figure out how to focus on the game, rather than the player."

His breath hitched audibly when he pulled a few inches back to look into my eyes. "Cam…"

I licked my lips with care. "I know what's distracting me. And you know it, too."

His eyebrows trembled briefly before he surrendered into a small frown. "Aren't you getting the message from the universe?" His voice was thinner than ever as he asked this. "It keeps interrupting us."

I allowed myself the liberty of grazing the side of his torso with my fingertips. "I know you're stubborn enough to listen to the universe."

Riley hesitated a moment, then melted into my arms and allowed our torsos to press tightly. He surrendered himself to me when I took a step forward, pinning him against the locker he'd only just shut. When he had nowhere else to go, he lifted his chin a little and closed his eyes as if to say, "Do whatever you want to me."

My lips sealed over his. The kiss radiated white heat that clouded my mind. Maybe there were higher forces at play, pulling us apart, but I didn't care. So far, the only thing that had ever torn us apart had been of my own making. I first needed to conquer that before I could worry over divine intervention.

For now, at least, I wouldn't worry about anything. Despite our best efforts, Riley and I collided in this violent and beautiful culmination of a month of resentment and raw, unprocessed feelings. We put them aside, just now, and I savored every moment of this kiss. I savored the way he shivered all over and how his breaths were shallow when he inhaled with my lips still on his.

The kiss stopped when he pulled back an inch and

pressed his brow against mine. "You think this will make us play any better?"

"I don't know," I admitted. "At least we'll know for sure."

He hesitated a moment, lips hovering over mine. Then, as if he cuffed it with his hand, he made my heart trip when he spoke next. "Don't lock your shower cabin."

I needed to hold my breath so I wouldn't gasp. Only now that it was a reality did I feel what a rift had existed between my wishes and my expectations.

Before I left him, I leaned in again, pressing my weight hard against his body until my crotch sank into his and our torsos sealed together. I was merciless in the way I kissed him, filling his mouth with my tongue and letting him feel my throbs against his cock.

Airless, Riley pushed me back and licked his lips.

I held his gaze a moment longer, then walked away to wait for him in the shower. The rest of my clothes marked a trail to the cabin at the far end and I couldn't believe this was happening.

Plenty of opportunity for something to stop us, I thought. It would be in line with how the last few days had gone. And yet, I found that flutters filled my stomach and tingling rose from my fingertips.

Riley Brooks. So many years later, it was still Riley Brooks who made me dizzy with lust and expectation. My heart was speeding up and my breaths were shallow when I turned the shower on. Water cooled me down until I heard his bare feet on the tiles. Another cabin door creaked and he turned the water on, then shut the door and quickly crossed the rest of the way to my cabin.

The door opened as he spoke. "Decoy." There was a ghost of a smile on his lips before he pulled the lower one between his teeth and dropped his gaze. His pupils dilated and ears perked as he unashamedly scanned my hard cock.

He tossed a condom with a cheeky smile and I caught it, then placed it on the small space carved into the tiled wall of the back of the shower cabin where shampoo and body wash normally stood.

"You carry these with you to practice?" I teased, arching an eyebrow at him.

Riley's cheeks were pink at the suggestion. "For emergencies."

I extended my arm and he placed his hand inside my palm, entering the shower while wearing his underwear. The first splash of water startled him just as I shut the door of the cabin and he flung himself back, pressing himself against the shower door. "Jesus, fuck. That's freezing."

I grabbed his wrists and lifted his arms high above his head, cutting off whatever else he'd meant to say. His eyes widened and he bit down on his lip again. "Is there nothing we can agree on?" I leaned into him until his cheeks were red at the feel of my hard cock against his abdomen. I moved my hips slowly and rubbed myself against him. I remembered the unbearable cloud of steam that always left his shower cabin and the stark contrast of what he was getting now stretched my lips into a grin.

"There might be a thing or two," he whispered, his words somehow distant. It was like he wasn't even thinking about talking, but ran it on autopilot. His hands closed into fists, though he couldn't move his arms from my strong grip. Instead, he inhaled deeply, his chest rising with expectation and eyes never leaving my face.

I was beyond words, too. The sensation of his cock pulsing at the slightest pressure squeezed the last of the oxygen out of my lungs and I released myself to the current. No reasoning remained in my head. No clear thought crossed my mind.

All I wished to do was to devour him.

To make him mine again.

If this ridiculous competition had any sort of ending, it would be with me winning and Riley gaining everything. There was no other way for us to function.

My mouth covered his and our tongues played and explored each other messily. When I crossed his wrists high against the shower cabin and gripped them with one hand, Riley gave a feeble swing of his hips in rebellion. The fucker was still wearing his white boxer-briefs, but we were soaked and they were starting to be see-through. And when I pulled back, I couldn't stop the smirk on my face at the sight of his cock desperately stretching the fabric thin.

I rested my other hand on his hip and buried my face in the crane of his neck, making him wiggle in protest and growl that I was tickling him. As if that would make me stop. He should have known better than to try. All it did was give me another little way to torment him.

My hand slipped from his hip to his cheek, cupping it and squeezing until he moaned right into my ear. I silenced him, sliding my lips over his and swallowing the rest of that moan.

His arms trembled and I could almost sense the searing in his muscles. Being the villain of this irresistible play, I didn't release him. Instead, I pulled his wrists higher until he had to push himself to the tips of his toes to keep up. My hand on his butt massaged him firmly, inching closer to the middle while his underwear stuck to his skin.

In an instant, the wet cotton irritated me so much that I released his arms and let him drop back to his flat feet only to grab his boxer-briefs and yank their edge over the curve of his ass. Sticky as they were now that they dripped with water, they folded in the front, pulling his hard cock a few inches down.

Riley whimpered, the back of his head bumping against the tiled wall.

Water pattered against my back as I stepped back to admire his physique. Every muscle was nicely defined and his skin was smooth and shiny now that it was wet. Perhaps I drooled for a moment, but the beads of water on our faces concealed that much.

Riley opened his eyes, the blueness in them striking when it wasn't so icy and filled with hatred. It was like he'd left those things outside the door and entered here with a ceasefire. He shivered, though I didn't think it was his body's reaction to the cold water.

It was like it took him great effort to form the next question. He licked his lips and looked at me meekly. "Have I been bad, Cam?"

My pulse doubled, but I kept my expression flat. "You have no idea, Riley," I said darkly. For five weeks, he had been snapping and pouting, but I had been accruing the payback without even knowing it. "On your knees," I commanded, watching the rebel regress in him as he immediately obeyed and slid down against the wall until he was kneeling, legs spread wide and his cock still trapped in the tangles of his underwear. His ass, though, was bare and sitting on his heels where his feet touched.

Riley looked up, his eyes seeming bigger and brighter, lips redder, and eyelashes longer. Water had rendered his hair honey brown rather than blond and his eyebrows arched when I placed my hand on one side of his face.

He reached for my cock and — fuck, it felt good — as soon as he wrapped his fingers around it, I held my breath. The first sensation of his hand on me threatened to push me over the edge. Everything about me was strung tight and stretched thin. I was like a balloon, one deep breath away from bursting.

My thumb feathered over his lips, leaving a wet trail where water trickled down my arm and hand and over his face. Where I touched them, his lips parted. And he was soon gaping, eyes pleading and mouth inviting. He tugged on my cock a little, enough to make him grunt with the need for the sweet release and force my feet to move.

I approached him and swallowed the words of praise. He deserved them for the eagerness, but I wasn't so quick to shower him with them. They would sound all the sweeter if he stewed in expectation.

The head of my cock was glistening with precum as much as it was with water. Riley rounded his mouth and reached up, sealing his lips around me and sucking the air out of his mouth. The sensation soared through my chest. The unbearable itch spread within me and I cupped the back of Riley's head with one hand, while leaning against the wall behind him with the other. Tipping myself forward, I leaned into him and explored his limits.

A few inches deeper, Riley winced and I stopped, giving him a chance to do what he liked. He seized the opportunity like he had been starving and craving it for a century. His head bobbed back and forth, taking my length a fraction of an inch deeper all the while looking right into my eyes. The look he was giving me, a mix of neediness and submissive fear were the winning combination that billowed the flames inside of me.

When I thrust my hips forward, holding the back of his head firmly, he whimpered over the length of my cock, the vibrations feeling so fucking fantastic. And when I jerked myself closer still, he choked, his eyes flashing and eyebrows twisting. Each little move we made squeezed my chest tighter. I curled my toes and grabbed his head with both hands, pulling him down my length just to feel a little more of the wet warmth of his mouth and the constricting of his throat. Every filthy little act brought me closer to the red zone and to Riley himself, who slapped my thighs with both hands, then held onto me while I fucked his pretty face.

His hands clawed their way up to my stomach, my abs steely and tense with exertion.

Riley relaxed his throat at last, letting me reach far to the back of it. His breathing was cut off abruptly and he glared at me, three quarters of my dick buried in his sexy mouth, and I held myself there for an excruciating moment.

When the muscles in his throat tightened again, I pulled out, grinning at the way my cock glistened with his saliva.

He breathed in deeply and wiped his chin and eyes, then blinked at me. "I deserve it," he said. It wasn't a defeatist acceptance. It was an invitation, a dare, and a provocation. His eyes had never shone brighter than when he opened his mouth again and I made myself welcome.

Every little move of his tongue against the rim of my cock's head tickled me as he sucked it and savored it, worshiping it with appetite. He wrapped one hand around the base of my dick and the other set on his own crotch.

"Tsk." It was a warning he understood, wincing but obeying. His hand moved well away from his cock. "That's right," I murmured, grabbing a fistful of his wet hair and yanking him down my length. "You're mine, Riley, to do what I want."

His cheeks might have turned red, but he wasn't embarrassed to do just that. He swallowed me, his mouth gaping wide and throat letting me deep inside. His voice came and stopped quickly, cut off with my thickness stuffing him. He stared at me from down there, letting flashes of rebellion and panic swap. It was on the second one that I pulled back and let him breathe.

A moment later, I was grabbing Riley under his arms and lifting him up, soothing his mouth with kisses he embraced and welcomed. My scent on his lips and tongue turned me on so hard that I couldn't resist reaching for his bare ass. I massaged his cheeks, grinding them together, spreading them apart, and squeezing them so hard that Riley moaned into my mouth.

I pulled back and spun him around, pressing his defined pecs against the wall and dropping on my knees with the sole mission to lift Riley all the way to heaven's gates. Up there, he would be turned back, no doubt, for all the sinful things I was about to do to him.

I pulled his underwear a little lower, still keeping them on his cock, but baring his ass completely. I spread his cheeks wide and savored a choked whimper that escaped his throat. When it passed, I buried my face between his cheeks and licked him gently, at first. It was sudden enough that he tensed, but moments later, Riley relaxed and pushed his ass back, pressing hard against my face.

His right hand fell to the back of my head and he held me there, my nose and mouth buried deep, my tongue working his tight, pink hole. I sucked and licked and slurped like a madman, not giving a damn about the embarrassing sounds I made as I devoured him. My tongue probed him, pushing hard against his hole until I felt him tighten and relax. And when I lifted my hands off his cheeks, then let them fall with a loud, wet slap, it hardly even scratched our shared, filthy fantasies. But the small shower cabin wasn't the ideal space to toss him over my knee and show him where he belonged.

Instead, I worked him with my tongue long and hard, then pressed my index finger against his hole and circled it several times. Slick and ready, he accepted me as soon as I added the faintest bit of extra pressure, entering him a bare inch before I felt him clench. I paused, waiting for him to relax, and getting precisely what I wanted. He thrust his butt back, his hole loosening and my finger sliding a little deeper. As if he couldn't stand the idea of not being in control, he grabbed my wrist and held me steady, panting against the tiled wall separating the stalls. He exhaled with a groan as he pulled my hand closer, my finger entering him to the last knuckle.

"Fuck," Riley grunted and I leaned in, licking his rim above my finger while turning my fist clockwise. His groaning grew faint and high-pitched as I pulled my finger back, almost all the way, before sliding in again, harder, and stretching him gently.

Riley was rising on his toes with each thrust of my fist; one hand around my wrist but lacking control, the other pressed against the wall. When I looked up, his head was lifted, his mouth open, but his voice wasn't passing through his throat. Instead, he was breathing through his mouth, air flowing in and out of him silently so as not to draw any accidental attention to what was happening here.

My stomach leaped with nervousness and thrill. We were in a locker room shower, for fuck's sake. It was empty, yeah, but we had no idea for how long. The sense of danger made it all the sweeter.

His breath hitched and his voice cracked. "Jesus, Cam..." His words were tortured, voice thin. "Fuck me or I'll cry."

I pulled my finger out, sliding my tongue over his hole a few more times as it pulsed. "Needy," I pointed out.

"Screw you," he rasped, though venom was gone from his voice.

My hand dropped on his ass before he could know what was coming. He yelped and broke my no-touching rule when his hand shot down to his trapped cock and rubbed.

"Stop that," I commanded and received a pained whimper in return, followed by total obedience.

I was up on my feet effortlessly. I watched Riley's breathing steady a little while I grabbed the condom and slipped it on. The slippery lube on it stayed on my fingers and I dragged them over his hole as I stepped behind him.

Riley didn't need me to direct him. We had always functioned like clockwork. It was always a dance we had flawlessly perfected, the two of us. Riley spread his legs and folded his arms between the wall and his head, surrendering himself to my mercy. And I positioned myself behind him, pressing the small of his back to ease it in for him. When he thrust his butt back, I settled my hard cock between his cheeks and held back shivers of my own while sliding through. I was feeling every little bit of him as I did this. The familiarity of Riley's body, no matter how much he changed and had grown in the time apart, resurfaced to the forefront of my mind and I stepped into the tide of his appeal.

I wrapped my fingers around the base of my cock and pressed the tip against his hole. He tightened by reflex and I leaned in to kiss his neck. It wasn't just a gentle peck of lips on skin, but a sensual kiss that slowly morphed into a bite. It raised his hackles for sure, but he relaxed his entrance and I pushed myself a little deeper.

The choked cry stopped me and I let him take over for a moment. Wiggling his hips, Riley pulled away from me, then returned to impale himself on my hard length. His arms unfolded and he set his hands on my hips, controlling my movements. When I grabbed him by his hips and yanked him back a little, he stopped me, but didn't pull fully away from me. Instead, he waited and adjusted, getting used to the sensation.

It was in that moment that I realized it had been a while for both of us, and not just me. Slowing down even more, I settled myself inside him and felt as tension left his muscles. Whatever pain there had been, it was fading now. He embraced me and pushed his ass back on me, letting me enter him an inch deeper.

"Now, you're mine," I growled and wrapped his arms behind his back, crossing his wrists and holding them in my left hand. Trapped, helpless, Riley found himself in his favorite position.

I wondered, for the briefest of moments, if anyone knew how desperate he was to be controlled like this.

Had other guys done this to him, too? Blind jealousy flooded my system and I pushed those thoughts away.

He wasn't truly mine.

I had nothing to be jealous of.

But heart and reason disagreed on it. And my heart was as possessive as ever.

My free hand traveled to his abdomen and I pressed him, pulling him on myself until his cheeks slapped hard against my crotch and he cried out with unfiltered ecstasy. He was still leaning against the wall, his upper chest plastered against the smooth tile, while I filled him and stretched him mercilessly. He was grinding the wall just as I was grinding him. My boy-toy; my wannabe captain and chief; my biggest adversary and my first true crush.

I felt his hole stretching around me and his soul tearing with the years of simmering resentment and the fulfillment of all our wishes in the moment. The two pieces of a grotesque puzzle that still fit in perfectly. Rage and lust; rivalry and companionship.

The deeper I explored him and the harder I rammed him, the closer to him I felt. It was like taking out the anger we had been carrying for weeks and putting it somewhere where it actually made me feel better. It wasn't simply sex. It never could be just that. This was sex with Riley. It was its own category.

I released his arms and Riley slammed his hands against the wall, scraping and clawing as he fought down his moans and cries. He chewed his lip to keep himself quiet, whimpering through his nose all the while.

My hands found his hips and I jerked him up, lifting him off his feet, and burying myself all the way until my balls ached with pressure. The weight of his body ensured he was impaled on me completely, so when I bounced him and pulled back, his body returned to mine.

I fucked Riley until the cold water couldn't catch up with washing away the sweat off my back. My arms were searing and my legs shaking, but I rammed him all the same. Sending bursts upon bursts of air out of his lungs.

He panted for more and hummed every time my cock rubbed against his prostate, his hole relaxing, then winking tightly around my base.

When Riley was on his feet again, he whimpered hard and murmured a plea. "...me come...let me...come...I need to..."

I found the rhythm that was driving us both crazy, sticking to it as I edged him closer and closer. He knew better than to touch himself without my spoken approval. But he didn't know he wasn't getting it. I had learned a trick or two in our time apart and I held him still, his torso bent forward a little, back arched.

I brought the intensity down a little, but the pace quickened. Hitting that spot that rendered him an unintelligible mess was the highlight of my day.

I swiped my left hand over his crotch, untangling the underwear and freeing his cock. It sprang out and I lifted Riley's torso upright, slamming my chest and abs together with his back and fucking him just the same. His moans were uncontrolled and rising, now, but I didn't stop him. I penetrated him, rubbing his sweet spot until one of his arms rose to clutch the back of my head and the other gripped my hip. He clawed at me, stiffening all over, and choking on a long moan that stopped abruptly.

Everything about him was tense, his hole clenching tight around my cock and pulsing rapidly, his breaths short and shallow, his fingers twitching and digging into my hip. He came in blows that spread his white heat all over the tiled wall of the stall, then whimpered: "Keep going."

I did, teetering on the very edge, as he forced his hole to loosen and embrace me. His orgasm was still thundering through him a few moments later, then he urged me to speed up.

I did and Riley grabbed his cock, spilling a litany of filth over his lips, crying that he was coming again.

Those few short words at the end, combined with the sensation of his body tipping over into another orgasm mere seconds after the first, removed every stop I'd had in me. My balls tightened and I slammed into him, kicking the last few squirts of cum out of him and dragging a few more fragile sighs out of his throat. My cock pulsed inside of him, filling the condom to dripping after such a long and unplanned abstinence.

When I was done, air finally flowed through my mouth and nose again, flooding my burning lungs and lifting my chest. I held Riley in a crushing bear hug, twitching and jerking all over, shaking and thrusting my hips forward only to receive a pained cry in return.

I settled myself inside of him, still, leaning in to kiss his nape and raise goosebumps on his skin wherever my breath touched it.

"Fuck..." Riley gasped. "Fuck..."

I couldn't even say that much. As the shivering passed, I felt myself sliding out of Riley. He inhaled deeply as I did. I took the condom off my softening cock and tossed it on the shelf to dispose of later. Riley turned around and faced me, his face pink and eyes mischievous.

His breaths were still uneven, as were mine, when he stepped toward me and let the water pour over his face.

He seemed to completely forget how much he hated showers that were anything but boiling. He batted his long, wet lashes at me. "You better fucking play well on Wednesday," he said, his voice tight with amusement and restrained laughter.

A side of my mouth cocked up in a lopsided grin. "What if I don't?"

He shrugged. It was an oddly elegant move with someone so broad-shouldered as Riley. "Let's worry about that if we fail."

And right now, I felt like I could totally sign up for that.

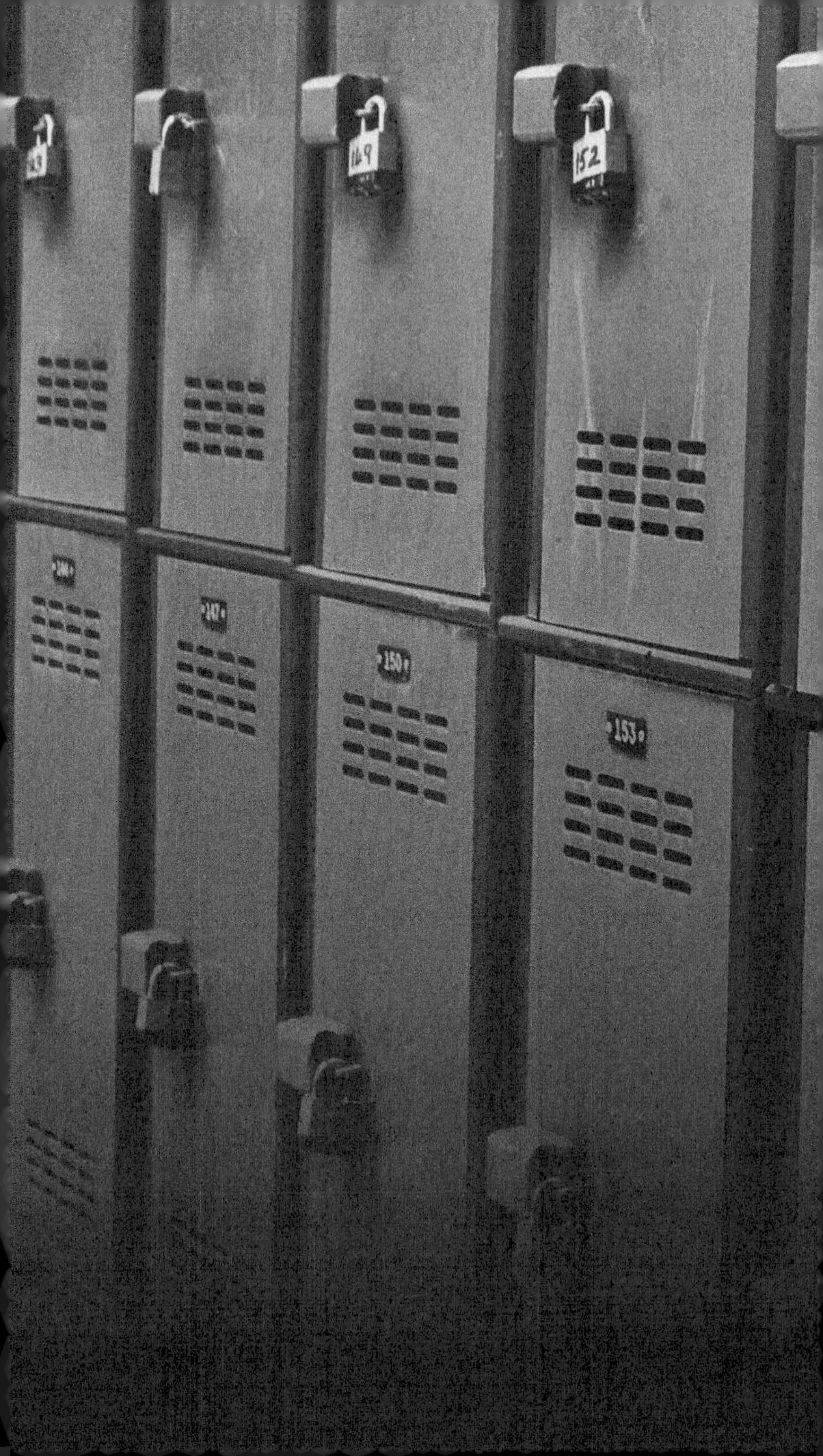
149
152
150
153

NINE

Riley

I awoke with a peculiar sense that I had dreamed that last twenty-four hours. Caden was still fast asleep when I writhed out of my bed, muscles in my legs tight and aching. My ass was sore and my heartbeat matched no rhythm I had ever heard. *If I'm shit on the ice tomorrow, it won't be 'cos of Cameron distracting me*, I thought as I wobbled to the bathroom.

The tingling sensation that was spreading through my lower abdomen was a welcome change of the status quo. I'd spent half the summer back home, where life consisted of cooking meals and cleaning dishes after eating, Sunday mass, and an everlasting sense of being out of place. The strained relationship I had with my family was like quicksand. The harder I tried to break free of their expectations, the more they sucked me in. To say the second half of my summer had been a dry and lonely one would be an understatement.

But even then, surrounded by all my memories of Cameron, I hadn't, in my wildest dreams, dared to imagine he would have me again. Especially not in a place like a locker room shower. Jesus Christ, we had to be crazy.

Just horny, my voice of reason, still waking up, supplied.

There was that, too, but it wasn't the biggest reason why we'd ended where we had. Cameron knew me. It was clear to me, especially yesterday, that he knew me like nobody else. Every little kink and every insecurity, he sniffed them out and spun them around.

However much he drove me crazy with his easy dismissal of my authority on the team or the depth of my feelings for all the shit that had gone down between us, I had a weakness for Cameron Martinez.

There were certain people you never totally moved on from. Your first crush. The first one that got away. And to me, Cameron was both of those. I didn't love it, but it was as true as anything.

I splashed my face with warm water, brushed my teeth, then put my running clothes on before quietly sneaking out of the room and the house. Part of me hoped, suddenly and stupidly, to run into him on my way out. In truth, it was a relief that I didn't. These flares of hope were infused with lust and that never sharpened your mind.

That morning, I ran like hell. I ran to loosen the knots in my muscles. And I ran from the tangled thoughts that tugged on my mind this way and that. I ran because I couldn't stand still and let the perfect storm of feelings pull me down.

By the time I circled the entire campus, I knew one thing for sure. We had given in to a temptation that had been building for weeks. It didn't have to mean anything.

I had more than enough reason to doubt it meant anything at all to Cameron.

Did it feel fucking fantastic? Hell yeah it did.

Did that mean something changed? Probably not. At best, we had a truce. A nice little ceasefire with the added bonus of a double orgasm in the shower. And holy Mother of God, that had been an explosive serving of delight.

When sweat covered me and my lungs stung with the cool morning air at each breath, I returned to the team house. I had just enough time to shower, grab a bite, and get ready for lectures. And in that time, I only encountered Sawyer and Caden in the house, both of whom were oblivious to the fact that I'd gone to shower with the enemy.

Though I kept looking over my shoulder, as if something would happen if only I spotted him, this entire day lacked Cameron. All until the evening when I found him in the basement, playing *Fallen Order* solo while a couple other guys made noise around the soccer table.

I feigned interest in the soccer match all the while looking at Cam's long neck. He was so deeply invested in the game of our teenage years that walking up to him and intruding felt like sacrilege. To us, that game had been the only thing that was ever holy. That and the shrine of lust we had made of my bed every Sunday morning.

I knew I had a ticket to hell, if my parents turned out to be right all along. It didn't matter. I carried it in my breast pocket. Even if it had ended where I'd thought it had, I always felt like it was worth it. The many hours Cameron and I had spent together were still locked up in a hidden compartment of my heart. Untouchable, but there.

Tyler scored the last point and Sebastian called the end to the soccer game, then they all filed out of the basement to take care of their notes from their lectures. All of us were here on a hockey scholarship, but that entailed maintaining passing marks everywhere else. And while mine had all been flying colors for the past three years, not all of my teammates were so dedicated. I often wondered why I bothered. My family had never seemed particularly pleased with my grades.

"And yet, you are still chasing a pipe dream," Dad had said the last time I had shown him my transcripts.

"A brilliant mind," Mom had added sadly. "Wasted potential."

My mood soured a little and I shoved my parents right the fuck out of my mind, then looked at the boss fight Cameron was struggling with. "The hell? I remember a time when you passed that one on your first try."

The fact that he didn't even flinch or look at me told me he had been aware of me all along. "I wasted my health boosters," he muttered.

"Excuses," I accused him and joined him on the sofa. "Your fingers are rusty."

Just as his character died again, Cameron turned his head slowly to me and gave me a grim look. "I don't remember you complaining about my fingers yesterday, Riley."

My eyes widened in shock and heat rose to my face. "I..."

"Exactly," he said after I stammered some more. "Now, stop distracting me or I'll have to shut you up myself." His game was loading and he was fully focused on the screen, but the suggestion of his words made hope zing through my chest like a shooting star.

If he joked about it, maybe he felt like a second time was a possibility.

"Ah," he mused, glancing at me ever so briefly when I inhaled through my quickly constricting throat. "I've made you horny. My apologies."

My nostrils flared and I narrowed my eyes at him. "You haven't."

"Sure, sure, sure." He was handling the controller like a pro, his thumbs swiping across the buttons, his index fingers bent over the top. The controller vibrated hard in his hands, lighting up each time he received a blow from the boss he was fighting. "You're just blushing because of the heat."

"I'm not blushing," I insisted heatedly.

He snorted and shook his head, tilting the controller like that gave him an advantage. "Now, you're being a brat who's asking for it."

"Asking for what?" I played dumb. "I'm not even sure what we're talking about."

Cameron threw his head back and laughed out loud, getting killed in the process. "Pick a lane, Brooks. Are we flirting or are we not?"

I swallowed, my mind spinning a little, and the familiar sense of needles pricking me through my insides. "Let's see how we do tomorrow, first, huh?"

Cameron dropped the controller to the other side of him, then threw an arm over the back of the sofa, facing me. His gray sweatpants were the bane of my evening, especially now that he lifted and bent one of his legs, sat on his foot, and shamelessly allowed me to look at the rising bulge. "Is that how it is? We play a good game, then reap the rewards in the shower?"

"Erm... That's not exactly what I meant." I bit my lip, fighting the urge to undress him with my eyes. The taunting, while we were clothed, did more harm than good. It annoyed me to pieces. "Why don't you stop tormenting me and play that game?"

"There's no better game than tormenting you, Riley," he said in an amused tone, picking up the controller again and shifting away from me. "It's full-immersion, open-world, state of the art stuff."

No matter the teasing that made me wrinkle my nose and growl at him, something had shifted between us. No wonder. Taking his big dick so unashamedly in the shower was bound to push the needle a wee little bit.

The miracle happened on Wednesday evening, when Coach Murray pinned us with a steely look that brought the temperature down in the already freezing rink. He didn't need to say the words for Cam and me to know our asses were on the line tonight.

Coach put us on the same team for the scrimmage, accompanied by Beckett on the left wing. If Cam had any reservations about being put on the right wing instead of center, he didn't voice them. For once, he let me take the lead without throwing a tantrum. Perhaps because he knew my leash was short and firmly in his hands since Monday. Me leading our team to victory didn't take anything away from his massive ego when he was the one who brought the captain to his knees.

For the first time since my blood had curdled in the basement upon seeing Cameron after three years of silence, we played the fuck out of this game. Somewhere along the way, magic was born again. Beckett, always cockier than skilled, was still a strong player for the team, although I would have preferred Caden on my left side.

It was Cameron, however, who carried the magic of this game.

He committed to his position and worked the offense against Caden's team. They were unified behind the assistant captain as they had been for the better part of this season. Aside from his eye rolls at Beckett, Caden had no enemies, rivals, or distractions. He had been carrying the burden of my role all this time and his team fought well for it.

But I had Cameron on my side today, which made all the difference so long as we played like one. And that we did. He was generous with sliding the puck my way instead of trying to take everyone on by himself. But, as I evaded Caden's attempt at a body check and slipped the puck back to Cam, I realized that it hadn't been just him.

Last week, I would have rather lost the puck to Caden and gotten checked, then to let Cameron score an extra point, no matter which team he played for.

I was the asshole, too.

Dammit. Moments of reflection such as these were better left for the quiet hours of a sleepless night. My heart was full of something fuzzy and weird when I realized that we could, in fact, be a team. We could work together.

And that was the moment when Sebastian slammed me against the boards and I went down laughing and crying at the same time. The impact knocked me off my skates and I flailed, sliding down until I was sprawling on ice, seeing that I had been effectively contained from fighting back Caden's offense. Cam, who had the shot to foil Caden's plans, wavered when he saw me sprawling and gasping for air. He missed the chance because his gaze lingered on me for too long. And when he rushed after Caden it was too late, but he left me filled with warmth despite a stupid and sentimental loss of a point.

Later, Sebastian marched up to me to hug me for not taking the blow so lightly, but I had barely been aware of anything except Cameron's horrified expression upon seeing me down. He had doubtlessly wondered if I'd broken something.

I should have thanked Sebastian, but I merely slapped his shoulder and told him that was the fun of the game. I'd always loved the physicality in hockey. I'd never gotten big enough to play football, but I'd never cared for it as much. I belong on the ice, my blades sliding and scraping, a stick in my hand. It was like Spartans fighting the Vikings if the game was good. There was a sense of battle and unity, today more than ever, that filled me with the feeling I had lacked most of my life.

Belonging.

This was my place. These were my people.

Cameron's outward attitude hadn't changed in the locker room. He was still quiet, brooding, almost suspicious. He did, however, search me for one naughty, sparkling instant, as we filed into the showers. He was entering the very same stall we had been in two days ago.

It exhilarated me, even though I picked a distant stall for myself, to think he was hinting at repeating it. Maybe that was exactly what we had needed. A way to vent without killing each other so that we could play properly.

Just as we all dried and dressed in the locker room — me, struggling to look anywhere but at Cameron's bare body — Coach entered. Most of the guys had left by then, but the few that remained decided to stick around and hear what Coach Murray had to say.

The clap that echoed against the walls made my head spin. For a moment, I thought he was being sarcastic. I couldn't understand why. This was the best I'd played in ages and Cam had given it his all. "Well, boys... You did it."

The weight that dropped off my chest was accented when Cam grabbed my shoulder and gave me a friendly shake. I didn't believe it for a second, but it was still reassuring to feel his hand on my body, even if it was as innocent as touching my shoulder.

"Whatever it was that you did, keep doing it," Coach said.

I was too stunned to speak and the temperature of my face was rocketing. Cam, though, pulled on his unbelievably innocent smile. "That we will, Coach. We sure will."

If anyone heard the dripping sex-appeal in Cam's voice, they weren't swayed by it. As for me... Well, I was struggling to stay on my feet. Sometimes, ice was better than solid ground.

But Cam's words echoed through my head long after we returned to the house and all went back to our own worries. Caden announced he was going out with a friend and wouldn't bite the bait no matter how much I was asking if it was a date. He wouldn't deny it, either.

When I stayed all alone, the room seemed to shrink around me rather than expand. I was pacing, thinking of how assured Cameron was when he said those words. Like it was a given. Like there was no way he could be wrong.

It excited me so much that he would just assume I would run to his heels at a single whistle. It fucking blinded me. And it looked to me like I was the most comfortable when there was an iron grip around me, squeezing air out of my lungs and threatening to crush me.

Even now, I was fighting for every breath. The glimpse into the wrongness of my desires made me bite my lip hard, right where I'd cut it not that long ago.

Before I knew what I was doing, I found myself getting out of my room and marching downstairs to Cameron's. I knocked once, hard, and heard him clear his throat. It was an invitation enough for me, so I walked in and shut the door. "What was that all about?" I demanded, annoyed with myself.

"What?" he asked.

"You know what. Telling Coach we'd keep doing whatever it takes to keep winning." A small frown creased the space between my eyebrows as I cocked my head in waiting.

Cameron lifted his eyebrows. "Are you for real?" he asked, incredulous. And when I gave no answer, he scoffed. "Sorry, then. Didn't mean to presume."

I looked around his room for the first time. There were a few trophies. One of them was from high school and I was there when he'd won it. But his words confused me and I stopped looking around and pierced him with a confused look. "Wait, what?"

Cameron hopped off his bed and walked up to me, crossing his arms at his chest, just one pace away. "Didn't expect that, did you?"

"Um... I... No."

"Did you want to fight a little, first?" His tone was serious, but I could see the amusement glowing behind his eyes.

"Actually, kind of." I had no choice but to admit it. It wasn't until he pointed it out that I realized a fight was exactly what I was baiting for. A fight, then making up. Because I wanted it. I wanted it more than I knew how to describe.

But I couldn't just get it.

It needed to feel hard-earned and dangerous and terrible in the best of ways.

Cameron bit his lip and nodded. "Alright. Since you insist on being a needy little brat, you're leaving me no choice but to cut you off."

The severity with which he spoke startled me. "Cut me off?"

"You heard me," Cam said in his flattest, most contemptuous voice. "I'm revoking your access to my dick."

"That's rich, assuming I want to have anything to do with you." My tone was growing heated, but my heart was jittery.

Cameron lifted one corner of his lips and let his arms drop, stepping heavily toward me until his face was inches away from mine. "Prove me wrong, Brooks. You came here with a purpose. Don't pretend to be coy when you're not. I can read you like a book."

My throat was tightening fast and my stomach was filling with butterflies. Holy shit. If this was a kink, I didn't know what to call it. But I knew I liked it. In part, it was like looking at something grotesque and bizarre that you couldn't decide if it was disgusting or beautiful. It was appealing, though. "You don't read, Cam," I wheezed.

"Don't pretend like you know me," Cameron

snapped, setting his hands on my hips and pushing me against the door of his room.

Breath hitched in my throat and I was lost. I was gone down the stream of lust. I melted into him, viciously clawing at his tight T-shirt, sticking to the sides of his torso. It was like a prelude to a wrestling match, but with a much happier ending.

And Cameron played his part beyond all my wildest expectations.

TEN

Cameron

Static energy filled the cold air of the rink. Chatter and cheers, as well as boos, ricocheted against the icy surface and the metal roof. The arena was filled with spectators, all of the avid fans of one team or the other.

The long awaited game that would open this season was finally on.

Though our training only felt like real practice over the last week or so, optimism had filled the locker room and the entire team was skating out with complete determination to take the win tonight.

"Alright, guys," Riley had told us before we had left the locker room. He had only briefly glanced at me, as though prolonged eye contact would cause us to shed our clothes and reveal to everyone how exactly we had been smoothing out our differences. "I can feel the victory." The team had clacked their sticks against the floor and hooted. "This season, we have the best team so far and you all know it. We've done our drills. We've had our scrimmages. It's time to show those Blizzard wusses what it means to be an Arctic Titan." The cheers had intensified. Riley, glowing with pride, continued. "If we win this one, we'll win the rest of the season, boys."

And while there had been no way to predict anything even close to that, the optimism had spread through the Titans. Now, we were still feeling electric as we readied for the game to begin.

Around me, it was all unfolding in a familiar way, but my attention drifted away from the ceremonies and to the guy I called my captain. His helmet covered his sun-kissed hair, but I could see it before my eyes if I only tried. I could feel its silkiness between my fingers and smell the lavender of his shampoo.

So when Jonah Hamilton, the Breakers' captain, hard checked Riley close to the end of the first period, my vision narrowed and I discovered myself filled with rage. Riley was fine, but I observed a moment where Jonah grabbed Riley's jersey and said something that made Riley pause for a moment too long. While he quickly returned to his senses, I filed the moment in my memory to discuss it later. I was busy, right now, chasing after the puck. Caden and Beckett, who seemed to be rolling their eyes at one another whenever their feet were on solid ground, played well as a team. The puck was sliding between them while I covered them from the enemy attacks, and Beckett scored the single point for our team in the first period, evening us out with the Breakers.

The intermission came as a relief. The strain of the first period of the first competitive match was durable, but the feeling that Riley had been unjustly threatened made my brain slow down just enough to give the enemy a slight advantage.

I skated across the rink to catch up with Riley, but

Jonah reached him first, grinning like a cocky fool after he threw an arm over Riley's shoulders. "Ever thought of studying hard and doing something you're actually good at, Ry?"

Whiteness of my own anger blinded me and I reached Riley's other side. I pretended I needed to speak to him as a teammate, so I slapped his right shoulder and carelessly pushed Jonah's arm away. "Need a word, Cap," I said. Riley was red after Jonah's remark and I pulled him to a side. "The fuck was that all about?"

"It's just Hamilton. He's like that." But Riley's voice was tight with hurt.

A growl rose from my throat.

"Leave it, Cam," Riley said. "He's an idiot."

"We'll see about that," I muttered, but Riley spun to face me.

"I mean it," he said, his blue gaze intense, like he was looking into my very soul. "He's an asshole, but I can put up with him."

I shrugged. "Sure. Fine. He's all yours." But a desperate need to put that jerk in his place was welling inside of me. It was good to be off ice for the next fifteen minutes and get my head together. We hydrated and listened to Coach Murray lay out the plans for the second period. Riley absent-mindedly rubbed his shoulder, which had slammed against the boards when Jonah had checked him and I felt myself reaching a decision that was completely based on feelings and not even a little on reason.

The problem with me was that I carried rage deep inside myself. In California, I had excelled because I had been, as Coach had put it, surrounded with mediocre players. That rage had nowhere to go except in aggressive, meaningless hookups. But even before Santa Barbara, I had been a quietly angry person. I had carried this anger in me since I could remember. Anger at my parents and the flying fucking saucers that would smash against the walls. Anger at the smell of booze filling the house at noon. Anger at feeling like Riley was doing me favors when he let me in to hide from the Sunday shouting matches in my own house.

Years had helped me hide it better, but it had never truly gone away.

And Jonah Hamilton painted a big, red target on himself when he told Riley to do something other than hockey. I could take a hard check on ice. We had all signed up for getting physical and leaving the rink with bruises. But to prod Riley where it hurt the most... Not on my fucking watch.

The second period was a bloodthirsty battle all over the rink. Few got through without bruising and I found myself in the thick of it. We scraped the icy surface with our blades and chipped our sticks. We struggled and skirmished. Nobody would leave the rink without feeling like they had meandered uselessly during this period. For twenty minutes, sweat poured over our bodies, then cooled down with the freezing temperatures. Jonah evaded me, though I was coy about seeking him out.

Riley was gliding through the center, heeding Coach Murray's advice, and matching each point the Breakers scored with one of our own. In this period, a true sense of kinship emerged among our entire team. It was something I hadn't truly felt since high school. In California, it had been hard to develop a bond with the team where nobody had their heart really set on hockey. Not like these guys, at least.

When Riley and I charged, breaking through the enemy defenses, followed by Caden, Beckett, and Sebastian, all of whom supported us without a question, I finally found it. That which I had been looking for all these years. It came from a short glance Riley and I exchanged. A quick grin and a rising sense of adventure.

I felt like I finally belonged somewhere.

For a moment. A semester. A year. My place was here.

And while Jonah remained out of my reach for the entire second period, it was in the final five minutes of the last period that he triggered my full wrath. Breakers were leading with a single point, like most of the game, and Riley was scrambling to organize our offense while increasingly under attack.

Just now, in the heat of the battle, I was filled with unwavering loyalty to our captain, and the team felt as much. No discord or rift existed among the Titans when we focused on swaying the course of the game. I skated shoulder to shoulder with Riley when Hamilton went on the defensive and crossed Riley's path.

I didn't know what he wanted to do.

My tunnel vision only allowed me to be aware of Riley's hurt feelings and the trigger of his life-long anxiety. When Hamilton yelled, "Just stop embarrassing yourself, asshole," the beast in me was unleashed.

I changed course in an instant, crossing paths in front of Riley and slamming Hamilton against the boards. It gave the Titans a good chance to slide through the Breakers' defenses and score the point that evened us out, but it also gave me a chance to press my forearm against Hamilton's collarbones and stare into his eyes. "Don't you fucking dare speak to him like that again. Don't even fucking look at him. Do you hear me?" I shoved the guy once, hard, against the boards and then pushed him away. When Jonah snarled at me, I slowed down and faced him.

"What the fuck is your problem?" he demanded.

"You are." The bark left my throat as my anger stalled the game.

"You'll fucking pay for this," Hamilton said and skated away.

I turned to meet Riley's gaze. He was looking at me questioningly, although around us mess and mayhem were intensifying.

I sneered and shook my head. "Only I get to call you 'asshole.'" My gaze remained locked to his.

Riley gave it a moment, the corners of his lips ticking up ever so slightly, and nodded. His airy voice came as if he was in awe. Or too exhausted to fight me. "Okay."

After that, we parted to the opposite sides of the rink, employing every trick we could think of to score the leading point before the end of the period. It would make for a clean victory that would open the season and set our spirits high for the rest of this year.

It would also look great on our record. I knew how quickly a year could pass. In no time, scouts would be swarming the rinks and looking for talented players like me. Or Riley, for that matter.

It didn't need to be a competition between us. Not if playing together for the win opened more doors to a brighter future.

But, as that thought crossed my mind, another followed. In eight months, we would be looking for our individual futures. There was no guarantee our paths would cross again any time soon. Worse still, the likelihood of us going in different directions was almost a given. How else would this story end? How else, if not with me and Riley going to different sides of the country, never standing a chance against geography?

The thought of this undefined, unnamed, and unexplained thing we had ending flooded me so much that I was almost numb to the rapturous cheers that filled the rink when Riley scored the winning point, with the help of his loyal assistant captain and the guy who held this team together while Riley and I took pleasure in hating each other this past month.

But seeing the glowing pride on Riley's face when he removed his helmet and was surrounded by most of our team that hailed him the winner, made my heart pound faster and louder. It grew in my chest and such warmth filled it that I needed to look away or the jig would be up.

I would congratulate him in a way he understood best. Later. Unlike all of them, practically lifting Riley to their shoulders, I knew what our captain really wanted. I knew what filled him with joy.

I had been doing it every other night for a week and I had no plans of slowing down. In fact, all I could see myself doing was luring Riley back to my room and throwing him a celebration party he couldn't resist.

As we left the rink, I spotted the wary stare of Jonah Hamilton, sulking over their defeat and glaring at me like I was enemy number one. It was fine by me. If I occupied the top spot, he'd be too distracted to meddle with Riley's sense of worth. And that was a victory of its own. He was skating away from his team and nearing me, so I slowed down.

"What do you want?" I growled at the fuckface.

He pretty much skated into me, stopping at the exact moment our bodies touched. "I want you to remember this face, asshole. 'Cause you'll be seeing a lot of it."

I grabbed his jersey with all the strength I had and pulled him closer, our helmets nearly slamming into one another. "Not around Riley Brooks, I won't."

Jonah snorted with a truckload of contempt. "We'll see about that." The look of mischief in his eyes told me to watch out for the fucker.

I pushed him away, nearly tipping him out of balance. He rubbed the spot on his chest where my hand applied the most pressure, then turned away from me, muttering profanities.

While tonight we partied as a team, I treated Riley to his private party the next day. Two days later, he returned, frustrated by his history professor, and took the fight to me until I shut him up the only way I could. Days were passing swifter than I could keep track of them and Riley kept returning to me much like the way I had been coming to him, all those years earlier.

Nothing else changed. We never spoke of what this meant or where it was leading us. When the quiet knock came to my door just before midnight every few days, it never startled me. It was always the moment when my mind blanked and I allowed myself to dive into the hours of pleasure without considering the consequences.

Just for a little while, nothing else mattered. Especially not when we kept winning. And even when we lost a match, we would give the opponents hell.

Though I knew good things couldn't last — like peace in my childhood household or the thrills of sharing Sundays with Riley during our senior year of high school — I was adamant about never questioning this one good thing. We enjoyed those moments which we could steal away. Outside those little bubbles of an alternate reality, Riley and I behaved much like any other pair of teammates. And if there was a disagreement, we both let it go, filing it as something to resolve the next time he visited.

We did little resolving when we were alone, though. Much like our reluctance to talk about the meaning of these encounters, we rarely talked about the issues we ran into. There was only me, Riley, and the heat that burned brighter with each encounter.

And for a few weeks of this fall, it truly felt like a truce.

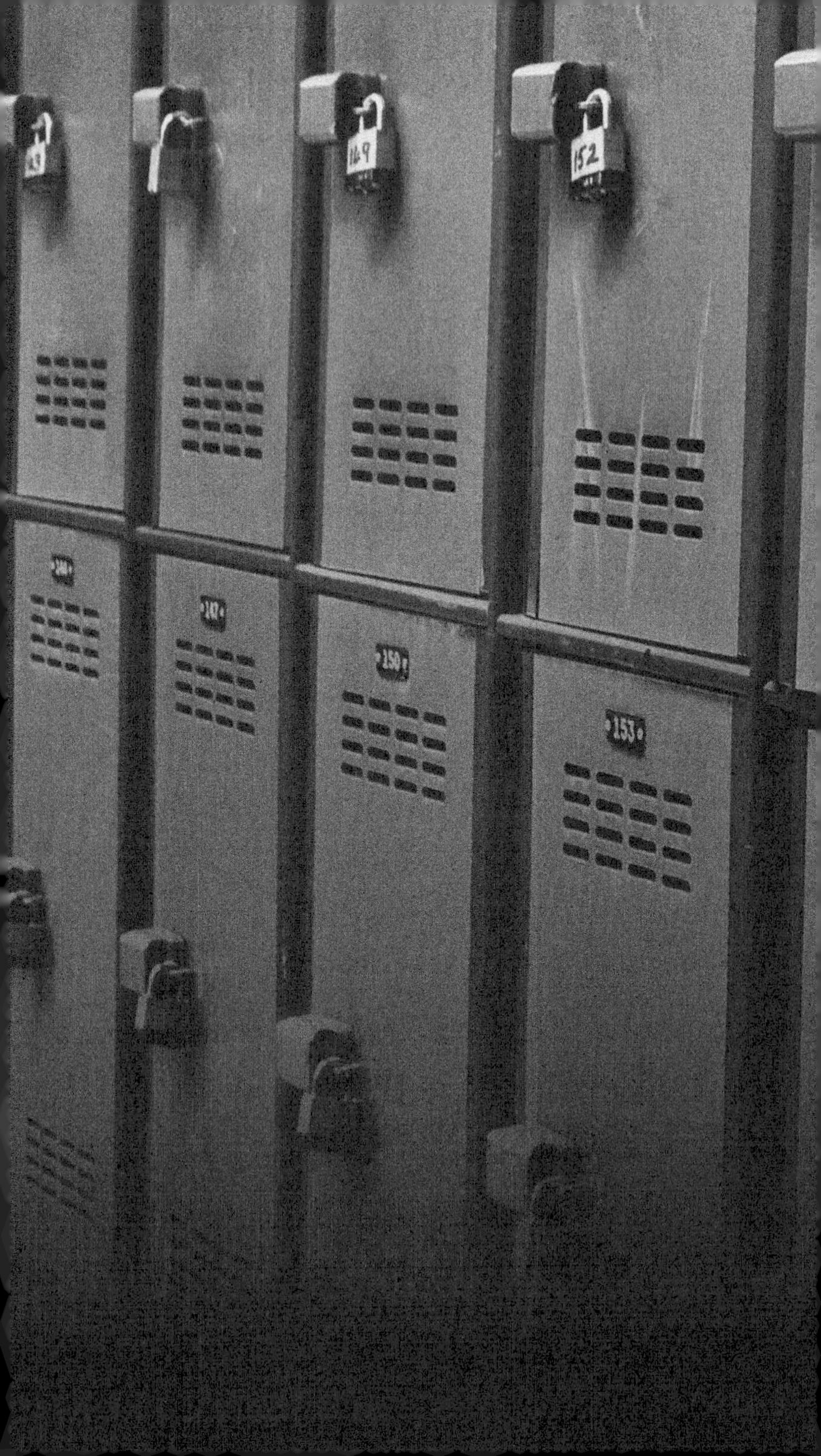
149
152
150
153

ELEVEN

Riley

THE FINAL DAYS BEFORE THE WINTER BREAK found us licking our wounds and hurrying to pass the end-of-semester exams. We played the last game of the period in Chicago and returned to Detroit with broken hearts and low spirits.

I found Sawyer in a corner in the basement, practically banging his head against the wall, a physics book hanging from one hand on the verge of slipping. "I'm never gonna make it. Never gonna make it." He finally turned around, red-eyed from sleepless nights, and leaned against the wall. "I'm done, man." He didn't say it directly to me, but more like he was speaking to an imaginary person comforting him.

"Sawyer?" I asked and glanced over at the couch where Cam was playing *Fallen Order* relentlessly. His slow and rusty thumbs had finally regained most of their skill. "Are you alright, buddy?"

"Am I alright?" Sawyer scoffed. "Jesus, Cap, I'm toast."

"Dude," I sighed. "Is it really that bad?"

Sawyer rubbed his eyes with one hand, the other releasing the textbook to smash against the floor. "There's no way I can pass this. And then I won't be able to catch up. And then I'll fail this goddamn course and lose my scholarship..."

"Is he spiraling?" Cameron asked from the sofa, glancing over his shoulder.

"I've got it," I said, not too kindly. Though I had given myself over to him in every physical way there was, Cameron and I kept our guards up whenever we weren't alone in his room. "Listen, I know a guy who knows a guy," I told Sawyer. It was a long shot, but I couldn't let my goalie despair and leave campus for Christmas in this state. "We can hook you up with that guy, Noah What's-His-Name. He tutored half the football team last year and nobody failed."

Sawyer looked at me like I was speaking of employing a poltergeist to teach him physics. "You're fucking kidding," he said. "Noah Foster quit tutoring 'dumb jocks' according to all the competitive nerds on campus, Cap. He's prepping geeks for national competitions now. Have you seen the line in front of his room every weekend?"

"I..." I scratched the back of my head. "I didn't realize that."

"I can see that," Sawyer said, voice clipped. Cameron apparently found that amusing since he was currently chuckling. I ignored him and focused on my goalie. "I never realized you were a quitter," I said, harsher. It was another long shot, but Sawyer hadn't reacted well to pampering and compassion. "The Sawyer I know grabs life by the balls and makes his own rules. If you want to pass this course next semester, you'll get Noah's help.

And if you want Noah's help, you'll march in there and convince him to help you."

Sawyer blinked twice, like he was emerging from a trance, opened his mouth, then closed it firmly and nodded.

"Do you hear me?" I all but shook him by the shoulders.

"Yeah, uh... Yeah, I hear you, Cap. Grab life by the balls." He nodded again, firmer, and bent down to pick up his textbook.

"Good," I said in the end. "Make sure you do that as soon as you're back from break."

"Aye, aye, Captain." Sawyer saluted me and drew toward the door. "Merry Christmas, guys."

"Same to you," I said.

Silence filled the room briefly as Cameron and I remained the last two souls in here. Then, dramatic music began playing on the TV and the clicking of the controller clued me in. Cameron was in a heated boss fight and getting himself killed by the time I turned around and started toward the sofa.

After everything, I still feared speaking to him. This feeling of dread had been present in high school, too. I could remember assuming, but never voicing my thoughts. I could remember dreaming up a future for us and never asking what he thought. God, I had been a moron. And I remained one, apparently.

It was so much easier to pout and receive the punishment — or reward, depending on who you asked — than to ask him anything even remotely personal. And it wasn't even Cameron I feared. In all my life, I had never been as close to anyone as I had been to Cam back then. But to ask a question and receive a negative answer terrified me after years of rejection and casual dismissal.

Great job, Dad, I thought. And, as I recognized where the fear stemmed from, I inhaled and let the smallest of my many questions leave my lips. "Christmas plans?" My voice was barely louder than a whisper as insecurities welled within me. Would he think I was clingy for asking? Would he think I was asking him to stay with me?

I barked at myself, a shield of anger protecting me until I forced myself to cool off.

Cameron was utterly unfazed. His snort of contempt said it all. But it wasn't directed at me. I could see it in his eyes as he dropped them from the screen where his character had just gotten killed. "You?"

I shrugged. How much truth was too much? How open is too open? "Not really."

Cameron looked at me fully for the first time this evening. "Aren't you going home?"

"I don't think so," I admitted.

"Your folks are gonna be bummed out." He set the controller on the cluttered coffee table in front of us, then shifted toward me. "They love Christmas."

It pained me how little he actually knew about my family. "They're obsessed with Jesus, not with Santa. And I don't fit in."

Cam nodded a little, like he understood everything and nothing at the same time. "That bad?"

"Coming out made it…not worse, but not better, either." I heard the words as they left my lips and realized I was forming sentences from thoughts that had long lived in my mind, but had never been spoken aloud.

"How so?" Cam asked. "Did they say something hurtful?"

"Not exactly," I said. "They didn't say anything. That's the part that bothers me, ya know? They just sort of nodded, said the mandatory happy wishes, and ceased asking me about my love life. Before that, they kept pestering me about having a secret girlfriend and so on. Afterwards? Nada. Not once did they ask me if I had a boyfriend. It's hockey all over again. They disapprove, sure, but it's not the quiet sort of disapproval. They just gave up on me. First in my profession, then in my romantic life. The closest they ever got to commenting was when they hinted my brother would be the only one to give them grandchildren."

"Oh, shit," Cameron muttered.

"Yeah." It was more a sigh than speech.

We sat in silence for a time, then Cameron licked his lips and inhaled reluctantly. "To answer the question, no. I've got no plans for Christmas."

"You're not going home?" I asked.

He ogled me like I was speaking in tongues. "Riley, I haven't been there in over three years."

"What? Not once?" I asked.

Cameron slouched slightly. I almost missed it, except that he suddenly appeared smaller in every way. "You know what they're like," he said.

I knew vaguely. We had never covered the details. Cameron had never wanted to talk about it and I had never been brave enough to insist. "I'm not sure I do."

He thought about this for a moment, then closed his eyes like he was giving up. "Of course. I never…" He pulled his eyelids back up and directed his blazing brown gaze at me. "I never let you in."

Words died on my tongue.

Cameron sank into the back of the sofa and dropped his

gaze lower on my face, then at my hands sitting uselessly in my lap. "They never got along, Mom and Dad. Like, never ever. Since I could remember, they were fuming in different corners of the house. It was like growing up in a minefield. I had to stay neutral, you know? I had to be careful where I went while they were fighting. For years, it was just words aimed at hurting the other one and me running away from the crossfire. But Dad accused Mom of turning me against him and…" His voice stopped abruptly and I realized I had been holding my breath. Cameron blinked. "I never knew he saw me like that. That I was against him? What the fuck? But that doesn't matter. They soon started throwing plates against the walls. Not at each other, but not aimlessly, either. Plates, cutlery, framed photos. All that shit was always broken at my place. Mom broke my computer screen. The only one I had until I moved away. Dad broke my first trophy. It's in my room now. I glued it back together. And this gigantic *Empire Strikes Back* puzzle I put together…" He smiled like he was revisiting a very fond memory. But the smile soured. "I came back from your place one time, way before we…" I knew what he meant, so I just nodded for him to move the conversation along. "Yeah, er. I returned and found the puzzle scattered because they were fighting over my interests and Mom spitefully tore it apart because Dad accused her of indoctrinating me with puzzles. He was venomous. She wanted to prove him wrong even if it ripped me the fuck apart." His growl faded out and I could see anger rising.

"Jesus, that's so messed up," I whispered. "I had no idea it was that bad." I had my suspicions. He had angrily shown up on my doorstep when I was alone far too many times for me to completely miss the hints. But I hadn't truly been there for him. "I wish I knew, then," I admitted.

"Tsk. I'm glad you didn't. That angry, eighteen-year-old Cam couldn't stand compassion, Riley." He was as blunt as I'd ever heard him with this. I had been his escape when he had needed it.

What did that make me, now? That was a question I didn't dare to ask. "But the adult Cameron deals with it better, huh?"

"Better?" He shrugged indecisively. "I don't know if this is better, but it's different."

I found that my left hand was restlessly touching my left knee. My nails were scraping along my jeans and I wanted to reach out to him with that hand, to take his, to make him feel better. As if touching his hand could make anything better. As if all those years of rage could be swept away with hand holding.

But I wanted to try, at least.

At that moment, the basement door opened, and Caden called. "Cap? You down there?"

"Yeah," I said, balling my fists now that the moment was over. Cameron reached for the controller and lost himself in the game before I even turned around to look at Caden. "'Sup?"

"Just... Merry Christmas," Caden said with a smile. "To both of you. I'm on my way out."

I hopped off the sofa and hugged my roommate goodbye, wished him a good time back home, and decided to leave Cameron to the game while I wandered around the quickly emptying team house.

Everyone had somewhere to go. Everyone had someone to be with. And, as I indulged in my pathetic feelings of loneliness, I realized that I also had someone to be with for Christmas. And he was downstairs.

We had the entire house to ourselves.

And holy shit if that didn't make me smile.

OUR CHRISTMAS EVE WAS MET WITH FEW festive traditions. We had a full fridge of Coke and the entire day snowed enough to leave us holed up in the house. The dinner I prepared was amateurish at best, coming from various frozen packages that needed baking, boiling, or microwaving. But when Cameron appeared at the door to his room and saw me toiling away in the kitchen, his deep chuckle made my skin prickle. "What are you doing?"

I wiped my hands against my apron. "Can't talk. Ruining Christmas dinner."

"I see that," Cameron said, swaggering out of his room and leaning against the huge kitchen island that separated me from the rest of the ground floor. "Is that mashed potatoes?"

A grin escaped me before I could suspend it. "Er...it's the instant kind."

"Brilliant," Cameron said and I couldn't decide if he was being sarcastic or not.

"It's the best I can do. Sorry." I stirred it as it bubbled on the stove, but the timer dinged and I had no idea what it had been timing. I checked the microwave, where an apple pie was defrosting, then decided it had to be our turkey in the oven. I hadn't gotten us a whole turkey. We'd never finish it. Instead, I just got the best parts. The gravy was off the shelf, too, so I didn't have to make anything from a recipe. "Last year, I was all alone, and it was good enough. Can't claim I got any better."

"You were here last Christmas?" Cameron asked, concern touching his voice for the briefest of moments.

I wanted to challenge the accusation in his tone, but I couldn't find any. It was strange. We hadn't bickered in hours. Maybe days. "Yeah," I replied simply. "I go home during summer, but prefer being alone than, you know, in a crowd where I'm invisible."

Cameron said nothing and I felt like I had overshared. Damn my tongue. For a while, this silence left me to simmer. "This place is eerie when there's no one around."

"I like it," I blurted.

Cam tilted his head to one side and examined my entire body, head to toe and back, while I filled the place with the scent of roasted turkey drumsticks and fanned the traces of smoke off the tray that I set on the kitchen island. "It would only get better if you wore less under that apron," he said with complete seriousness.

I arched an eyebrow. "If you ask nicely."

"Never gonna happen." Cam laughed out loud and continued smiling when his laughter died down. It was infectious and I found myself smiling when I turned away and pulled the apple pie from the microwave. I had never enjoyed Christmas in my entire life. My family had piled guilt all over it, removing the childish joy I might've had if there had ever been any talk of Santa or gifts. Speaking of which, I had one for Cameron. It was up in my room and I reminded myself not to forget to give it to him.

We ate in the big dining area of the ground floor that was between the large sofas on one end and the kitchen on the other. Cameron was quiet, although he commented that it was the best Christmas dinner he'd had in years.

I didn't buy it. "Just because you were alone in California, but I'll take it."

"Who told you I was alone?" he asked, his voice awfully suggestive.

My cheeks heated and I looked at his cheeky smile. "Er...I just assumed. I mean. Obviously. It doesn't matter. I mean, it doesn't matter if you were alone or had company. Or what kind of...company. Oh my god, please make me stop talking."

"You're rambling," Cameron said gently, obeying my final request.

I wanted to fall through the floor. Jealousy was a treacherous thing. I hadn't seen Cameron once in those three years. By all accounts, we were never going to see each other again. And yet, the thought of Cameron spending Christmas with someone else — even if they couldn't prepare dinner as well as me, apparently — ate at me from the inside. "I just want to say, it's cool. You can say shit like that."

"I know I can," he said confidently, playing games with me. Finally, he cracked a smile. "You're so red, I can't even keep my face straight. No, dummy, I wasn't having Christmas dates in California. It was with just a bunch of teammates."

I blinked a few times, licked my lips, and cleared my throat. "Sure. But...if you *had* Christmas dates, that would be totally normal."

"Sure it would. And still, you turned into a Red Riley-icious." He didn't even crack a smile at that. Instead, he shoved mashed potatoes into his mouth while I wanted to spontaneously combust.

After we had so much pie that Gluttony went, "Bro... Bring it down a notch," we washed it all down with a bit of cheap, bottom-shelf red wine while lounging on one of the large sofas downstairs. The decorative fireplace had a small pile of logs and twigs on one side and all the poking, dusting, and cleaning equipment you'd imagine on the other.

Cameron checked it out and asked if I thought it worked.

"We've never lit a fire in there," I replied.

His ears perked and eyes narrowed in mischief. I knew that look. That look made me feel like a naughty teen. I didn't even need him to gesture with his head or speak. I got up at the same time Cameron leaned into the fireplace and we both looked up its massive chimney. The thing was, you couldn't see anything. But there was a good, drafty feel in the air. It was getting pulled up and sucked out of the house.

In no time, Cameron had found paper in his room and began piling twigs on the hearth. When he lit it with a candle that had been flickering on the mantel all evening, the fire seemed like it would fail. The suction of the chimney almost killed it, but a few sparks glowed bright and the twigs kindled. Soon, the twigs were burning at full blaze and Cameron was adding the dry pieces of firewood that had been on the right side of the fireplace since before I moved in.

While he did that, I retreated quietly to my room and pulled out Cameron's gift from under the bed. As I made my way back, I felt dumber than a teenager in love. He didn't want gifts from me, right? It wasn't even appropriate. We were just fucking in order to play better as a team.

But the story he'd told me the other day had stuck

with me and I was already standing behind him with a box wrapped in Christmas paper. Cam turned around from the fire, visibly pleased with himself, only to meet my cringing face. "Wh-what's that?"

"I, uh, nothing. I got you something. It's stupid." *Stop fucking talking*, I barked internally. When hatred wasn't on hand to use as a shield, I was a yapping idiot. I blew out a breath of air and thrust the box forward. "It's okay if you hate it."

Cameron wagged his finger. "Hold on a minute." He hopped around me and practically leaped into his room, then hurried back. The red bag with elves dressed in green and thick white snowflakes was much smaller than the box I was holding, but the self-satisfying look on Cameron's face beat mine by a mile. "I figured, since we're all alone, I might as well get you a little something, too."

He set the bag on the table and grabbed the box from me playfully. "I'll go first." We sat down and Cam placed the box in his lap. He ripped the wrapping paper without a second thought and I wished I could rewind time and make all of this never happen because he frowned at the box when it was revealed.

I should have known. Getting him a fucking thousand-piece *Star Wars* puzzle was the surest way to poke a wound that had never truly healed. What the hell had I been thinking? I wondered how long it would take me to freeze if I just walked the fuck out of the house right now.

I held my breath as Cameron finished ripping the paper from all sides of the puzzle. "Riley," he said quietly, his voice deep and hoarse.

"Sorry," I said, scooting away from him. "I wasn't thinking..."

But I didn't get to say anything else. The swiftness with which Cam seized my sweater and cut the flow of words from my mouth terrified me until I felt the heat of his lips on mine and the wetness of his tongue enter my mouth.

I surrendered to the first kiss we shared in days and air slowly drained out of me. His hands were on each side of my face and he kissed me deeply and thoroughly like we would never get a chance again. *Great. Just what I need to think about right now. The finite amount of time we have left*. I pushed these thoughts aside just to savor the sweetness of his lips and tongue.

And when Cam pulled back, I shivered in need of more. "Wh…"

"This is the best gift ever," he whispered. Before I could even let the words sink in, he snatched the small bag from the table, then apparently changed his mind again and gave it to me. "This feels way too silly now, but maybe we can still put it to good use. Either way, you win Christmas, Riley."

I took the paper bag while grinning to myself like a school boy. He loved it. He freaking loved it. It was a huge risk, but the *Empire Strikes Back* movie poster puzzle was the only thing I could think of getting him. I hadn't realized what a gamble it was until it paid off.

I opened the colorful bag and my heart leaped as much as my cock sprang and air drained from me again. My throat tied and I wheezed as I pulled this single, plain object out. This was as much a gift for him as it was for me, but I wouldn't complain one bit. Or I would, but just enough to force him to use it.

It was a table tennis paddle with a big, flat, semi-circle and a nicely carved handle, finely sanded and polished. I could already feel it. I could hear it meeting my flesh. "Wow," I managed, my throat relaxing a little.

"Oh, you love it. Good." Cam grinned. When I looked up questioningly, he shook his head. "You're turning red, Riley. And not in the place I want to redden."

My eyes widened briefly as I turned the bat in my hand. He wanted to redden my cheeks? I'd go for it. I would go all the way. "Alright," I said matter-of-factly, then thrust the bat to him. "We'll play with my gift first."

"Now?" he asked, faltering only for a moment.

That was all the opening I needed to slide into my character. "Unless you're chickening out."

He startled, then frowned and assumed the other half of the role we played.

I went on. "You'll have to fight for it. I'm not just a toy waiting around for you. Come and take it."

The frown deepened on his face and he pushed himself a little closer to me, spinning the tennis paddle. "You are what I say you are, Riley. Remember?"

"Ohmyfuck," I blurted, strangled by my own body. I blinked twice at Cameron as he slammed the flat surface of the paddle against his open palm and winced.

"Stings," he mused, then swirled the paddle in his hand again. "Now, be a good boy, and stand up."

I didn't need to be told twice. But as I rose, I felt myself swelling and hardening. The bulge that formed in my sweatpants was pronounced enough to drag out a chuckle from Cameron. But there was nothing funny about this. The sinister sounds he made in his throat as I straightened sent shivers down my spine.

Cameron tossed the bat on the sofa and set his hands squarely on my hips, then looked up from his sitting position. Even so, he looked imposing and larger than the universe. He seemed to have me wrapped around his finger.

Being at his mercy was equally sexy as it was dangerous. To have him control me, possess me, and claim me aggressively in his unique fashion was the fulfillment of all my wet dreams. And yet, being his to play around with meant I was his to discard, too.

I hushed myself when Cameron spoke. "You're so fucking horny, Riley," he said, almost like he was scolding me. "All the goddamn time." There was a trace of humor in his voice as he sucked his teeth and shook his head in mock disapproval. "What will I ever do with you?" The hypothetical question dulled in my mind because, at the same time, Cam pulled my sweatpants over my ass, revealing a pair of briefs and cupping my firm, round butt. The front side was still fairly up, hooked over my hard cock.

I'd made it easy for him without even knowing. The drawstring on my sweats was untied like with all the shorts I'd worn the last summer we had spent together.

His touch was cool against my bare skin as he slid his hands down my legs, pulling my sweatpants lower. "Take them off," he commanded in a clipped tone. "Leave the briefs on."

I exhaled a shuddering breath of air, then did as I was told. Just as I bent to step out of my sweatpants, Cameron got up. The annoying two inches of height he had on me seemed like miles after I straightened and looked up into his eyes.

Cameron placed his hand gently on my face, then moved it around until it was at the back of my head. There, he closed his fist abruptly and a sliver of pain stung my scalp. He yanked my head back until I bared my teeth and growled up at him. But that seemed to amuse him. Like I was a puppy attempting to bark or bite.

"Are you seriously resisting me, Riley?" he asked, incredulous and sexy as all hell.

In reply, I reached forward and grabbed his long-sleeved T-shirt. I closed my fists around the soft fabric on the sides of his torso, earning a tighter grip on my hair. We were deadlocked in this bearhug, threatening to rip each other apart any moment. He lived for a little bit of resistance, and I loved seeing how far I could push him. We had always been like atoms in a fission bomb, igniting and splitting one another's very core. The devastation we threatened everything with was unimaginable. And yet, I was struggling to breathe and my cock was throbbing harder with each little move of his hand.

Cameron used his other hand to grab the bottom edge of my sweater. His move was so swift and clean that I barely knew what was happening before my arms flew up and the sweater disappeared. It fell in a heap somewhere behind me and Cameron stepped back to look at me.

I stood still, letting my chest rise and expand with a deep breath of air. The glare I directed at my lover was as much staged as everything else we did to one another, but I could feel it. Coating the desire and lust between us, the vengeful and aggressive roles we played were almost real. They were almost alter egos we carried deep inside of us.

"Are you gonna be good for me?" he asked, his gaze kissing every inch of my muscled torso.

"Was I ever?" I retorted, instinctively flexing my muscles like a real show off.

"Tsk." Cameron narrowed his eyes and let his gaze

linger on the massive bulge inside my briefs. "Get down on your knees," he said, gesturing with his head at the sofa.

I hesitated for a short while. "So you can make my ass red?" A tiny note of contempt touched my voice, but the fire in me blazed so hot that it was a wonder I could stand still at all.

"You deserve it, Riley," he said, wielding so much power with nothing more but his smoky tone. "Walking in here with that bubble-butt, putting me through hell, asking for it…"

My breath hitched and my lips parted a little.

"You sexy little fuck," Cameron said and it sure as hell got me to turn around and slide down onto the sofa, my knees sinking into the seat and arms folding over the back of it. My chest rested against my arms and I shuddered as I inhaled.

Cameron was slow and deliberate in his movement. He positioned himself behind me, pressing his fully dressed crotch against my ass. Then, he placed his hands on my hips and yanked me back against him. His soft sweatpants let the hardness of his cock rut against me. He swiped his thumbs along the edges of my briefs, tucking all of the fabric between my cheeks and baring my skin for the things he wished to do to me.

I was so fucking desperate to feel the bat on my flesh that I couldn't contain a whimper. It broke out of me at the slightest touch of his palm against my body.

"Christ, Riley, you're shaking," Cam said, his voice considerably softer.

I inhaled a deep breath of air and held it for a short while. "Hurt me, Cam," I whispered, harsher than I'd meant to, and bit my lip as I sensed him lean over for the paddle. Its smooth surface was beautiful on the skin of my cheeks. Cameron traced my butt with the tennis paddle, sending waves upon waves of chills up my spine. He pressed his free hand down on the small of my back, bending me until my ass was perched up for him.

"Your skin is so smooth," he said, purring with pleasure. "It's almost a shame to…"

The paddle slapped me hard and fast before I even knew he would do it. I yelped, digging my fingers into the sofa's soft back. "Fuck," I grunted.

"…make it so red and bruised," Cam continued uninterrupted. "But my boy is needy."

This time, I was ready, and he only got a strangled growl from me when the flat wood spanked my other cheek. The stinging spread all over my ass and the sensitivity to touch increased by a hundredfold. The smooth circling of the paddle over my skin was no longer just that, but a totally heightened experience.

"He likes to feel pain," Cameron went on, sliding the paddle in a circular motion over my right cheek.

I could tell he was holding back and dipping his toe in first, testing what his ingenious device was capable of. When he spanked my right cheek again, I whimpered into the fold of my arm. Burning spread several inches around the place he had struck and he fast soothed the hurt.

"He likes when I punish him," Cameron said, voice dropping lower, then landing another blow on the same side that made every muscle in my body cramp. I choked on a cry that never left my throat, but I was still far from the maximum I could take.

And Cameron knew it. He knew it so fucking well. In truth, he was the one who served obediently and I was the one coming out on top.

He slid his bare hand gently between my legs, cupping my tightly packed balls and pressing two fingers along the length of my trapped cock. He did it for a single purpose that I saw through right away. And it was the hottest fucking thing I knew.

When he spanked me on the left side, every inch of me pulsed, and Cameron hissed with pleasure as he felt my cock throb.

"My boy likes to play dirty," he said finally, lifting the paddle and tightening his grip on my cock and balls, just short of making me uncomfortable. And when the blow landed, my head sprung up and I yelped, sweat breaking over my back and brow.

"Harder, you fucker," I demanded.

"Easy, boy," he grunted back at me.

"Coward." The accusation, no matter how fictitious, still irked him enough to prove me wrong. Cam spanked me three times in a row, draining all the air out of me and leaving me shaking. He pulled back abruptly, hooking his finger under my briefs where they were tightly folded along my cleft. I could feel his knuckle brush against my pulsing hole and I shivered.

"Coward, huh?" he asked, slowly pulling the fabric of my underwear higher along my ass, tightening it over my cock and balls until I whimpered.

One of my hands shot down, desperate to free my cock of the pressure, but Cameron dropped the paddle against my ass again and it made me grab the sofa with all my might.

"Tsk," he said. "No touching."

I moaned in protest, but that was the extent of my abilities. Sweat beaded on my forehead, then trickled down my temples.

He pulled my briefs into my crease ferociously tight and the strength in his arm meant he would soon either lift me off the sofa or tear the fabric apart. I heard myself moaning, pleading with him for a little more, a little harder, but my words were a jumbled mess.

Cameron understood me, though. He knew that every ounce of pressure he applied and every bit of me he wrung was a promise of a brighter, harder, and more destructive finale. At long last, I could be loud. I could cry all I liked and he could spew filth without a care in the world.

We were all alone in the house and the realization freed me to spill a litany of filth back at him when he spanked me harder and faster. He held my underwear in his entire fist, now, yanking it up and rubbing my cock by extension, spanking me with the toy as much as he did with his hand when the toy became obsolete.

His skin on mine and the dirty slapping sounds filled me with lava that needed to erupt.

Finally, I disobeyed and rested my head on the back of the sofa, but thrust my arms back and found his hips. When I pulled him in, his crotch pressed firmly against my ass and I felt his hardness. "Fuck me, Cam," I begged, my voice frail and my entire body a glistening mess of sweat and fiery sensations.

Cameron stepped back. "Where's your phone, Riley?"

"Table." The fractured word required all my strength.

"Stay like that," he said and lifted my phone off the table. The sound of the camera app taking photos made my chest so tight it felt like it was collapsing in on itself. My heart tripped and hurried to catch up, losing every trace of rhythm. Cameron photographed the results of the abuse I begged for and tossed the phone onto the sofa before returning to stand behind me. "Now, I'm going to fuck the hell out of you, boy."

It was a wonder I didn't faint right there and then. He yanked my briefs down and my cock sprang and slapped my stomach once with the force of this move. The wetness of my precum didn't surprise me one bit when it cooled on my skin. The burning, tingling sensation on my ass turned me on so much that my brain felt out of balance.

Cam left my briefs around my knees and forbade me from moving around. I could hear him undressing, tossing his clothes left and right. Then, he grabbed my cheeks and sank to his knees.

His tongue was another wonder for the erotic world. Cameron was merciless in applying it to heighten every sensation and every trace of pleasure a person could feel. The gradually increasing pressure and the smooth, wet heat of his tongue on my most sensitive parts made me whimper and thrust my butt back. The sensation was almost like it tickled, somewhere deep inside of me, and I could imagine only one way to reach it and make it go away. My hand moved to the back of his head and I pressed him, his lips sealing around my rim and sucking me, then pressing the tip of his tongue so hard it was almost like he was trying to fuck me with it. Again and again, he changed methods abruptly, making my heart leap and my eyes roll back.

And when he pressed his finger against my hole, I was desperate to feel it breach me, enter me, and explore me. He did just that, but excruciatingly slowly, like he wanted me to beg louder and harder.

When he finally pulled back, I was more ready than I had ever been. "I want you on your back, Riley," he said.

In the months that had passed and the nights we had spent together, I had always tried to bury my head in his pillow to silence myself, then let him ride me from behind until we were both spent. But now, without a care in the world, I could have him like this.

I rolled back and fell flat over the sofa, incapable of controlling my exhausted muscles. I lay down and spread my legs, my cock flat on my stomach, glistening with silvery precum.

Cam towered over me, chiseled like a marble statue and beautiful like the first ray of golden sunlight after a dreadful nightmare. He was so hard that his cock stood at full mast, his sack heavy and full. I could feel the lust coursing through his veins just from the way his breath left him unevenly.

He stroked himself carefully, biting his lip as he examined the sweaty mess that my body was. "Christ, you're beautiful when you're dirty."

Then, I would be dirty. Pressing my left hand on my chest, I held his gaze and dragged my right hand down between my legs. He'd made me so slick that it was as easy as breathing. My index finger traced my rim and I adjusted a little to spread my cheeks, then filled myself with one, then two fingers.

Cameron observed intently, his chest pausing at a full breath, his ears perking and his pupils dilating. "Filthy boy," he purred, reaching down and holding my hand for me. His firm, merciless moves made my fingers fill me faster and harder until I was sliding them in and out as easily as blinking.

I could tell my mouth and eyebrows were contorting

in an ecstasy of joy and pleasure. I wiggled on the sofa, my body restless and needing something more. And just as I wanted him the most, Cam pulled back and bent down for his sweatpants, found a condom in his pocket, unwrapped it, and slipped it on within a few heartbeats.

I let my fingers slide out of me, my hole closing and tightening in their wake as I waited. Cameron knelt between my legs, stroking himself with the condom's lube and pure spit, just the way I liked it. The tip of his cock pressed my taint and I lifted my hips a little, letting it reach my hole.

"Ready?" he asked.

I nodded. It was impossible for me to utter a word at this point. The sensations were splashing through my chest and I couldn't untangle any of the jumbled controls over my body. It was best to let the master do what he did best.

Cameron sank into me gently, feeling for every trace of resistance, and looking intently into my eyes. He paused several times at the first sign of wincing, but I encouraged him to sink deeper with my hands on his hips. As he did, my voice flowed out of my tightening throat and my lips parted wide.

He entered me deeper and I clenched by instinct, savoring a little victory at the pained expression on his face.

"Fuck, that's tight," he growled, thrusting his hips forward and pressing his cock hard against my prostate.

I relaxed by the sheer force of will, pushing back hard and letting him slide in easier. And when he was deep enough, he let me look into his eyes for one frozen moment in time, then began to ram me like a beast.

My legs wrapped around his waist and my hands

brushed lightly over his fast hips while he leaned all of his body down on his hands, pressing against my broad chest with his weight. He fucked me like it was our last night together and he wished for me to always remember. He fucked me like I was a single-use hole made just for his pleasure. And it was the role I played the best.

When he leaned in and pressed his lips hard against mine, the sounds cut off and I realized how loudly I had been moaning. To kiss him while he filled me and connected our bodies and our souls was the greatest form of pleasure I had ever known. Never had a hookup brought me even close to feeling this safe, this close to another being, and this accepted for the freakish kink of loving to hurt. He kissed me deeply and fucked me harder, the naughty sounds of our bodies clashing filling my ears while my moans filled Cameron's mouth.

His balls pressed hard against my cheeks whenever he rammed me deep and I sighed into him with every breath he squeezed out of me.

When he lifted his torso, he was a gorgeous giant in possession of both my body and my soul. My heart beat in unison with his and I found myself falling hard for him in this instant of eye contact. Everything I had been willfully ignoring for months finally filled me to the brim and made itself known. How had I survived the last three years apart at all? How had I lived with the belief I would never see him again? Obviously, we belonged here, coiling and tangling, bringing each other to the climax that shattered my universe.

Cam lifted my legs, fucking me at a steady, merciless pace, and I hooked my ankles behind his neck. With the pure strength of an athlete, Cameron knelt straight as an arrow and lifted me with him. Each time he impaled me, precum dripped onto my stomach. Cam thumbed it roughly over my skin, then brought it to my lips. And if I hadn't already been at the gates of hell, he would have sent me there, now. I sucked his thumb into my mouth and tasted the salty precum with all the vigor I had in me.

He fucked me harder, pushing me into the sofa and leaning down. He bent my legs so that my heels were on his chest. He folded me over myself, towering above the ball my body formed. My knees were well above my head and my dick was some inches away from my face, but my ass was spread for Cameron who filled me from above. The angle gave him a chance to bury himself balls deep in me and do it loudly.

"Are you gonna be good for me?" he asked, unruly locks of black hair falling over his sweaty brow. He pressed his hands against my chest, then inched them closer together until he was holding me by my neck. I was about to lose it.

"Yes," I moaned. "I'll be good."

"You sure about that?" he asked.

Flutters filled me on top of everything. "I'll do anything," I gasped.

He quickened his pace, massaging my prostate with his cock relentlessly. He looked into my eyes and spoke the single hottest request I had ever received. "Come for me, Riley. Come in your mouth."

I inhaled sharply, but quickly grabbed my cock, having to reach around my own bent leg to get to it. My mouth opened wide, my tongue sliding out. With a keen eye, Cameron observed every moment of my obedience playing out. He gazed, filling me and edging me, stretching me so much that taking all of him felt no different than if I was fingering myself, except that his cock could play with the spot that made me want to laugh and cry at the same time. It was driving me blind with lust by the time I began stroking myself, lapping at empty air and breathing through my wide open mouth.

"Harder, Riley," he commanded and I obeyed.

I fisted my cock harder until my orgasm welled in me and exploded through my chest, stomach, and groin at the same time. Everything lost balance as my balls tightened and I tipped over the edge. I no longer had the chance to force myself to stay relaxed and open for Cam. Instead, like all my muscles, my hole tightened around the base of Cameron's cock, contorting his pretty face in a mixture of pleasure and pain.

Cum squirted in white strings of heat out of my cock, splattering my face and trickling down into my mouth. A week of waiting for this tour of heaven and hell made for a relentless stream of hot whiteness, pumping out of me for seconds upon delicious seconds. The sweet and salty flavor coated my tongue, more of the hotness filling my mouth until I felt it trickling down my throat.

"Give it to me," Cameron whispered, leaning down and pressing his lips against mine. Though he caught me by surprise and my body functioned on sheer instinct, making me swallow a good deal of my own load, Cameron's tongue reached deep into my mouth and he shared the fruits of our sins with me.

I whimpered into his mouth as he swallowed my cum, each thrust of his hips sending an electrical current to the furthest parts of my body. My toes curled and my eyes rolled back as Cameron licked my lips and face for every trace of my orgasm he could lap up.

And when he grunted and throbbed deep inside of me, I clenched harder still, grabbing all of his body and pulling it close to mine. Sweat mixed on our bodies while air drained from Cameron and he filled the condom. And when he tried to pull out, I wouldn't let him. I held him, feeling him inside of me and savoring every last moment I could drag out of this.

"Fuck, Riley," he whispered over my stained lips. His cock eventually slid out and we shifted so that he could lie half on top and half next to me. He looked into my eyes, then kissed the very tip of my nose. "Are you alright?"

"Alright?" I murmured. "I'm never gonna be the same again."

He chuckled, then laughed, then laughed some more. His lips pressed over mine and we kissed, laughing in waves.

And the longer I held him, the more I wanted to keep him right there. I wanted our lives to look no different than this. A merry fire on a snowy night and the heat of our sinful natures binding us together.

Why did it ever have to change?

TWELVE

Cameron

THE PUZZLE WAS NOTHING LIKE THE ONE I'D had as a teen, which made it infinitely better. I was enthralled with putting it together. Riley and I spent countless silent hours working on it for the next several weeks. The festivities thundered around us and the few days of privacy we had, we spent wisely. Well, maybe not wisely, per se, but we definitely didn't waste any.

It was only when the house was full of hockey players who had been treated to a few too many homemade meals and needed extra training and conditioning that Riley and I retreated to the privacy of my room for puzzle assembly.

The luckiest thing of all was the lack of interest on Caden's part. He never asked, as far as I knew, where Riley was in those hours between ten in the evening and two in the morning. And we never made a sound. Riley was well familiar with the feel of my pillow between his teeth. So, time was passing. And though everyone said this winter was dragging, to me it was all just snippets in a fever dream. Flashes of joy and lust, followed by deep, immovable loneliness.

It's you, I thought once while we were working on the corner of the puzzle that featured the *Millennium Falcon*. I glanced at Riley who was so lost in his work that he wasn't even aware of my gaze. *You're the piece I was missing*. The loneliness that had haunted me for three years in California had come out of nowhere. It had crawled into my bed and into my heart within weeks of arriving there. I'd thought, foolishly, that it was just a reaction to a big change. I had never traveled far and for so long before. I had never been that alone. But, as I met people and formed so-called friendships, my sense of isolation had only deepened.

It had run so deep that when Coach Murray reached out with an offer, I accepted it without thinking. To return to my home state and be near something familiar was all that kept me from going crazy in the final few months.

And I had known, all that time, that returning to visit my parents was not something I would do any time soon. Worse still, I had known that facing Riley after leaving for three years would be painful.

What had never crossed my mind was this. The longing for home was satisfied when we sprawled out on my floor like those school boys we had once been. When we found the missing pieces and finished each other's threads, revealing more of Han or Leia.

When Riley and I had first gotten together, *Fallen Order* had been the newest game on the market and every gamer geek, myself included, had gone crazy for it. The friendship that had, for years, existed between Riley and me only deepened and reformed when we began playing the game together. Then, when we stopped playing as much with his console and discovered there were some interesting activities we could be doing instead, it had been akin to forging two souls together in the deepest core of our Sun.

It confused me to my core how I ever thought that leaving that behind was a bargain. Especially now, when I found myself looking at Riley and leaning in to kiss him.

Day after day, week after week, Riley captained the Titans and Coach Murray grew bigger with pride. "My best boys," he started calling the entire team.

Winter gave way to spring at the very end of February when oddly warm winds swept most of the snow away. The team toured the state and won all the crucial battles against everyone who was foolish enough to think they stood a chance against us. The Breakers occasionally played against us in a friendly match and we won as many as we lost to them. But nothing could hinder our joint determination to win the state cup and get the championship Riley deserved.

To watch him come into his own was like growing up all over again. Riley Brooks, the true captain, and the natural-born leader. But then, at night, he would knock meekly and enter my den. He would shrug away all the responsibility of his daily life and I would take over.

"You are mine," I told him one night. "Don't you ever forget that." After that, he left with an odd air of sadness. I marked it and filed it away to ask him about it later. But, the truth was, I didn't need to ask much.

We had been doing this crazy, risky thing for a long time now, and we had never spoken about its meaning. What would we do in a few months, when the clock neared midnight, and the ball had to end?

I knew I deserved an NHL contract. I had been born with a stick in my hands and a puck in the center of my vision. Chasing it was all I knew how to do. I was good at it, and even better when I played shoulder to shoulder with Riley. I could follow well when I believed in the leader and I knew, deep in my heart, that spending my life on the ice was not something to negotiate.

And as scouts swarmed the benches in the coming weeks, and as Coach Murray kept motivating us with the tales of the NHL searching for young talent in generations before ours, it grew larger. This knowledge that Riley and I were skating together now because the race track was heading in the same direction. But we wouldn't do so forever. To expect that would be to expect an easy way of capturing lightning in a bottle.

Odds were stacked against us as more and more games took place. The better we played, the more likely the outcome was. We'd get drafted, each to his own, and life would take over once again.

Perhaps, someday, we might face off on opposing sides of the ice. And even that would be lucky. At least I'd get to see him.

The reality truly crashed one Monday evening in early March. We had just showered after drills because the Breakers had discovered a small weakness in our defense maneuvers which the wingers could assist but never before had. Drills were productive and even my blazing ass managed to play along and assume a brief defensive position to subvert the enemy's expectations.

Riley glanced at me guilelessly, not hinting at anything at all, but it was enough to increase my temperature and make me thirst after him. He'd pulled his hoodie over his bare torso and pretended to ignore me before he filed out with most of the team. He would come tonight, I knew it.

To my surprise, Coach Murray walked into our locker room and called for me. "I need to talk to you privately," he said.

Beckett made a mock horrified expression signaling I was in trouble. Sawyer was pouting in his corner, probably hating his life because he was still struggling with physics despite getting tutored according to the last report we had from him. Caden didn't pry, so if he assumed anything, he didn't engage. Avery was on his way out and received an approving tap from Coach Murray for today's drills. He wasn't an active player that often, but he was a good backup and today was one of the moments he got to shine.

"I'll be right there, Coach," I said and finished dressing, then followed Coach Murray to his office down the long hall. In there was a man I had seen in passing at a few of our games.

I slowed down abruptly as I entered. The man wore an iron-pressed shirt and elegant pants together with a larger-than-life smile on his face. "Ah, you must be Cameron Martinez."

"Yeah, that's me," I said suspiciously. "What's all this about?"

Coach Murray gestured for me to sit. I walked up to the chair in front of Coach's desk and waited a moment, then sat when Coach and the man sat down, too. "I'm sorry if this caught you by surprise. We didn't mean to gang up on you. My name is Jason Manning."

The realization clicked in the back of my mind half a second before Mr. Manning finished introducing himself. Of course. I knew his face. I knew his name. He was among the top ten agents in the country. Jason Manning was almost legendary among aspiring hockey players and I really should have recognized him right away.

I wanted to slap my forehead.

"You know me," Mr. Manning said with a pleased smile. His salt and pepper hair was slowly receding from his forehead and his eyebrows were bushy, but kindly. There was something deeply knowing in his green eyes, which combined well with the stark lines on his face that gave him a somewhat hardened look. I couldn't exactly pinpoint his age, but he was definitely still short of fifty, and in the years of work, he had acquired a high status among the NHL teams and aspiring players alike. "That's good to see."

"I...I do, I know you. I don't know why it took me so long," I blurted, trying to force my brain to work through all the reasons Jason Manning would be meeting with me. There was only one reason I could think of, but it was too surreal to believe in it.

"It's the beard," Mr. Manning said.

That was when my brain made the other connection. I had never seen him without his short, elegant beard until now. We shared a brief laugh and Coach Murray cleared his throat. "Martinez, Jason has been keeping an eye on your progress."

"Erm..." I lifted my eyebrows. "That's good. Right?"

Another short laugh passed between us and Mr. Manning leaned a little closer. "It's too soon to speak of things like interest among coaches, you see. Whatever little whispers are flying around are too faint and distilled to give any credence. However, I was surprised to discover that you haven't signed on with an agent already."

I held my breath for a moment, then decided admitting the truth was my safest bet. "I've spent three years playing at SBU in California. We didn't exactly make waves."

Coach Murray snorted. "You can say that again. I happened to watch a game by chance, then stayed for another by design. That team didn't deserve your talent, Martinez."

I wasn't going to badmouth the team I spent three years with, but...he was right. I smiled politely and gave a little shrug.

"So, you enlisted the promising future star yourself," Mr. Manning concluded.

I would be a liar if I said I was numb to flattery. To be seen as the promising future star of hockey was very near to the fulfillment of all my hopes and dreams.

"Indeed. And it was the best damn decision I made in ages," Coach Murray said.

I smiled at that, too, but a sense of dread filled me sooner than I was able to process it. I hurried to speak. "I'm only as good as the coach that trains me and the captain that leads the team."

When I looked at Coach Murray, he seemed well pleased with the first part of that sentence, but even more so with the last.

"That would be Riley Brooks," Mr. Manning said.

"Yes, Sir." Tightness in my chest awfully resembled anxiety.

Mr. Manning nodded. "I've had the pleasure of meeting Riley before."

I didn't let my surprise show. He'd never mentioned it. I was sure he had his reasons, so I simply waited for the conversation to move along.

"Like I said, talking about specific teams right now is

almost pointless. Drafting won't start for some time. But I'm sure you're aware that scouts have been watching the Titans intently and your name has been coming up in certain circles. It's good that you are familiar with the West Coast already." Mr. Manning smiled so brightly at the hint that there was a West Coast team interested in me, but my stomach felt hollow.

I had only just gotten a sense of home again. I had only just found something I enjoyed in my life that didn't involve ice and skates and brutal physical combat. No matter how much I loved the sport, my life had been a desolate desert in all the years of isolation. Would an offer so lucrative and life-changing come at the cost of ripping me away from the first place where I felt like I belonged? When I closed my eyes and imagined that place, it wasn't a location. It didn't have mountains and lakes or cities and towns. It was Riley's blue gaze. It was Riley's lips on mine and his heated breath washing over my neck whenever I made him feel particularly good.

"The West Coast is...amazing," I said, fighting against the fear choking me. This was it, right? This was the thing I had been hoping for my entire teenage and adult life.

"What I would like you to do, Cameron, is to keep my card and consider joining forces with me. I feel lucky enough to have been in the presence of several people mentioning your name, then to discover you are still not represented by someone who would protect your interests and fight tooth and nail to get you the best deal there is."

The knot in my throat was the result of far too many emotions swirling around me at once. I was beaming with pride that I had accomplished this much, no matter the amount of sweat and blood it had taken. I was desperate to stay in my small bubble for a while longer and slow down the passage of time if I could, just to earn a few more nights with Riley. And I was moved by the prospect of having an experienced fighter representing my interests at the big table.

I took the card from Jason Manning and thanked him.

"Remember this, if you will. You are a talented and devoted player, Cameron. You deserve the freedom to focus on your skill and on doing what you love. That is the best I can offer all the players I represent." Then, he went on dropping names that I was well familiar with. Jason Manning represented some of the country's biggest stars. Not only were they the highest paid hockey players, but they were the living legends that had inspired me as a boy.

"This is definitely something I'll think of a lot," I admitted. "I'm, uh, honestly just very surprised that you know of me, Mr. Manning."

"The pleasure and honor are all mine, my friend. Call me Jason," he said.

"Thank you. Jason." I tucked his card inside my pocket and mused aloud. "The West Coast."

Jason laughed. "Could be. Could very well be."

When we shook hands and I left the office, I was buzzing with excitement that I wanted to share. Except…I couldn't. It had a sharp edge of finality to it. I headed down the hallway and spotted Caden leaving at the door on the far end, then made my way after him at my own pace.

I guarded my thoughts as I left the building and headed to the team house. I couldn't just spill this excitement to Riley's face and flaunt my ticket to the West

Coast again. Wouldn't that be the final blow to the little bit of happiness we had managed to carve out for ourselves?

Even though we both knew this was just a fling to pass the time and help us vent, I also wanted it to be so much more than that. But I couldn't let myself imagine a future like that. If I did, it would be as though I wrote off my own future that I had worked so hard for. And his, too. Separately or together, we had far too much to lose.

So, when I got to the team house, I kept to myself in my room and waited for him. And when Riley knocked around ten that night, I didn't hesitate. I leaped at him and kissed him, ruining every chance at having a conversation that we might have had.

We made out until our faces were sore and Riley was so horny that he was humping my leg in desperation. "Need you. Want you. Can't stop this."

I replied with all the same words, blocking out all other thoughts. They were true. I needed him and I wanted him, too. I couldn't stop kissing him. If I did, I would have to tell him about Jason. And he would take it as well as he could. It would be betrayal all over again. And yet, it had been inevitable from the start.

I grabbed him and led him to my bed. "Tonight, you're going to ride me," I told him. "You'll be good for me and you'll ride me until you come."

His eyes were glazed with lust as he listened, following my lead and immersing himself in our game of passion. We undressed and pleasured each other in all the ways we could. Then, he did what he had been told. Sitting down on me, he rested his hands on my chest and rode me cowboy-style until we fucked each other's brains out and were left in a sweaty heap of gasping bodies. I hugged him for a long time after we'd thrown ourselves over the edge of our orgasms and soared in delight. I held him so hard that even breathing was hard, let alone talking.

And in all that, we somehow did the unimaginable.

We fell asleep in my room.

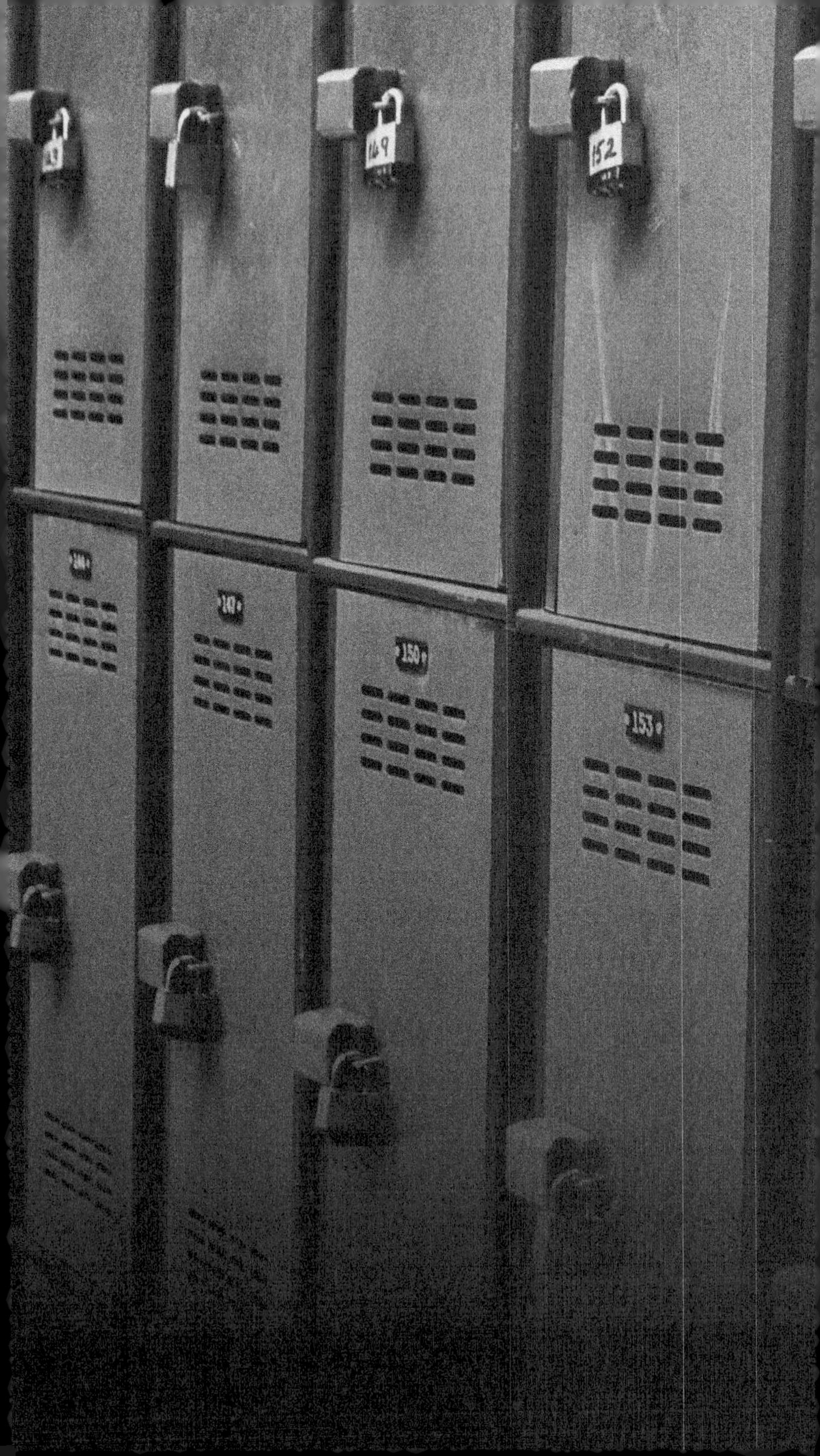
149
152
150
153

THIRTEEN

Riley

"Shit." I jerked awake at the beam of sunlight heating up my goddamn eyeballs. In the same instant, I specifically did not remember ever moving back upstairs to my room. The arms around my naked body were another clue that this was not my own bed. And then, the heated body of my lover wrapped all over me was really what gave Cameron away. "Cam," I hissed. "We overslept."

Cameron's room was inconveniently positioned just next to the kitchen and the common area. I could hear the clinking of cutlery in bowls and the footsteps outside the room. Our teammates were just there and the moment this door opened, they would sure as hell see me walking out.

"What?" Cam murmured.

"It's morning," I said, panic touching my voice. "We fell asleep. Dammit."

I got up first, no matter how much it pained me to leave the warmth our bodies had created under the sheets. Naked and dazed, it took me a moment to find my clothes and put them on. Cameron followed, reluctantly leaving the bed and also getting dressed. His hair was unruly as fuck from the pillow and from the action last night in which he'd been lying on his back for a solid forty minutes.

He was cute as a disgruntled kitten now, but I didn't have time for that. I went for the door and took the knob. Several voices were loudly talking outside.

We had been getting significant glances now and then, but we'd just tossed that to the oddness in the change of our behavior toward one another. Cameron and I had stopped bickering. And while I was sure Caden had his suspicions, he and I rarely spoke of intimate things and he knew how to keep a secret if he knew one. But the rest of them hadn't picked up on it just yet.

And now, we were screwed.

"I'm coming with you," Cameron offered bravely.

"Chivalry lives," I replied, my grimness matching his bravery. "Let's just get it over with, alright?"

"Aye, aye, Captain," Cam said.

We opened the door to dead silence. Every spoon stopped midway to its designated mouth and every pair of eyeballs moved to find two messy-haired, sleepy, and blatantly well-satisfied in the sex department guys filing out of Cam's room.

We stopped at the door and waited numbly as the silence drowned the room.

"God fucking dammit." Sawyer stomped his foot hard and pushed a hand into his pocket, pulled out a small wad of cash, and counted a couple of bills which he crumpled into balls and threw at Avery.

Avery, in turn, hooted. "I fucking knew it. Pay up,

bitches." He collected the bills shamelessly, then thrust his hands out for others.

Several growly guys were muttering their annoyance.

Horrified as much as I was, I couldn't stop gaping at the scene that played out before us. Cameron and I quietly filed out of the room to the overall disapproval of one half of our team and the cheers and applause from the other half. Sebastian glared at us. "You couldn't keep it in your pants, could you?" There was a slight hint of a smirk on his lips as he handed some cash to Tyler.

"Hold on, hold on, hold on," hurried Avery. "How long has this been going on?"

I crossed my arms over my chest. "I have *no* idea what this is all about."

"Drop the act, Cap. Your shirt is inside out. How long?" Avery demanded, so fucking smug. "September?"

Cameron was the one to give in and nod.

Avery clapped his hands and walked up to Tyler with an even less bearable smirk on his face. "Now *you* pay up."

Tyler rolled his eyes. "Fuck. I really thought it was Christmas."

"Wait, let me get this straight," I said. "You've all been betting on us fucking?"

Avery shook his head. "No. Of course not. Are you crazy? That's not how betting works. Only half of us were betting on you fucking. The other half are losers."

"Go fuck yourself," Sawyer said. "I really thought I had a nose for these things."

"Do you even know how disrespectful that is?" I asked, but try as I may, I couldn't hide the smile that was lighting up my face. They had all speculated about this. That had to mean there was something real about this thing Cameron and I had. Right? There was something here if the entire, mostly straight team of hockey jocks picked up on it.

"Oh boo-hoo," Avery said. "Let me wipe your crybaby tears with all this cash." He laughed out loud and I couldn't stop my own laughter from breaking out.

"Asshole." I punched his shoulder playfully.

By the kitchen island, I spotted Caden. It was his heavy gaze that drew my attention. When our eyes met, he gave a little nod and the faintest ghost of a smile.

I smiled back at him, but a sense of foreboding filled me sooner than I could keep up with my own thoughts. By the time I replied something to Avery and Sawyer, who were in a heated argument with Tyler detailing the entire timeline of my rivalry with Cameron, Caden had disappeared from the common area.

I tossed it aside and made my way to the fridge to grab some breakfast. Laughs and questions that had no place being asked among friends were filling the room. Which one was the bottom? Had we ever done it in other rooms? Was there preferential treatment on ice?

"I'm not answering that. I'm not answering that, either. And so long as nobody's seducing Coach Murray, I don't see how there would be any conflict of interest." I said no more than that. But those answers pretty much gave the truth away.

Tyler was the one to point at the sofa with eerie precision. "I bet it's that spot where Sebastian just sat."

"Ew. What? No way. Why'd you even say that?" Sebastian scooted to the actual spot from Christmas Eve.

"Nobody noticed they'd built a fire in here?" Tyler asked. "That's why I was sure it was Christmas. Damn. All that money."

"Don't weep," Avery suggested. "I'll buy you an ice cream. It's only fifty bucks, anyway."

Tyler shrugged and decided to accept the consolation prize while my cheeks burned like our Christmas fire. Cameron, however, joined me at the kitchen island and wore a little smile of his own. "Twenty years ago, this would have been unimaginable."

"Hm, yeah, no sense of decorum or honor among these guys," I said, purposefully misunderstanding his meaning. The truth was, it was an incredible thing. A team of athletes that made a bloodthirsty sport their entire life, was so unfazed by two of their teammates fucking all over their shared house that it really felt like our society had progressed this morning.

Cameron and I ate and evaded the increasingly personal questions thrown our way, replying with bewildered looks and questions of our own. "How the fuck do you even know what a rusty trombone means?" I gawked at Sawyer.

He shrugged. "I'm a man of the world, my friend. I've been around the block." He ran a heavily inked hand through his pitch-black hair and let a messy arch form over his forehead, then assumed his resting bitch face. Then he asked if the Czech hunter was a real thing and fuck if I knew what to say to that.

The mess of the morning gave way to the business of the day. I never got a chance to sit down — or, preferably, lie down — with Cameron to unpack all the excitement of the morning. And I never got to check in with Caden, either. Instead, we were all dragged to different faculty buildings for lectures. The schedules only allowed us all to reconvene at night and by that time, I was so tired that

I first headed to my room to shower and crash in bed for a few minutes.

Caden was at his desk when I entered the room. He looked at me over his shoulder and the same sense of loss crossed his face.

Dread filled me more acutely this time. I feared I knew what this could be. But I'd never gotten a hint from him. I'd never even seen him look at me like that. I was certain he was seeing other guys, too.

I mean, Caden was hot. He was tall and his thick, floppy curls gave him the look of a Greek statue of an ideal athlete. But I'd never been drawn to him. Even at my loneliest, last year, Caden had been my friend, but little else.

So when he looked at me sadly like this, I didn't know what to do. I didn't know how to react or what to say to him. I slowed down, shut the door, and frowned a little. "Are you alright?"

"Me? Yeah. Why?" he asked. Again, the way he looked at me was like death was following me.

"It's just…you're being kinda…I dunno." *Dammit.* I inhaled and parsed through my thoughts. "You looked kinda sad since Cam and I left his room this morning."

He cringed. "It's nothing. I just…" His eyebrows contorted and he looked properly pained.

I saw this wasn't something a few words would solve, so I walked up to the other desk and sat on my chair, then turned on it to face Caden. "You can tell me whatever's bothering you, you know that, right?"

"I know. It's just that…" He sighed. "Don't get me wrong, Cap. I'm happy for you. You've had a shitty deal of the hand for the last few years. I'm glad you and

Cameron are clicking. But the West Coast and all that. I guess I'm just sad that it can't go on forever like this."

I frowned when I lost his trail of thoughts. "What does the West Coast have to do with anything? He's been back since August."

Caden slouched. Everything about him got smaller as he closed his eyes in regret. Whatever it was, he was just admitting a blunder to himself. Slowly, he opened his eyes. "Shit." It was a whisper. "You don't know."

"I don't know...what?" I made a goofy, confused smile and shook my head in expectation.

"Fuck. Listen, it's really none of my business. I overheard something I wasn't supposed to hear. And maybe I'm wrong. I wasn't there in the room when they talked. I just passed by the door that was a little ajar." He was blurting words fast and I waved my hand to stop him.

"I get it. You weren't eavesdropping. But what happened?" I asked.

"Erm." Caden forced a short silence, then gave in. "That agent, Manning — you know him — was talking to Cam in Coach Murray's office. I don't know what they said, but it sounded like he was signing on to represent Cameron. Or would, soon. And he was saying something about West Coast teams wanting Cameron, but nothing's certain yet."

"Oh," I said, keeping my tone cool if I couldn't keep the heat of surprise out of my face. My mind spun but I nodded shortly. "That? That's good news, right?"

"Is it?" Caden asked. There was no venom in his tone. He was only doing this to protect a friend, but I couldn't stand the idea of being weak and needing protection. Even from a friend.

"Course it is," I insisted, my voice pitched higher.

"We knew this was just a...college thing. You can't have relationships and hockey, right?" Suddenly, it was too hard to talk. My eyes stung and my mind spun faster. "So...we're good?"

"Yeah," Caden said, obviously taken aback by my reaction. "Of course we're good."

I slapped his shoulder. It was the least I could do to show him some encouragement for being on my side. But I couldn't let myself break down here and now. I couldn't sit still and attempt to process these thoughts around anyone. "Anyway," I said, keeping my tone flat because my voice was shaky and about to crack. "I came to change. I think I'll go for a quick run. Didn't get a chance this morning, ya know?"

I did change, quickly, hiding my face from Caden who sat quietly and waited for me to leave. And when I did, I shut the door and rushed down the stairs. As I walked out of the house, my vision blurred, but I trudged on. The ground was wet from the last snow that had melted a few days earlier and the rain that had fallen yesterday, but it wasn't so slippery that I couldn't jog and clear my head.

But as I stepped onto the path, I saw him. The first and last love of my life. The guy who'd left me once before and made me swear off falling in love again. It was timely, in fact, that I learned this piece of information today. I only wished I had known it yesterday.

Cameron smiled at me and gestured with his chin. A silent, 'What's up?'

I couldn't control the frown that broke over my face as I marched on and bumped my shoulder against his. He stepped aside quickly.

"What the hell?" he called after me as I walked off the

path in front of our house and stepped onto the paved road that would take me all around Northwood. "Riley?"

I didn't stay to hear his calls after that. I broke into a jog and disappeared into the night. I needed to cool off. I needed to sort through my thoughts. I needed to get my heart to beat in some kind of rhythm.

It was lucky that I had learned my lesson early on. *You will always be left behind*. It was lucky that I was so good at hockey that my future was safe. I had agents vying for my attention and the drafting period coming up. I was going to do just fine.

I didn't need some guy to make me feel whole, even if he was the only one I had ever cared for. Those you kept the closest to your heart hurt you the worst. He would leave me. Of course he would. It was all fun and games in his room until he had a ticket out of his boring life again. I was a passing piece of entertainment, to be used however the fuck Cameron Martinez wanted. And though it was the role I had adored playing up until now, it wasn't something I would weep over again.

I wasn't going to let him break my heart again, either.

I wasn't going to sacrifice my own future and leave the agents waiting for my response. Because committing now, meant accepting the reality of our future. Which was nothing. There was no future for us.

I'd baited Manning and Hawke and Richards to wait for my call because I couldn't accept the fact that we would be drafted in a few months. I couldn't bring myself to sign that goddamn piece of paper and have someone work to take me away from this universe.

But I was a sentimental child in all of this. Instead of using reason, I always let my heart and imagination rule over me.

No more.

I needed to accept that our future was hockey. I needed to accept that Cameron and I had no way to ensure we could stay together even if we wanted to. And if he was so willing to jump ship and head back to the West Coast, he probably didn't give a fuck about me now any more than he had three years ago.

Cameron Martinez only thought about himself. And he was the smart one between the two of us. I should have taken that trick out of his book a long time ago.

All of this was one big mistake.

I ran like hell.

FOURTEEN

Cameron
———

I BARGED INTO THE HOUSE TO TOSS MY backpack and laptop bag into my room. As I headed across the common area, Caden Jones was leaning against the kitchen island opening up a bottle of water. He looked at me for a moment, then lifted his chin in greeting.

"Congrats, man," he said.

"On what?" My voice was so sour that I was sure he could half taste it.

"Er...the agent. And that West Coast team." He stretched his lips into a smile. "I know nothing's sure yet, but that's really good news."

My mind raced as I stared at this guy. "You..." I blinked once and Caden froze. I dropped my backpack on the floor. "You told him about my meeting. You heard me talk to Jason Manning. You fucking rat."

Caden's horror was genuine, but my torment was much worse so I didn't have time for pity. "Wh-what did I do? Oh God, what happened?"

"You ruined everything," I hissed and dropped my

laptop bag next to my backpack, then ran out of the house. I ran after him along the usual route he took in the mornings. Not nearly often enough, I had joined Riley for his morning jogs. In the mornings, you could at least see where your feet were landing.

I had always been far better at skating than running, but I did it anyway. "Riley," I called into the dark. The lamp post shed some light over the paved street, but not nearly enough for me to see much into the distance. "Riley!"

Cold air filled my lungs as I breathed deeper and deeper, burning me from the inside as my body worked to retain its temperature. I raced like lightning and finally spotted him down the lane.

"Riley, wait!" My voice was hoarse after breathing in too much cold air through my open mouth. Dammit, running was way harder than sliding along smooth ice. "Please."

Riley stopped and spun furiously enough that I regretted coming after him. Would it have been better if I'd waited for him to cool down? Probably, but I needed to make him understand. "What do you want? A goodbye kiss?"

"What are you talking about?" I demanded, my own temper rising.

"Spare me," he said darkly. "If you're gonna pretend you don't know what this is about, you can just fuck back off to California right now."

"Jesus." Anger filled me and I stepped up closer to him. "It's not like that. I just met with the guy. You met with him, too."

Riley shook his head. "It's not the same."

"How so? I just took his fucking card. What did you

do that's so different? Say no? It's fucking unfair that you're this angry with me." I stopped and waited for him to say something, but his lips curved down and he shook his head some more.

"I'm not angry, Cam," he said softly and I could hear the door to his heart shut and lock. "I'm being stupid. We both know where we're headed. I'm getting worked up over nothing, because I knew this would happen, Cam." He chewed his lower lip for a moment, then shrugged. "We were doomed from the start."

"Are you fucking kidding me?" I asked, louder than I had wished to. "Riley, we've been doing this for months. Are you just...dropping it? Because I met with an agent? I didn't even know there was a meeting."

"Nah," Riley said, voice breaking. "I'm saying we've been making a mistake for months. Don't tell me you imagined a bright future where we just lived happily ever after." The bitterness in his tone bruised me more than I had expected.

"I...don't know. I don't know what I imagined." It wasn't exactly your usual happy ending that I saw for us. I knew, deep down, where life was taking us. "I just wanted to enjoy the time we had."

He narrowed his eyes at that and I knew I'd said the worst possible thing ever. "Time we had? Jesus, Cam. We could have had years. Literal years. No. I'm done with this. It's time to grow the fuck up."

"Riley, please don't do this," I said, desperation mixing with my temper. "You know what we're like. We should...be together when we can. You know? We should..."

"Just because we have the same kink, it doesn't mean we should be risking the rest of our lives for it, Cam. I'm done." Tears not only welled in his eyes, but in mine, too. "You should pursue the West Coast or East Coast or whichever fucking coast you prefer. And I'll see whatever's the best offer on the table for me. We were gonna do this all along, right? Why fucking pretend? Why live in false hope when this was always going to be the endgame?" He wagged his finger between us at the last question and I stepped closer to him.

"Because it's good," I snapped. "It feels fucking good to have you while we're still here. I don't know what's gonna happen tomorrow. I don't know where we're gonna end up. All I know is this, seeing you makes me feel better when I'm down." Tears rolled down my cheeks and I wiped them away furiously.

Riley's lips contorted until he forced some calm back into his face. "And to go through this again in a month or two...nah. It's not worth it, Cam. Better just move on. Sign on with Manning and I'll make sure to choose another one so we can go as far apart as we can."

If we don't I'll never get over you, I thought.

Much like he had never gotten over me in all the years. "Jesus, Riley," I whispered.

"Don't," he said and stepped back. "Just move on, Cam. Of all people, you should have the easiest time doing that."

As he stepped back, anger flared in me at that jab. "Don't be an asshole."

"Tsk. Just being brutally honest," he said. "And minding my own business."

"Fine." The word tore out of me like the dirtiest curse ever put to sound. I spun away from him and marched back, concealing the further oncoming tears with throaty growls. I didn't go directly to the house. Instead, I walked around, as far from Riley's jogging route as I could think of.

Riley had just broken up with me. Ah, but it probably didn't qualify as a breakup. We'd only been fucking for a few months and we had been public about it for slightly longer than a catnap.

It felt like a breakup.

It felt like shit.

My heart was sinking and sinking and whenever I thought it had crashed at the bottom, it only fell through it and sank further. My stomach was restless, yet it felt hollow and bottomless. My eyes stung with the saltiness of my tears as much as the cold breeze rising over campus.

It wasn't just heartbreak. It was hardly that when we'd built our entire relationship on running away from serious conversations. But it was the profound sense of loss that ripped my soul right out of my chest.

It was the loneliness that had only ever taken a little nap and was now well rested to resume its job of tormenting me until the end of my days.

I could see it. I could see myself as a washed up hockey player who'd had all this potential and had lost it somewhere along the way when his will to live left him. I could see myself failing at everything all of the time.

I could see myself sitting in some place I called home, feeling nothing, and speaking to no one. I would be alone. Always and forever, I would lick my wounds and wonder what had ever happened with that Riley Brooks who I'd placed in the center of my world for a short while.

But I got exactly what I had coming. I'd done this to him. I'd taught him this trick. It was only fair that he would pull the same card on me when the clock struck midnight.

I made my way back to the house, where I spent the next two days barely leaving my room. The only time I actually left for any sort of commitment was for drills. And there, I was as clumsy as a puppy placed on ice for the first time in his life. I was as useful to the team as a drunk man without a day's training in hockey. And Riley...

Seeing him made me seethe with rage, but I wasn't fooling anyone. Rage was a thin veil covering the abyss of bitter pain that was hard to conceal and even harder to ignore. We saw very little of one another that night as well as on Friday. But each day that passed failed to do what the old adage promised. It only hurt more, not less.

It hurt more to live next to him.

It hurt more to eat my food.

It hurt to fail at hockey and I only had myself to blame for all of that.

While I did attend the lectures on Thursday and Friday, I was a ghost who haunted the amphitheaters rather than an attentive student. My professors droned on and on about things I couldn't care less about and I wasted all of my energy on pretending I was fine. And when I did see Riley, I needed to put in twice as much effort in seeming alright.

He, for his part, seemed just fine. He would see me and that was acknowledgment enough.

I hated it.

I hated every goddamn tiny little bit of it. We acted like strangers after all this time. And I wondered if this was what he felt like after I'd left.

Time slowed down at last. It was all I had ever wanted, but not like this. It seemed to be grinding to a halt every so often. Nights were endless now that they were lonely and lectures lasted entire semesters. Even the time spent in the house where Riley was only a staircase and two doors away from me stretched out indefinitely. Showers after practice and the walks from the rink to our house all doubled or even tripled their lengths.

But I had nothing to enjoy. Nothing for my memory to soak up for those times that would come after. We already were in the after times. This was the rest of my life even if I hadn't graduated.

It had been deeply stupid of me to imagine we would shake hands and part ways upon graduating. I should have known the pressure in the cooker would become critical far sooner.

But even so, as the week trudged on, I had one thing going for me even if I wasn't aware of it. I had the consolation that neither of us had moved on. And while I ended up calling Jason Manning to reaffirm my eagerness to have him represent me when the time came, I still felt like I had at that moment when Riley had spilled all those words into my face.

I kept my head high and pushed on. Loneliness was going to shroud me either way. I might as well make something out of the rest of my life. And if I sounded like a brat, swearing never to play with another toy because the one I wanted was taken away, then so be it. But I wasn't going to search for another human being who fit so well next to me. I wasn't going to put myself through the insufferable torture of getting to know someone's prickly sides just to make sure they complemented my prickly parts. Hell no. I'd had a real shot at it with Riley once before, and I'd thrown it away.

To have had the fugue to our old relationship was a blessing enough.

I'd never expected this much at all.

And so my mind went back and forth. I was grateful and hateful. I was mad and glad. I was hopeful of the future and I detested the thought of it lacking Riley. And in all that time, I had to put up with courteous nods exchanged between us when we were in a crowd. I had to suffer through the awkward silences of all these guys who'd been betting on our relationship one day and shrugging at its demise the next. And the worst of all, I had to suffer through the nights when all I did was stare at the door and expect him to knock one last time.

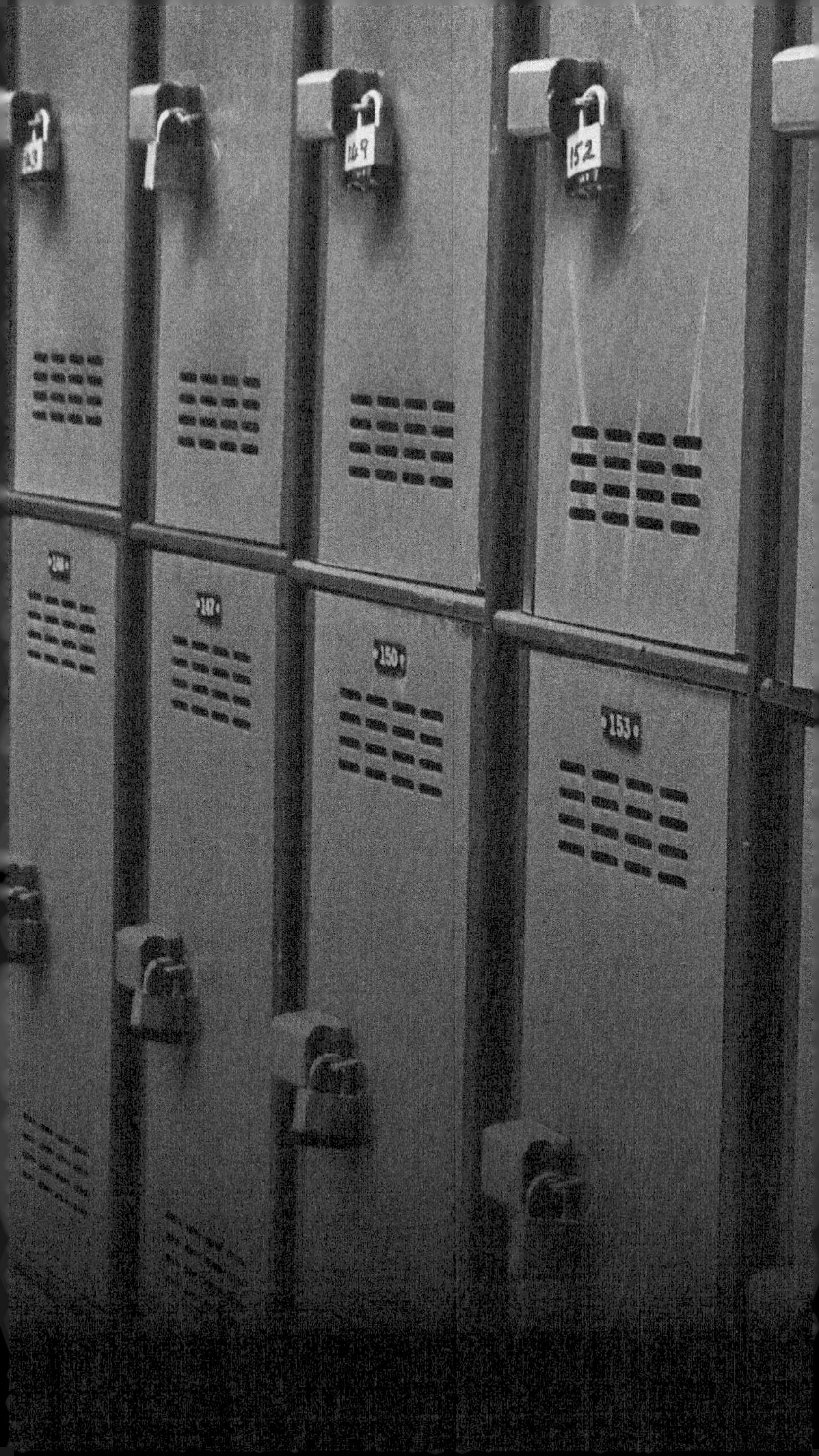
149
152
150
153

FIFTEEN

Riley

IN A LITTLE LESS THAN TWO WEEKS FOLLOWING whatever the equivalent of a breakup was when we hadn't actually been dating, nothing seemed any better. Although Caden apologized to me three million times and received the same answer each time, he still persisted. And I kept telling him he had done me a favor, but he felt responsible for my misery.

That was why he dragged me to a frat party on the first Saturday of April. We dressed in smart casual clothes and made our way to the frat house at the edge of campus. It was loud by the time we got there and promised to only get louder. And while I sensed a great deal of reluctance in Caden, who rarely did social occasions like this, I was secretly glad we came. It was good to pretend life was all normal again.

It was a blatant lie, mind you, but it was nice to fake a semblance of normalcy. Stiff as he was in this unnatural surrounding, Caden managed to bring us beer in plastic cups and frown upon discovering how cheap and crappy frat house beer from a keg was. It made me laugh, which was a novelty as of late.

"You know, I really didn't think I was meddling," Caden said.

"Jeez, dude, you really have to drop it." I threw my arm over his shoulders in a friendly hug. "I told you..."

"I know," he said. "I did you a favor and so on. But you have no idea what he looked like when he realized what I'd done. He was furious."

I didn't know what to say to that. "Water under the bridge, then," I muttered numbly.

"Shit," Caden said abruptly, looking at the door on the far side of the frat house. Cold washed over me when I realized Cam would probably come here, too. I looked over my shoulder and, for a moment, didn't know why Caden had reacted the way he had. Then I saw him. Jonah Fucking Hamilton. But just as I turned back to Caden to roll my eyes, I spotted a twink freshman approaching us and laying eyes on Caden.

"You know him?" I asked discreetly.

"Er..." Caden ogled me with a guilty expression. "I don't want to rub it in. It's just that I've been, you know, seeing..."

I tapped his shoulder shortly. "Go for it, buddy."

The freshman orbited us while keeping his eye on Caden until I stepped a little to the side. He then rounded on Caden with all of the interest your first year at college allowed you to express. Caden seemed to bask in the attention and I was genuinely happy for him.

My happiness went out like a candlelight on a breeze when I turned away from the lovebirds and was face to face with the Breakers' captain and my professional rival. "Jonah," I said sourly.

"Riley," he replied, mimicking my tone for laughs. His satellite friend detached and drifted into the mass. "Whatcha drinking?"

"Not arsenic, I'm sad to say," I admitted.

"Mm. That saddens us all. Still considering hockey?" He was expressionless as he spoke, his deep brown gaze reminiscent of another brown look I loved receiving. Fuck. They actually looked a little alike. And the resemblance made me want to stick around and hear this asshole out.

"Last I checked, the Titans are leading by two games, my nemesis." I pressed the edge of the plastic cup to my lips and smirked as I took a sip.

"Beginner's luck. You are a beginner, are you not? You play like one." The cheeky smile he shared made it safe to laugh. "Come. They have better beer in the back."

"What's wrong with Bud Light?" I protested.

Jonah shot me a look of pure contempt. "Same thing that's wrong with your technique. It's bland, unoriginal, and falls flat."

"You are, without a doubt, the biggest asshole I've ever met," I said and promptly followed my nemesis to the back of the room where there was a mini fridge stacked with cans of craft beer. I was intrigued.

"It's just the way I flirt," he said, cracking his beer open and some sloshing to the floor right away.

I snorted. "Is that what we're doing? Flirting?" Not that I was interested. Curious? Maybe a tiny little bit. For the fun of it. For the novelty. For the sheer power to distract me for a moment.

"The word on the street is, you're dating someone already. But also, the word is *you're not*." He shrugged and leaned against the wall, eyes on me without a sign of wavering. "You seem troubled."

Of all the things I could consider doing, telling Jonah Hamilton about my love life was definitely the least likely to happen. "I'm just suffering from all the attention agents are paying me these days."

"Oh, you have an agent? Is it the janitor? Did he say he knew a guy who knew a guy?" Jonah laughed.

"If you call this flirting, I'll bet money you're still a virgin." I tried the beer he had given me. It was arsenic free, but it was bitter enough to make me wish it was otherwise. Except, after a couple of sips, it grew on me.

"Virgin?" He threw his head back and roared. "Bottoms love a bad boy, Riley."

"Whoa, you're assuming a whole lot there," I said for playfulness' sake.

"Yes. Correctly though, am I right?" His smile was so self-satisfied that I had to roll my eyes. And concede that he was right. Dammit. It only made him laugh louder. "Tell me about those agents. Are they really flocking around you?"

"They sure like a winner," I said. "But don't worry. Your time will come, too." When he was silent, feigning emotional wounds and a broken heart, I sighed. "I've had three offers so far. Not exactly the craziest, but they're solid guys. Manning, Hawke, Richards."

"Manning," Jonah said with raised eyebrows. "Why are you even thinking about it?"

Because he'll represent the man who broke my heart. I shrugged. "Hawke is brilliant. He represents Nate Partridge and I'm sure he'll scoop my winger, Beckett, as soon as Beckett's a little more seasoned."

"Nate's famous because he's Nate, not because

Hawke made anything out of him. The first two teams Partridge played for were a travesty." Jonah said matter-of-factly.

"And the reason he climbed the ranks," I said in a tone that all but suggested a big, 'Duh.'

"I mean, if you wanna risk capturing that lightning, be my guest. Nothing helps me fall asleep as well as seeing you flat on your ass." He laughed a little. "I'm not here to give you career advice, but..."

"Right," I interrupted. "You're here to flirt. Great job so far."

He winked and I rolled my eyes. The thing was, the smallest spark of something that might turn into interest kindled in me. And it was quickly drowned out with sadness that this wasn't Cameron I was bickering with. "And what about Richards?" Jonah asked.

"A good choice. Steady. Well connected. Respected." I ran out of things to say about Richards.

Jonah, however, did not. He ticked them on his fingers. "Old-school. Irrelevant. Outdated. Well overdue for retirement. You're looking at a trophy of another time, my friend. He would have done wonders for your dad."

"My dad is a doctor," I said bitterly.

"Congratulations to the world. So happy for him." The nonchalant way he spoke made me laugh and I buried that laughter in the can of craft beer. Beneath the bitterness of the hops was a strong aroma of cranberries and I wasn't sure how I felt about it.

Jonah looked over my shoulder and at the window, then leaned in a little too much and I squirmed.

His breath was hot when he spoke. "It's raining."

I twisted away from him and he must have noticed because he pulled back and eyed me.

I looked away and had another sip of my beer.

"How come you're not a doctor, too?" he asked. "Isn't that how it works?"

"It's definitely not how it works," I protested, glad to change the course of our conversation. Then, quieter, I added: "My older brother is a doctor like our dad."

Jonah threw his head back and laughed out loud, but as he calmed, he shifted his weight and appeared a few inches closer to me.

"Who let you in?" I asked abruptly. "You're not a Northwood student. The party's invite only."

He snorted. "I'm the star captain of Detroit's oldest college hockey team. I'm on all invite lists."

I laughed at that. "A lot of big words, there, buddy. Maybe try getting yourself into the Northwood library and check a dictionary."

"Maybe we should sneak in there right now," he suggested.

And while the thought itself was a fun one, the image in my head ripped my heart into pieces. It was me and Cameron doing precisely what Jonah suggested. If there was something in this whole world that I wanted, it was for everything to be different. I wanted the proximity Cam offered when he was with me. I wanted possessive jealousy that sprawled from him whenever there was another guy near me. I wanted the protectiveness when someone — Jonah, for one — checked me against the boards.

And I'd thrown them all away months too soon. But it was for the better.

I just had to keep telling that to myself and maybe I would start believing it someday.

Jonah cocked his head. "What are you thinking about?"

"Nothing."

He stepped closer to me leaning against the wall so that his arm was hanging and his hand touched my shoulder. I scooted an inch away and found myself in the corner, only able to climb the mini fridge or push the guy away. And he hadn't done anything to deserve that. In fact, he had offered a respite from self-pity that I had so badly needed.

But then the back of his finger caressed my cheek and I had to stop this. "Listen…"

"Right, right," Jonah said, laughing. "You're dating, but not really. Sorry."

"Um, that's not it," I said. "I don't belong to someone. I have a working mind and free will, you know?"

He nodded like he understood, then acted like he hadn't heard a word I said. "I'm game for whatever, though." He finished his can while mine was three quarters full, then reached over me and set it on the mini fridge. When he was done, he lingered there, pinning me against the wall and looking at me challengingly.

"Okay," I said. "You're game, but I'm not." I wasn't sure if I frowned. I wasn't even sure if I made any expression at all. I did wince, for the briefest of moments. Jonah was straightening, but he wasn't moving away from me.

"You just need to get into the mood," Jonah said, a smirk stretching his lips.

"Er, I think I was clear," I said, pushing him back with the tip of my index finger.

He lifted his arm and rested his elbow on my shoulder, bringing his face up close. But after that, everything was happening way too quickly to keep up. A hand slapped down on Jonah's shoulder and we both startled.

"Didn't I tell you to stay the fuck away from him?" The growl sent chills down my spine. That same hand spun Jonah around easily and revealed its owner when Jonah staggered.

"Fuck off," Jonah barked, anger flushing across his face the moment he recognized Cameron.

Cam's fist was closed and flying through the air just as Jonah started to speak. Whatever Jonah's 'Mother...' meant, he never got to finish it because Cameron's fist kissed his pearly white teeth and sent him crashing into three guys who stood a few feet away.

"Jesus. Fuck." My voice broke from me in horror, exaggerated to conceal the relief I felt that Jonah was no longer leaning into me and joy at my protector being Cameron after all. "Don't... Fuck!"

Jonah leaped when the three guys stood him upright but failed to hold him back. He tackled Cameron to the ground, but the amount of booze he'd had somewhere before coming to the party had made him slow and dazed. "I told you to remember this face. And it's owner is now going to fuck you up."

While Jonah managed to hit Cameron's nose with his forehead, probably by accident, Cameron was quickly on top of Jonah, pinning him to the ground and sharing a couple of not-too-harsh blows to send a message. But when Jonah spat at Cam, it bought him just enough time to throw Cam off and try climbing on top of him. "And I told you never to go near him again, you pathetic piece of shit."

A crowd formed within seconds and I realized I was

getting pushed back by guys who tried to separate Cam and Jonah. I felt like a fucking coward, but it had happened too quickly.

While there were a bunch of guys pulling Cam back and containing him, the two who were supposed to do the same to Jonah failed. He tore free and jumped on Cameron while he was defenseless, punching him once in the eye and splitting his eyebrow enough to send blood pouring down his cheek.

My feet worked as I watched the only guy I'd ever loved get punched. I tried to push through the crowd, but it grew denser and it managed to stop Jonah from attacking Cameron.

"Get them out. Both of them. Out. Now!" Someone was yelling while a few guys were able to grab Jonah and drag him outside, practically throwing him out the door.

I hurried around the other half of the crowd, grabbing a kitchen towel someone had been carrying. I managed to stop them from throwing Cam out right away and pressed the cloth to his eyebrow.

"It's fine," Cam growled, wincing at my touch.

"It's not." I dabbed him methodically, then pressed the cloth hard against the eyebrow to stop the bleeding.

"I'm not kidding. Out!" The guy shouting was sending bunches of people outside as the fight sparked more skirmishes. The guy who'd come with Jonah was leaving with his arms raised in defense and a pissed expression on his face. He was ruffled, too. "You too, buddy." This was said to one of us, but it didn't matter which.

Cam marched outside before I could help him and I followed. "Fine, fine. We're leaving."

"Seriously. Animals." The frat guy shut the door as soon as we stepped outside into the rain. Jonah and his friend had already disappeared somewhere and only Cam and I remained.

Rain soaked my hair and shirt within moments as we walked a few paces away from the noise of the house, then stopped. We watched one another with passionate fury and more hurts than you could unpack in a lifetime. Cam hid half his expression behind the balled up cloth over his brow, his other eye never leaving my face.

"What in the hell are you doing?" I finally spat.

"What the fuck do you mean?" he demanded.

I jerked my head left and right. "Getting into fights like that." My voice carried a metallic quality of anger.

"I was protecting your ass from a creep." His voice was tight, too. Anger was swelling in us both, but the fury of the fight was fading.

"Did I ask you to protect my ass?" I returned fire at this reckless, temperamental man. Infuriating. Fiery. Completely incapable of thinking things through. "You don't know the guy. He could have had a hidden knife." I stepped toward him, almost tempted to tackle him myself for taking such foolish risks. Instead, I balled my fists and grounded myself firmly in front of Cam.

"If he did, I'm twice as glad I got him first," Cam barked.

"Jesus," I sighed. "I can defend myself." Except, I wanted to hold him and kiss him and hug him until he couldn't breathe for the very fact that he'd stepped in without thinking. And I wanted to slap him myself for it, too.

"I saw him touching you." The worry in his voice mixed with rage. "He made you uncomfortable. I could fucking see you."

I frowned, misunderstanding him intentionally.

"Why the fuck do you care who's touching me?"

This provoked a flare of fury brighter and more devastating than I had ever seen in him. "Why shouldn't I fucking care? That creep was making you uncomfortable and I stepped in. You're welcome."

"You don't get to be jealous, Cam," I said, my voice cracking at his name.

He applied more pressure on the wound and bared his teeth. "I'm not jealous, asshole. I'm trying to protect you." He breathed for a moment, the rain pattering down on both of us. "Besides, why shouldn't I be jealous? You left *me*."

"You're the one who left," I accused, a river of feelings swelling and cracking the dam. "Almost four years ago, Cam. You left and you fucking broke me to pieces." I found myself nearing him, bringing my face closer to his.

Cam pulled away the fist that was holding the kitchen cloth. Blood stained his handsome face. He was frowning much the way I was. No words came from him as he glared at me, nostrils flaring.

"What else was I supposed to do?" I asked, my tone bitter and dropping low. "I know what Cameron Martinez does when he gets a ticket out. Was I supposed to wait for you to dump my ass again?"

He shook his head jerkily, but I didn't let him speak.

"I swore to myself never to repeat the same mistake," I said, louder against the increasing splashing of rain against the puddles on the pavement. "I'll never be that naive kid again. Once was more than enough to teach me to guard my heart. So if you think I was going to keep building this house on quicksand, you're really fucking full of yourself."

"And your solution was to get back at me?" he

growled. "Real fucking rich, Riley."

I stepped forward, bumping my chest against his just enough to make his eyes narrow. "I wasn't getting back at you, asshole. You took your golden ticket when you could. Why shouldn't I put myself first, then?"

"I never said you shouldn't. But we could have talked about it. Instead, you just cut me out." He frowned, causing a small amount of fresh blood to trickle on the outer side of his eye.

"How is that any different than what you did to me?" I whispered, the same old feelings from years ago choking me now. I stared into his eyes as my own brimmed with rain and tears. "We're fucking cursed."

"Dammit, Riley," he said, biting his lip as the corners of his mouth pulled down. "I'm sorry. I'm so fucking sorry that I left. It was never about you. Except, when I left you, my entire life got worse." Cam looked down, partly in shame and partly to conceal his eyes from the downpour. "I thought we were too young. I didn't want to be *in love* with you because I saw in my own house how falling in love ended. Smashing the fucking plates so often that we ended up with a cupboard full of single-use plastic plates. I thought all couples got there in the end."

I bit my lip and waited, my heart splitting for the boy he had been.

"I just wanted to run away," he said in a hoarse whisper. "I just wanted a better life. But when I got there, I realized you were the only good thing I had in my world. But it was too late."

"You could have..." I choked on the words and never finished that sentence.

"Called?" He shook his head. "Christ, Riley. I was so embarrassed that I failed. I left the only person I ever cared about for nothing. Do you even know what that does to you?"

I couldn't wrap my mind around it. All of me caught onto the fact that I had been the only person he'd ever cared about.

"I lost my chance with you, then," he said. "There was no going back. Until Coach Murray invited me. I knew, Riley. I fucking knew you were the captain and I knew we'd be at each other's necks *because* we had some unresolved issues. But I still jumped at the opportunity before he had a chance to even finish his sentence. It's like this massive black hole inside of me was finally filled when I saw myself coming back." He shook his head, pulling away from me by a few inches. "It took me longer to see it, but I feel like part of me knew it. Part of me knew that you were what made me feel whole."

Rain poured over my face, concealing my tears well enough now that they streamed down my cheeks. "What are you saying?"

"I don't know," he said, moving his shoulders and arms in a big, open shrug. "Maybe that you're way stronger than I could ever be. I left you for three years and look at you. The best fucking thing that happened to hockey in the entire tri-state region. And me? Not even two weeks and I'm a wreck, Riley. I can't stop thinking about you. I can't live with the guilt of leaving you behind when you were all I needed. You were all that made me happy then and I abandoned you. I didn't know better, I swear. I'd never make the same mistake again."

"Cam," I whispered, far too choked with emotions to speak. "But we're going to get drafted. What if...?" I trailed off.

"So?" he asked. "I don't care how it works. I just want

to be with you. Do you hear me?" He stepped closer, his wet clothes touching mine and rain pouring down on us. "That's my condition, Riley. I'll make everything else work. Somehow. But I have to be with you."

My mouth worked silently for a moment or two. "Why?" I managed.

"Because I love you," he said. It dropped between us like an anvil and I wanted to rewind the clock and hear him say it for the first time again. My heart tripped and he looked into my eyes. "I love you, Riley. I love you more than I have ever loved anyone else. And more than I could ever love a sport. It's you, then everything else."

"I love you, too," I whispered, grabbing his wet shirt and pressing my lips hard against his. The only energy left in me went into minding his split eyebrow while I kissed him, his mouth hot on my cold lips. We kissed deeply as we shivered, both with excitement and grief over the fight we'd had. Guilt and rage faded away under the blazing light of this kiss.

"Do you really?" He whispered after we kissed, placing his hands on my face and his brow against mine.

"You know I do," I said. "I have always loved you, Cam. Since we were boys tripping over our skates."

He laughed and sobbed at once. "I don't have a clue why you would, but I'm so happy that you love me, too."

I clung to him, my future rewritten in front of me. Us. Hockey. Jason Manning representing us both for the same state, if not the same team, or representing neither. Life together. Somewhere. Anywhere. "God, I love you."

"It took losing you twice for me to see it," he said. "But you, Riley, are what makes my life worth living. Everything else is just details." If he would risk it, I would risk it. I would follow him anywhere.

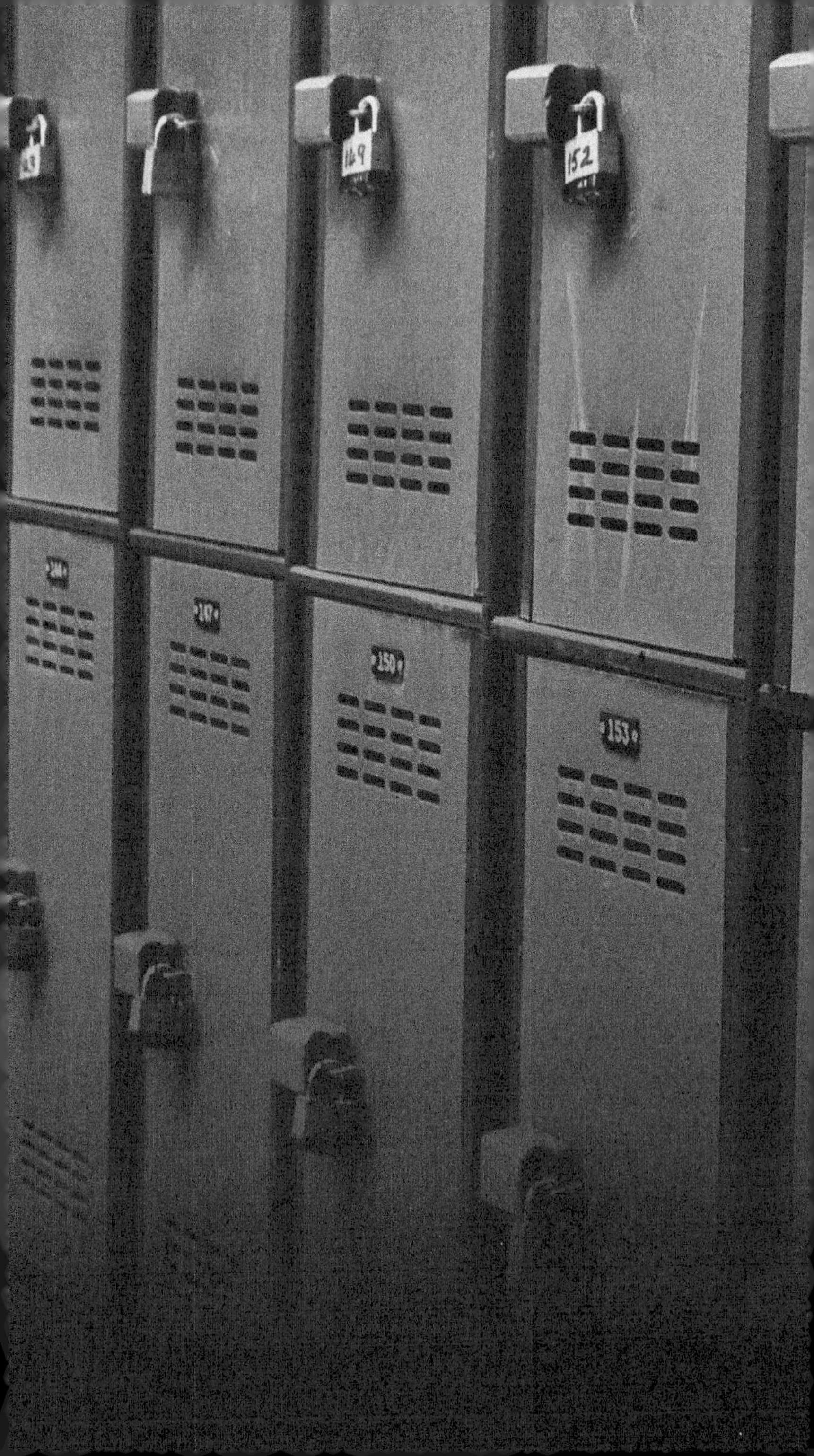
169
152
150
153

SIXTEEN

Cameron

Riley was in my arms as we found cover under the extended roof over the porch of the team house. He'd barely left my hold for the entire walk from the frat house. And now, as we tumbled up the few steps of the porch, my love spun around to face me.

The light in front of the house blinded me when it came on and Riley's breath hitched. "Oh," he managed.

"That bad?" I asked, trying to curve my eyebrows in question, but stopping it before I made it bleed again.

"It's just blood," he said, then took my hand and led me into the house. I had hoped to pin him against the door right here and kiss the life out of him, but his determination to take us inside was unmatched.

The house was empty. If anyone was in, they were in their rooms or the basement. I followed Riley across the ground floor and into my room, rather than his. He marched in like he owned the place, shut the door, then looked around. "Let's get you cleaned up," he said after a moment of thinking, then yanked me into the bathroom.

I followed obediently, discovering that being bossed

around by Riley wasn't the worst thing in the world. I looked forward to discovering things like this for many, many years to come. And when he shut the bathroom door, he sat me down on the closed toilet seat before proceeding to rummage through the medicine cabinet. He found some cotton pads that any hockey player would have plenty of, both in his bathroom and in every duffel bag he ever carried. Iodine was another necessity I had plenty of, both here and in my first aid kit.

I gritted my teeth as Riley methodically applied iodine-soaked cotton pads on my eyebrow and the stinging spread to my toes. "Motherfucker."

"Hush," Riley said. "You'll get to pay me back later."

I chuckled a little, focusing on not fainting with the stinging that somehow seemed to intensify, rather than melt away. It wasn't his fault I was in pain, but the promise of spanking him later helped distract me from my current torment.

There, just under the split eyebrow, the heat was rising steadily. "Did he get my eye?"

"No," Riley said simply, then squinted. "He got your cheekbone, but it's only a little bruised."

"Only," I mused.

I looked up at my soaked and dripping lover as he pouted and focused on cleaning me up. He bit his lip when the smallest of smirks trembled in the corners of his lips. He met my gaze briefly, then pursed his lips. "I do not condone violence," he said in a tight voice.

"But?" I managed to lift my other eyebrow without tearing the split one apart.

Riley was silent for a short while as if to say there were no buts. Then, like he was surrendering, he exhaled. "But you were so fucking hot."

I laughed in a low tone and swatted his hand away from my face. It was good enough. "You're freezing," I said, feeling the coolness of my own clothes, then his, too. I rose slowly, holding his gaze until he needed to look up at me. "Let me take care of you, now."

He forced out a little snort to conceal his excitement. "Is that all you ever think about?"

"My love, that's all either of us ever thinks about," I teased, then began undoing the buttons on his shirt, one by one, top to bottom. I revealed his sculpted chest and defined abs, his smooth skin prickling under my cool fingers. The fabric was sticking to his body until I finished the first part, then pulled his shirt over his shoulders and down his arms. He was wet and beautiful. "We gotta warm you up."

"Ah, yes. You're such a trooper," he joked.

"Just doing my duty, Captain." I pressed my hands on the small of his back and nudged him closer, leaning in to kiss the smirk off his face. "I love you, Riley."

He whimpered in reply, losing himself far in the land of pleasure already. And when my hands traveled around his waist to the button and zipper on his pants, he didn't protest. I undid both and lowered myself slowly down to my knees, pretending I was only there to help him undress. And when he stepped out of his pants, I simply remained on my knees.

His black boxer-briefs were wet, too, and stretching as he pitched a tent with his hardening cock. His fingers moved through my wet hair and I leaned in, pressing my heated lips hard against his stomach, kissing his abs inch by sexy inch.

Riley shuddered the harder I kissed him, parting my lips and letting my tongue slide out. I adored his body. I adored his sense of humor. I adored his anxieties and fears and his fiery, explosive nature. Every prickly little fault he clung to, I wanted a part of. Where I could help him lift the burdens unjustly placed on him, he could do the same in return.

I kissed him harder, hands cupping his ass and pulling him until he was grinding his hard cock against my upper chest. He rutted against me, holding his hands on the back of my head as I kissed and licked and sucked his muscled torso, rising to his chest and returning to the edge of his underwear.

And when I pulled the waistband over his big, firm butt, I looked up to find him dropping his head back and exhaling toward the ceiling. Every muscle in his body hardened visibly. Overhead lights cast shadows down to the ridges between his abs and the prickling rose along his skin once again. I continued pulling his underwear down slowly, revealing the smooth skin around the base of his cock and pulling his thickness down until he grunted.

Swiftly, I moved the waistband over the head of his dick and it sprung up.

"Ah, fuck," Riley whispered, then looked down. He was just in time to lock eyes with me as I opened my mouth and leaned in, then wrapped my lips around his length and survived a mini heart attack from the pure excitement of tasting him again.

I sucked him in as deep as I could, forcing my throat to relax little by little. He was always the more talented one in pleasuring me with his mouth, but I hoped my eagerness counted for something.

Grabbing his cheeks, I pushed him into my mouth, forcing a gasp and murmurs of filth to leave his sexy lips. The scent of green apples rose off his wet skin and the familiarity of his body wash was something I only now realized I loved in a way I had never loved a scent before. It crawled into my nostrils as I leaned deeper in, taking his hard cock down my throat and struggling to inhale but dying for it nonetheless.

"Fuck, Cam," he whimpered, pushing my head away gently. He throbbed in my mouth. "You'll make me come."

My lips remained around the tip of his dick and I allowed a little air into my mouth, relaxing the vacuum I'd created. I almost smiled but resisted. Instead, I sucked him softly for a while. His big balls hung heavy between his legs and I gave in to the temptation. I slid my hand off his butt and cupped his balls, playing gently with them while I teased the edge of his dick's head with my tongue. My thumb and index finger looped around his sack, trapping his swollen balls in my palm and increasing pressure both there and on his cock.

The moan that dragged out of Riley's lips was worth a million dollars. It rose higher and morphed into a whimper, culminating in his fingers that were twisting in my hair, pulling locks harshly, and his entire body rising higher on his toes.

I released him when his cock jerked violently and Riley hyperventilated. "You need to fuck me, Cam. Like, right fucking now." It was a cry and a plea and a command in equal parts.

I rose and pressed my lips against his, letting him taste himself on me for a few quick heartbeats before I pushed him away and undressed. I was swift about it, leaving my wet clothes in a pile and pulling the bathroom door open to file out with Riley. In the room, two lamps were on instead of the ceiling light, and I left it that way. The subdued orange glow warmed the images of our bodies.

There, I kissed him more. I kissed him harder and dirtier, letting my tongue explore every part of his mouth and battle his tongue in an attempt to do the same. Between us, our dicks were hard and trapped against our bodies, grinding roughly until Riley thrust one hand and took us both in a firm grip. He stroked us ferociously, friction driving me crazy with lust.

"Fuck me," he murmured into my mouth. "Fuck me, Cam, or I swear to God…"

I chuckled over his lips and grabbed his cheeks hard, pulling them apart and lifting him to the tips of his toes until he sang a little moaning sound and threw his head back. His voice choked as I thrust my hand between his cheeks and massaged his rim with two fingers. "You're so desperate for my dick," I said.

"Ya think?" But he didn't get to infuse those words with sarcasm because I pressed his hole and cut his words short. He choked up and tightened his fist around both our dicks, forcing me to take action.

I pushed him back almost like we were fighting and Riley breathed deeply, squaring his shoulders and glaring at me to move already.

I slowed down deliberately and crossed the room to my nightstand. I pulled the drawer open and turned to look at him over my shoulder. Riley had one hand around his cock, holding it but not stroking. The other one was behind his back, undoubtedly continuing the motions I had started between his cheeks. He had the sweetest, most excruciatingly pained expression on his glowing face that I had ever seen.

It softened my heart enough to lift the condom and

lube quicker than I'd intended and I prepared myself to give him the time of his life. And when I was done, I walked back to him with slick fingers and my cock at full mast in the condom.

Riley paused and waited for me, moving his hand away from his hole and letting me stand behind him. With only my index finger, I massaged him a little more, making him slick with plenty of excess lube.

Impatiently, my boy grabbed my hand and inserted my finger into himself, exhaling with relief. "Fucking stretch me, Cam. Please."

Something about his insistence to call me by that old nickname made me want to do everything he asked. He was relentless about holding onto the people we had been when we had first discovered the true extent of our relationship.

I filled him with one finger, then two, and ultimately three. Each finger I added made his voice rise and his hole tighten for a short while before relaxing. Stretching him was such a pleasure and such a way to make our souls connect. He was brave and strong about it, taking it as far as he could and trying for more even when I wavered and tried reining it in. His broad back leaned against my chest and I wrapped my left arm around his shoulders. He held onto my forearm with both his hands, arching his back and thrusting his ass onto my hand. With each push, he grunted, strangled, or told me all the dirty things he wanted me to do to him. "I want your dick, Cam, please. Fucking please."

I was already positioned right behind him, so I slipped my fingers out and whispered to him to stay relaxed for me. In an instant, my cock was sliding through my fist and sinking into Riley. I impaled him nearly halfway in, squeezing a deep, rumbling growl from his throat as he rose on his toes and shuddered all over. And when I paused, he wasn't done yet.

Instead, Riley waited a moment, held his breath, and pushed himself down on me until his butt cheeks squished hard against my groin.

"Holy shit." The words ripped from me and over his ear as I sank my teeth into his earlobe.

Riley was no longer capable of forming words. His voice was cracking and he cared none if we were overheard. It suited them well for making bets about our situation-ship. I held my arm firmly around his upper torso and Riley still clung onto it. My other hand went for his hip as I began to pull back and ram into him harder and faster, penetrating him deeper with each swing of my body against his. My front and his back were moving in synchrony. We ground against each other, my cock probing him deeper until he was relaxed and loose enough to allow me to slide in and out with little resistance and plenty of dirty, slapping sounds that matched Riley's tormented voice.

Rapturous moans and pleasure-soaked sighs filled the space around us as our bodies slammed against each other in an exercise of lust and endurance. Riley's fingernails dug into my forearm while I moved my other hand off his hip and to his groin. I felt his cock and balls settle between my thumb and palm. I felt the slickness of his precum trickling down his spear-straight thickness when I took him in my hand.

"Harder, you motherfucker. Just fuck me harder." The grunts riled me up so much that every sense of mercy fluttered away from me and I railed him until he was begging me to make him come.

We took two steps forward, never parting, and Riley lifted his right leg onto my desk, kneeling there as he bent forward. I released his torso and held his hips instead, massaging his prostate and making all his muscles tremble and bounce with the force I applied. Sweat was dripping off my brow and my breaths were shallow. And when Riley touched himself at last, I didn't stop him. I allowed him to stroke himself to his climax, grabbing a fistful of his hair and tugging his head back. He lifted his chin, pleading for me to keep doing everything just the way I was and, as we both neared it, I felt the shattering explosion of warmth spread through my chest. I fucking loved this man more than I loved life.

Riley whimpered as the movement from his hand intensified. His body froze and he spilled his cum all over my desk and floor, his hole clenching hard as I ravaged it and his muscles tensing. His voice cut off and I sped up, permitting myself to let go. And as soon as I did, my balls rose and I filled the condom, throbbing violently inside my boyfriend.

We were both shaking by the time I pulled myself out of him and pressed my fingers against his hole, soothing him with gentle moves that softened his voice. I led us to the bed, caressing all of his heated, sweaty body without a care in the world.

"You're mine," I whispered as we lay down together. "You're going to be mine until the end of time, Riley."

"My love, we both know who belongs to whom," he said cheekily.

I squeezed his bubble-butt and growled a warning at him, but he only threw his head back and laughed out loud. Then, he kissed the tip of my nose, then each of my eyes in turn. The bruise on my cheek was heated, but it was better after the kiss he placed on it. My split eyebrow was tight with my body repairing itself quickly, so I kept my expressions minimal. But I could kiss him back, so that was what I did. I kissed his lips and his chin, I kissed his cheeks and his Adam's apple. I kissed his forehead and his collarbones.

"It's gonna be a tough battle," Riley said in a low voice.

I thought about it. Sticking together through everything that was still to come wouldn't be easy. I never thought it would be. "Nothing's tougher than the time I spent without you." And when those words rolled out, I spilled all the other words. I told him of the soul-crushing loneliness in the thickest of crowds in Santa Barbara. I told him of friendships that were held together with duct tape and prayer because I was incapable of forming a bond. I told him how I'd returned blindly to Michigan as soon as Coach Murray had invited me. And I admitted that it had taken me months to realize that it had always been him. "I'm only ever really happy when I'm with you."

Riley kissed me twice and sighed. "I never realized it until you returned, either. But I haven't been happy since high school. Not truly." He breathed a moment, then blinked at me. "It's better like this, I think."

"How so?" I asked, but I had already figured as much.

"Now we know for certain," he said. He was very sure of his words. "If we hadn't lost the time we had, we would never know how much we belonged together."

There was no reward I was willing to claim if it came at the cost of losing him again. We'd tried that. And we would never try it again.

I would love him until my dying breath. And I would

force the entire world to reshape itself to comply with this rule. It was us, then the rest of the world.

"I swear," I whispered. "You will always be my number one. Everything else will come after that."

"I swear it, too," Riley said solemnly, sealing it with another kiss that merged our souls into one. Just the way they should be.

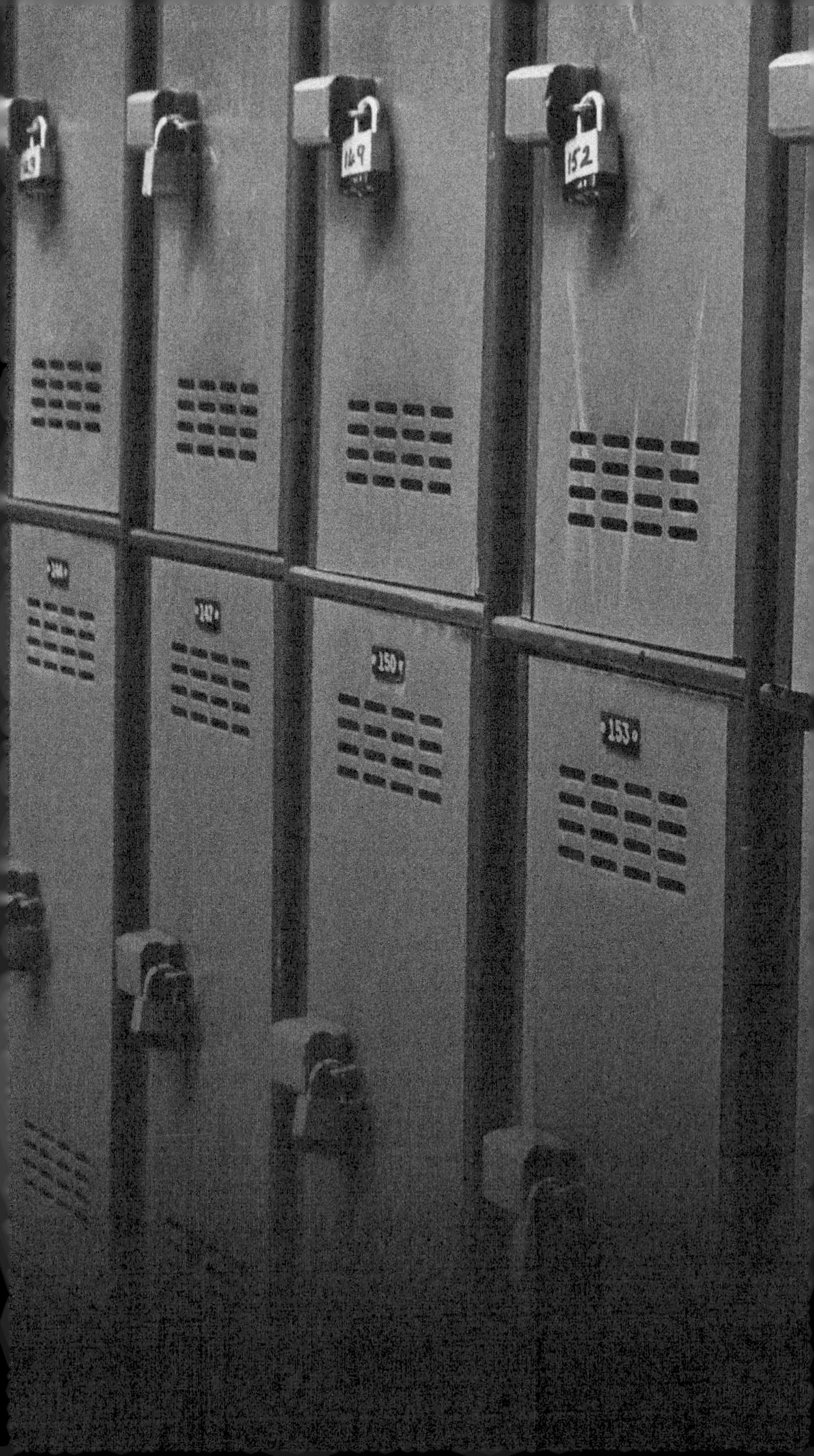
152
150
153

Epilogue

TWENTY MONTHS LATER

SOMETHING ABOUT THE COOL AIR BITING MY nostrils upon stepping outside made everything feel a little better. Cameron had told me that once, too, and it had been true ever since. We had gone through two winters together since he had first returned into my life and the third one was gathering high above us in the thick, leaden clouds that promised a heavy snowfall this afternoon.

Maybe it was the fact that I was always the most comfortable when I was on the ice. Maybe it was the burning furnace of passion that lived in my chest and required cold air to sustain me. And maybe it was the memory of our first Christmas together, with a thick blanket of snow outside and a merry fire in the common room, that had my heart leaping.

Cameron stepped out of the car a moment later and joined me where I was having my ideations. With his handsome body entering my field of vision, it pulled my focus to the reason we were outside in the first place. Then, Lizzy Jennings walked out of the neo-colonial house with a 'FOR SALE' sign displayed in the generous front yard. The house was painted the lightest shades of gray with an olive green accent on the window frames and shutters. Its dark gray roof tiles elevated the entire look. The porch wasn't much unlike the one at the team house where Cam and I had reconnected after three years of distance.

"Welcome," Lizzy said with a bright smile. Her hair was cut straight above her shoulders and her attire was casual and professional at the same time. She walked right down the stoney path to the sidewalk and extended her arm for handshakes.

"Thanks for seeing us," Cam said, apologetic that we couldn't come here any other day than Sunday.

"Please, I know how demanding your work is," Lizzy said to us both.

I doubted she knew the extent of it, but I appreciated hearing the words nonetheless. It was true that playing for the Spartans was taxing in many ways, but each morning, upon opening my eyes, I had the strongest urge to shout blessings from the top of my lungs. The luck Cameron and I had had in the drafting rounds, with the precise guidance of Jason Manning representing us, was something I never would have dared to hope for. I knew us coming out on top of the Frozen Four that last year helped us get what we wanted, too. It was the ridiculously happy ending to a story that nearly ended in its conception.

Our time was spread thin across practice and competitive matches, but we were together. It had taken a great deal of negotiations and Jason definitely employed witchcraft, but Cam and I had been playing for the same team for almost a year and a half. As we wanted to.

We were a team of two. We always had been. And when the Spartans gave us a chance to prove ourselves like a team, we damn well did. And the gamble paid off.

Lizzy ushered us into the house and talked of the type of wood that the pretty, white entrance door was made of. I only noticed the small, round window in the door and thought it was cute.

Inside, the space sprawled left and right with a staircase in the middle. Lizzy stopped us there by the door and explained when the house was built, when it was renovated, what sort of power consumption was average, how it was benchmarked against other houses, and what more could be done to improve the quality of life.

After that, she suggested that we should look around and ask any questions we might have. Though fully furnished, the current owners were happy to take anything we didn't need and offset it against the price of the property.

In truth, I couldn't see myself excluding anything that was already in the house. To our left was a spacious living room with a fireplace and a flat-screen TV mounted above it, a designer coffee table, and a sleek sofa and armchairs was a merger of some deep cozy-punk aesthetic brought into a contemporary setting. To the right, a kitchen and dining room were equipped with every amenity I could ever think of needing. After all, my cooking skills hardly surpassed microwaving a cake, but I was trying.

When Cam and I climbed the stairs to explore the smaller bedroom and the bathrooms, I took his hand in mine. "Is this for real?" I whispered.

"Which part?" he asked, pausing in the hallway toward the master bedroom. "The one where we're buying our first home? Or the one where we survived each other for the last two years?"

I punched his shoulder for that remark, but he wrapped his arms around me roughly and trapped me in his hold. As he bared his teeth, it turned me on pretty much instantly, but I forced myself to resist it. Instead, we indulged in a deep, long kiss that celebrated all we had gone through to get here.

And when we entered the master bedroom, I was sold. The large bed with tall, sleek bedposts and a see-through canopy above had an elegant headboard made up of thin wooden bars that were ideal for trapping my wrists whenever we wished to do so. The blue accent paint paired beautifully with the predominantly white room. Another TV was mounted to the wall across from the bed and the dark, laminated floor had a nice, small, wool carpet on the side. An ottoman was parked in one corner of the room and a reading chair was located in the other with a contemporary lamp hanging a little to the side of it. The walk-in closet allowed for more wardrobe than either of us had and the bathroom sported a large jacuzzi tub that promised to inspire more action than two horny lovebirds could possibly handle. Unless they were trained athletes, of course.

Stamina was a thing you practiced.

Cameron wrapped his arms around me from behind as we both gaped at the large bathroom. "I always knew we'd have this," he said.

"You did not." I glanced at him and found that he was serious.

"No, I totally did," he said. "Since we got together for

real. I knew this was it. Same team. Nice house. That ring around your finger."

By instinct, I touched the ring. My crazy, beautiful Cameron. After the first game we won with the Spartans, Cam told me to wait for everyone to leave. He wanted us to go back to the ice and so we did, elated with our victory and the promise we made when we joined the team. The rink was empty and we were young and dreamy. Our dreams were coming true day after day. And in the magic of the moment, when we were invincible, we skated across the rink just for the fun of it. Just for the laughs and the squeals of joy that we wished to share with one another. In all of that, having carried it throughout the game, Cameron had skated across the rink to the middle, and fell to one knee, offering me this beautiful, golden ring and asking me to marry him.

After years of pining and more years of loss, then the best year and a half of my life, there was nothing else to say but yes. He was mine and I was his. It was written that way in the stars.

"I always knew it," Cam insisted, tightening his hold on me. "When I told you that you would be my first in everything, this is what I meant. It's you and me, baby."

And it always was. My family was lukewarm about the wedding service and frosty about our drafting. His family had moved to another state without letting him know. And while they had been in touch to exchange contact information, neither side had ever truly reached out again.

But that was the thing everyone got wrong about family. Cameron was my family just like I was his. We came from groups of people with whom we had never fit in, but they shaped the puzzle pieces that we were. And we made the whole picture.

We built our family and we were giving it a home. With blood and sweat and passion that burned so bright it eviscerated everything that stood in its way.

"Stop being so adorable or I'll have you right here and now," I whispered, placing my hands over his on my lower abdomen.

He added a little more pressure and bit my ear for a short moment. "I'd have you anywhere, my love."

"Lizzy's waiting," I reminded him.

"Is that supposed to be a turn-off?" he joked.

I laughed and spun away from him, then pulled him in for a kiss. This was it. This was the house we would live in. This was the home we would make. And he was the only person on this entire planet I would ever want to do that with.

I kissed him without mercy or pause. I kissed him like it was the last chance I had.

And he kissed me back with equal passion.

I found myself holding the lapels of his jacket like the winds would take me away if I let go. He was the monolith of safety in my life and in times of change. Together, we embarked on this wild journey and together we could make it.

Cameron pulled back and looked into my eyes, fire blazing in those loving chestnuts and a smirk stretching his lips. We didn't need words when we slowly nodded to one another.

This was the one we would buy.

And today was the first day of the rest of our lives.

The End.

Author's Note

I'm so glad you've read *Crossing Blades* all the way to the end. Riley and Cameron were a fun pair to write.

If you enjoyed *Crossing Blades*, I would appreciate an Amazon or GoodReads review. They are priceless to indies like me and help readers decide whether to give this book a chance.

If you'd like to give me a shoutout on the internet, you can find me in all the usual places. Just look for Hayden Hall and you'll find me everywhere online.

If you enjoy college romances, I've got two complete series available on Amazon (and free with Kindle Unlimited). You can start with *Frat Brats of Santa Barbara*.

And if you would like early access, work-in-progress chapters, exclusive merch, bonus scene, and more, consider supporting me on Patreon: patreon.com/HaydenHall

And finally, if you would like to receive a free full-length novel (and sign up for a monthly magazine and book updates), you can do that here: https://BookHip.com/NDGCCQR

Love,
Hayden

Acknowledgments

It takes a village to write a book and I'm the luckiest author ever with the village that supports me.

All my love and thanks to Sabrina Hutchinson for pouring her time and effort into polishing my messy manuscripts so that you receive an actual novel.

My love, Xander, is the pillar of this entire operation and he deserves the world for keeping me on track. You've no idea how many deadlines I would be missing if he took a week off.

My Patrons are the best bunch of people ever. I love every single one of you and my mind is simply blown away by your generosity. You are taking my career to the next level and I can never thank you enough. Hopefully, some awesome art prints will begin to illustrate how grateful I am.

Angela Haddon is the brilliant designer to who I owe all the thanks and more for creating the drop-dead gorgeous cover art. Every detail and every step of the process were priceless to me.

And to you, my reader, I owe the biggest thanks of all. I hope to keep bringing you fun, sexy, and (sometimes) emotional stories for many years to come. And the fact that you are reading these makes sure that I can continue writing.

Love you all.

Also by Hayden Hall

Destined to Fail

Destructive Relations

Shameless Affairs

Explicit Transactions

Frat Brats of Santa Barbara

The Fake Boyfriends Debacle

The Royal Roommate Disaster

The Wrong Twin Dilemma

The Bitter Rivals Fiasco

The Accidental Honeymoon Catastrophe

The Bedroom Coach Contract

The Office Nemesis Calamity

College Boys of New Haven

The Nerd Jock Conundrum

The Three Hearts Equation

The Two Stars Collision

The No Strings Theory

The Geeky Jock Paradox

Standalones

Rescued: A Hurt Comfort Novel

Damaged: A Black Diamond Novel

About the Author

Gay. Sweet. Steamy.

Hayden Hall writes MM romance novels. He is a boyfriend, a globetrotter, and an avid romance reader.

Hayden's mission is to author a catalog of captivating and steamy MM romance novels which gather a devoted community around the Happily Ever Afters.

His stories are sweet with just the right amount of naughty.

You can find out more and get in touch with Hayden through his website at www.haydenhallwrites.com or one of the links below.

- amazon.com/stores/author/B08R5CSXYS
- patreon.com/HaydenHall
- instagram.com/authorhaydenhall
- facebook.com/hayden.hall.773

Printed in Great Britain
by Amazon